THE DEEP END

BOOK TWO OF THE JILL RHODES
MYSTERY/THRILLER SERIES

NINA ATWOOD

The Deep End: Book Two of the Jill Rhodes Mystery/Thriller Series

[E-book] ISBN-13: 978-1-7363470-6-5

[Print] ISBN-13: 978-1-7363470-7-2

TITLES BY NINA ATWOOD

The Expert Witness: Jill Rhodes Mystery/Thriller Series, Book One, is available on Amazon.

About Roxanne: A Psychological Thriller, is available on Amazon.

Free Fall: A Psychological Thriller, is available on Amazon.

Unlikely Return: A Novel, is available on Amazon.

For more of Nina's books, visit Nina's author page on Amazon.

Join Nina's VIP Reader Club for FREE fiction, notification of author inside stories plus upcoming titles in the series, and discounted book deals, here.

Copy/paste:

https://www.ninaatwoodauthor.com/freenovella/

Reward Special note: *If you introduce me to someone in the moviemaking industry [big screen, streaming content] that results in a signed contract and paid advance on any of my books, I will pay you a reward of $10,000.*

– Nina Atwood

Contact: nina@ninaatwoodauthor.com

lacking the capacity for verbal warnings, sent her a variety of somatic signals, escalating to a crescendo in a matter of seconds.

She almost stood up, envisioning herself running away. But her rational mind reigned in the impulse, telling her that would look ridiculous to her visitor. It would be unconscionably rude. Additionally, she couldn't imagine the end point. Where would she go? What would she do? No, there was something amiss, but it was nothing that couldn't be discussed and resolved, as she'd handled most of the difficulties life had served up over her many decades.

Later, she knew she'd rationalized a threatening situation to the point of no return. By the time she'd acknowledged the imminent danger, she'd lost any advantage. She fought back, but it was a feeble effort. She didn't have a lot of muscle mass left, and she'd never made it a priority to work out. All of her strength was in the sharpness of her mental acuity. But all that rational brain power had resulted in a mental machine that couldn't fully process personal danger.

As she struggled to draw air, the darkness closing in, she thought about how poorly she'd miscalculated the level of threat of the malevolent personality that had entered her life and the lives of those she loved. She gave it one last effort, her hand grasping for a nearby object. But it was too late, and she knew it.

PROLOGUE

At the sound of the doorbell, Linda looked up from her eBook reader and cocked her head. Glancing at her watch, she noted the time. She pulled her calendar out from under the morning newspaper, put on her readers, and moved her shaking finger carefully over the page. Nope, no one expected, not until later.

Most likely, it was a delivery. Since she couldn't even remember what she'd ordered from Amazon in the last couple of days, it wasn't anything she would miss too much. So, it could wait.

She picked up her eReader and continued reading, but the doorbell rang again. And again. Persistence on the part of the unexpected visitor gave her pause. Could this be her neighbor, Alvie? Perhaps she was early for their evening wine time. Her slightly hysterical friend down the hallway, whose insatiable need for validation of every life decision, periodically needed Linda's attention. Something trivial with her daughter, no doubt.

Linda took a wobbly sip of hot tea, trying to keep the slopping liquid from spilling. Alvie had a lovely daughter and three grandkids. Her daughter was a sweet young woman, as far as Linda could tell from the few times they'd met. But the looks of resignation and signs of extended patience she displayed around her mother told the true story. Alvie couldn't resist offering unsolicited advice, often in front of Linda, to the daughter's great chagrin. Everything from what she chose to wear that day— *maybe it's time to retire those jeans, dear*—to how to parent her children—*should they really be eating so much sugar?*

And the biggest issue of all. Alvie's daughter had apparently married the wrong guy, something that she couldn't let go of.

Now, there was another huge issue. For Alvie, it was an urgent crisis when her daughter informed her that they were moving a couple of miles further away. *I can't believe she's doing this to me! She knows I hate driving very far, especially if it involves freeways, and now, I can't just jump in the car and drive a few blocks, not anymore! What am I going to do? I've got to get this ridiculous notion out of her head. Those kids need their grammy nearby.*

This was foreign to Linda, as a mom who'd schooled herself many years ago to let go and recognize her children as fully formed adults who were living their own lives. Though, one could argue they weren't fully formed.

Linda sighed. Though she'd willingly and without resentment give her time to Alvie and others who needed her ear, she zealously safeguarded her 'me time.' Besides, Alvie was coming over that evening anyway. This was someone else, someone clearly lacking in the social graces to text or call in advance. She sighed and laid her eReader aside. Dean Koontz's latest chiller would have to wait.

Linda rose, fluffed her sadly thinning hair, pulled her top down a bit, and went to the door, first looking through the peep hole. She paused, giving herself a moment. Alvie could be a handful at times, but this visitor was Alvie times eight or maybe ten. Even so,

in the spirit of being polite, Linda opened the door and greeted her unexpected guest warmly.

They settled in Linda's living room. Her guest seemed even more agitated than usual, but then, that was to be expected, given the current circumstances. Completely understandable that there might be anxiety, a measure of fear of the unknown, when there's been a sudden life change.

Linda did her best to offer an open ear, empathy, comfort, and the occasional tidbits of advice to those who sought it. But her guest today wasn't interested in her advice or even a measure of empathy.

Though Linda had sensed something unpleasant about her guest in the past, something that ran darkly underneath the smiles, the occasional kind gesture, and the nice words, she'd never paid it much mind. She'd chalked it up to differences in personality, maybe in upbringing.

A sense of obligation enabled her to push aside her reservations. Instead, she'd put on her own smile and offered kind words wherever she could, as long as she didn't have to outright lie. Today, as always, she braced herself for the need to avoid the subtle manipulations, the attempts to draw her into any drama. It was exhausting, but she could handle it.

But as her guest made small talk, clearly avoiding the topic that had brought about the urgent doorbell rings and intrusion into her day, a small trickle of unease worked its way up Linda's spine. Warmth spread throughout her system, her body picking up something that her rational mind couldn't process quickly enough. Last, and most alarmingly, her heart rate dialed upward, and it was at that moment that her brain registered an alarm.

Linda's innate commitment to measured, polite behavior went to war with her internal early warning system. Her amygdala,

CHAPTER ONE

DAY ONE

Tim Hawkins, age 52, according to his intake form, wore a serious expression. Though his story might indicate otherwise, he was short on charm. He was married to his college sweetheart and had two children, one in college, the other married with a baby. He worked in operations for a company whose logo Jill knew well. She drove past it every day. His hands were carefully folded, and his legs crossed. He hardly moved as he calmly laid out his problem, the reason he sat in front of her.

"At this point, I don't know what to do. That's why I'm here. I'm seeking your opinion, your professional opinion," he said pointedly, as though her opinion might carry some sort of special insight or dispensation.

Dr. Jill Rhodes studied her newest patient. Inwardly, she sighed. This had been one of those days, one filled with patients who sought magical answers to their self-created problems. As a practicing psychologist, she knew there would always be these days. But if she were to be honest with herself, the truth was that she greatly preferred the kinds of sessions in which thoughtful, high-integrity people worked through emotionally laden issues such as divorce, death, or life transition. And did so with vulnerability and authenticity.

That, however, was the exception.

The real nature of her work was accepting the person in front of her, wherever he or she currently sat in his or her life journey. Whether that be in the throes of addiction, or the mess created by years of small, disastrous decisions, or with anxiety, depression, or some variety of personality disorder or neurosis.

People were messy, and she'd signed up for all of it.

"I can give you my opinion, but you won't like it," she told him.

"And that is?"

"I think you already know what the root of your problem is."

"The root of my problem? I have this woman I love, who I never expected to love, and I can't stop seeing her. I'm also in love with the woman I've been with for thirty-two years. I need you to help me make a choice."

For the first time, his calm demeanor broke just a bit. He reached up and touched his upper lip, which now held a small sheen of sweat.

She leaned in just a tad and slowed her speech, adopting a measured pace to allow the space to process new information. "I'm going to ask you something, and it will go against your natural inclination toward logic. I'd like you to try to answer without thinking or filtering too much. Can you give that a try?"

"Yes," he said, looking relieved.

"Okay. Here's the question. But first," she said, deliberately keeping him hanging, "an observation. You have two women who love you. You enjoy the benefits of two relationships. So far, everyone is enjoying your company, and there are no issues. Your wife doesn't know about the other woman, and so far, the other woman hasn't demanded you leave your wife for her. Do I have the full picture?" She kept her tone strictly factual.

She was schooled in the practice of holding the space around her patients without judgment. She recognized deeply that the flawed nature of people meant that there would be mistakes, errors in judgment, faulty decisions, and painful outcomes. After almost twelve years of practice, she knew this to be true for all human beings.

Including herself.

He nodded his head. "Yes."

"Okay. Now, here's the question. Why are you really here? It's all working for you. Why seek anyone else's opinion or advice?"

He closed his eyes briefly and touched his upper lip again. "I'm here because I don't feel good about what I'm doing. I know it's wrong. I'm afraid that at some point, someone is going to pressure me to do something about it. I just have this bad feeling—" He pulled at his collar.

"A bad feeling," she echoed. "How long have you felt this way, and how is it affecting you?"

"Weeks ago, that's when it started. I was on a business trip, and one night, I woke up, and my heart was pounding. I was sweating, and I felt like I couldn't breathe. I—I felt like I was going to die. I didn't know what to do. I almost called 9-1-1, but then it started going away. I didn't sleep anymore that night at all." He uncrossed his legs, clasped his hands, and began rubbing one thumb rapidly against the side of the other hand. "Uh, I'm not feeling so great," he said, as his face turned pale. "This has been happening more and more!"

"Tim, you're going to be okay."

Now, he gasped for air, and his eyes began to spin. "I can't breathe! Call 9-1-1! Oh, God!" His chest heaved with the effort to draw air.

"You're having a panic attack. Take deep breaths." Jill ran to her desk and reached into the nearby trash. Luckily, she'd just thrown away a fast-food bag. She grabbed it and gave it to Tim. "Here, breathe into this." She showed him how to close the opening over his mouth. He sucked in air and the bag collapsed. He expelled, and it expanded. Soon, his eyes stopped spinning. He set the bag down but close by.

She pointed to his chest. "Take your dominant hand, use the index and middle fingers, and tap just under your collarbone. Like this." She demonstrated. "It's an acupressure technique to reduce anxiety."

He followed her instructions and tapped. Gradually, his breathing slowed. "I'm fine now," he said when she questioned if he was able to continue. "But I still don't know what to do. Look, Dr. Rhodes, this isn't like me. I've always been very decisive."

"But not with this decision because it isn't logical. Let's take a step back and look at the bigger picture. Tell me what you really want. The outcome of all of this, down the road, in a year, or two, or five years."

"I just don't want to hurt anyone," he said. "If I could keep both of them happy, that would be great. But I don't think I can. I know what I should do. I should break up with Lucy, and that's it!" he said suddenly, vehemently. "I'll be happy with Leslie."

He stood and began pacing, raking his fingers through his sparse hair. "Why can't I just do that? Why does it feel so... impossible... to leave Lucy? When we're together, it feels so great; I feel so complete. She's my soulmate; I just know it. She's amazing, such an incredible lover, so good to me. But then I get home, and I'm with Leslie, and I can't stand the thought of leaving her, of hurting her. I feel like I'm going crazy!" He returned to the chair, sat down hard, and slumped over, rubbing his face.

"Lucy is your heroin, and no addict wants to give up the source of his high." She waited.

"What?! That's crazy! Lucy is a person, a human being!" Now his face reddened, and she noted the clenching of his fists.

"It feels so good, you don't want to stop," she continued, as if he hadn't spoken. "But you also know it's hurting you. The conflict inside you is escalating—the high of being with Lucy, the low of realizing you're hurting your wife and children, because sooner or later, this will catch up, and you could lose your family. That conflict is showing up physiologically because there's a short time horizon during which we can get away with living in a way that goes against our deepest values."

In her mind's eye, she could visualize the terrible meltdown between Tim and his wife, her pain, and the devastation to their family. It was her intuition, and it kicked in randomly. During those moments, she could clearly see the road being traveled by the person in front of her, see the final destination.

Of course, in this instance, it didn't take special insight to predict the outcome of an ill-fated affair.

He blew out air. "That's true. This isn't me. I'm not a liar. I'm not a cheater. How did this happen?"

"You took a hit of heroin one night on a business trip. You told yourself what addicts tell themselves. It's just once, just one time. It won't hurt. *It doesn't mean anything.*"

"Yes," he whispered, looking at the carpet. "I know I need to decide. I need to choose one of these two women, be truthful, and move on with my life." He looked up at Jill, his eyes pleading. "Tell me what to do so no one gets hurt."

9

"*No one gets hurt.* How can that be possible when there are two women, and one of them is going to be left with a painful breakup or divorce?"

"I don't know. I just need to know how I can handle this with very little or no pain. Neither of them deserves to be hurt."

Magical thinking. Wave your wand, Dr. Rhodes, and disappear the mess I've made of my life.

"Tim, I'm afraid you're seeking the wrong thing. There's no painless way out of the problem you have. Someone is going to get hurt. The panic attacks are telling you this."

"Maybe there's treatment for that. Maybe if I get better, if I don't get so scared, then I can figure out what to do. Can you give me a prescription for anxiety?"

"No. I'm not a medical doctor."

"Then I'll go see my family doctor and get something," he declared, but his voice lacked conviction.

"You can do that. Or you can face your problems and deal with them. Because if you medicate yourself, these problems will still be there later when you sober up. But here's the thing," she added, pausing.

He waited expectantly. "What is the *thing*?"

"You're living your life right now in a way that goes against your own values. If having a relationship with two different women at the same time was morally and personally congruent for you, you wouldn't be having panic attacks, and you wouldn't be here. Because there would be no secrets. It would all be out in the open, and the two women could choose for themselves with all the cards on the table."

"No secrets," he said, as though he'd tasted something foul.

"Secrets are like cancer. It starts small and grows over time. One day, you wake up and realize something is terribly wrong.

You find out you're going to need chemo, radiation, maybe surgery. It's going to hurt. You can't just wave a magic wand and your cancer disappears. Treatment is the only way to get well and move on with your life."

"Cancer," he whispered.

"And now, you have a choice. Continue treatment, deal with this head-on, and clean up your life. Or, you can hide from it, pretend it will magically clear up on its own, and take pills to numb yourself." She'd spoken that last part gently, knowing it was highly confrontational and could trigger defensiveness. "But I think you're here because you're ready to deal with it. And I believe you can."

He bowed his head over his knees and shielded his eyes with his hands. But she saw them anyway. The drip of tears as they fell between his knees landed on her carpet and signified the beginning of his healing.

There was nothing better to melt defenses and allow the opening for a new awareness than the cleansing power of tears. The kind of tears that come from the pain that has been sitting deep inside, unexpressed and unheard.

She gently pushed the tissue box closer to him on the table.

As soon as Tim left, Jill's door swung open. Lauren Glover, her assistant, stood there with raised eyebrows, one pierced, the other not. "There's someone here who isn't in your schedule. I—"

"Look for an opening and get them scheduled," Jill interrupted. "I've got to go meet my sister for lunch." She stood and grabbed her bag, but Lauren blocked her.

"Can you chill for just a second? She says she has an urgent matter to discuss, something about her partner's *death*." Lauren's face was flushed with excitement. She was easily stimulated by anything that broke up the tedious routine of paperwork for new clients, ushering people into Jill's office, and handling insurance. Lauren was a psychology student, no doubt with her own brilliant career ahead of her, but for now, she worked for Jill during the day, attending school at night. "You are *so* going to want to see this chick," she added.

"Okay, but just for a minute. Then you can handle her." Jill walked to the waiting room and stopped short in surprise.

"Hey, Dr. Rhodes. I'm so sorry to interrupt your day, but I really need to see you."

Roxanne Fairchild. Briefly, her patient a few months back. *Addicted. Obsessive and relentless.* But also, a brilliant attorney and successful at solving a decades-old, deeply personal mystery.

"Roxanne. It's good to see you." She greeted her former client warmly. "But I'm afraid I can't stay. I have another meeting away from the office." She nodded towards her assistant. "Lauren can make an appointment with you for another time."

"This won't take long, and I'm not here as a patient. I need your... other skills. It's about one of my law partners. He died recently, and I don't think it was an accident. Everyone else does, but I think something happened to him, and he—" Her eyes welled up, and she brushed away a tear. "Sorry. I'm a lot more emotional these days."

"Roxanne, I'm not really an investigator. I just got involved in—"

"I saw you," Roxanne interrupted. "On the news that night. And word travels fast around the courthouse, so I know you worked on the case of that kid who almost got prosecuted for murder. *Please.*"

Jill stood silently for a moment. Ultimately, too curious to pass up the opportunity to hear more, she relented. "All right. If you're willing to ride along, you can give me the story on the way to my lunch meeting. You'll have to figure out how to get back to your car. And no promises that I will be able to help, not until I know what it's about."

"*Thank you*," Roxanne said. "It's really important because I think someone is about to get away with murder."

CHAPTER TWO

Two days earlier

Roxanne sat on her patio, sipping an ice-cold gin martini, relishing the warmth spreading throughout her body as the deliciously intoxicating elixir took effect. She plucked out the two olives and popped them into her mouth. But they disappeared before she could chew and swallow, and she frowned, having missed out on the sharp flavor of the blue cheese stuffing.

Suddenly, shame washed over her. A small voice asked her, *what about Henry? What about the girls?* And then, she realized the stunning truth. She'd had over three hundred days of sobriety, now broken. *She'd fallen off the wagon.* And it was as if she'd never given it a thought.

A bee appeared out of nowhere and began buzzing around her. She tried to swat it away, but it dodged every effort. The bee drew closer, trying to land on her nose, and she panicked. She wriggled away from it, and everything else fell away as the bee loomed larger and larger.

Roxanne gasped, her eyes flying open. Her heart raced, but gradually, as she took deep breaths, it slowed. The bee buzzed again, and she realized it was her cellphone, tucked under her pillow, on vibrate. She pulled it out as she slipped out of bed, trying to avoid waking Henry, her amazing, long-suffering husband.

In the bathroom, she answered. "Hello. Do you have any idea what time it is?"

"Roxanne, I'm so sorry, but I'm calling about Cory. He's dead." It was Claire, her best friend and paralegal.

Cory Holloman, law partner and one-time nemesis. Dead? "That's impossible. I just saw him a few hours ago, and he was fine. Are you sure?"

"I'm very sure. Cory's wife called Richard to report it, and he called me." She sounded a bit choked up. Claire always found empathy for others, even for some of their clients who were arguably evil and unredeemable.

Richard Driscoll was the managing partner of the firm. He was a brilliant lawyer but not much of a manager, leaving most of the drudgery of that side of his role to Claire. "What happened, Claire? Was it a car accident?"

Her mind jumped to a DUI, but she didn't say it.

"No, nothing like that. They are saying it was an accidental drowning."

"Drowning? That doesn't make sense."

"I know, it's so weird. I can't really believe it myself. His wife, Erica, is the one who found him. I guess she was away at a spa, apparently, celebrating one of her girlfriends' birthdays. So, anyway, she was gone for a couple of days and got back home late Sunday evening. Cory wasn't home, or so she thought, so she went to bed, figuring Cory was out with his buddies like usual. She said he... well, never mind. But anyway—"

"Claire, focus!" Roxanne felt impatience rising. Claire had trouble getting to the point and was known for going off on tangents. She bit her tongue. "Sorry. I'm a little out of sorts. Please, go on."

"Sorry. It's just... I still can't believe it. Anyway, Erica went to bed but woke up a few hours later and realized Cory still wasn't there. She got up to look for him, but he wasn't anywhere in the house. She called his cell phone and heard it ringing in the family room. So, she went to get it. That's when she saw it... saw him. Out the sliding glass doors. Facedown in the swimming pool. Just floating there. *Oh, God.*" She sniffled. "What a terrible way to go. Drowning... all alone."

This wasn't real. It couldn't be true.

But it turned out to be true. By the time Roxanne got to Cory's house, his body had been taken to the morgue.

Current day

"I thought you said someone was going to get away with murder," Jill posed, glancing sideways at Roxanne. "But his death was accidental, right?" She did her best to navigate the mid-day Dallas traffic as she listened, but she was significantly distracted by Roxanne's story. And puzzled.

"Yes, according to the coroner who showed up that night. But there's something else... and I can't figure out why no one else thought about it. Cory was a champion swimmer in college. It's baffling, truly impossible, to think of him drowning. In his own pool."

"Okay, it's puzzling, but can't a good swimmer drown? Was he intoxicated? Maybe he hit his head somehow."

"I don't know all the details yet. But I'm telling you, something's not right."

Jill pulled into the parking lot of the restaurant and stopped the engine. "I don't understand, Roxanne. Why do you need my help? I'm sure you can get a copy of Cory's death certificate, maybe from his wife or through your connections. Maybe that will help you get a sense of closure."

Roxanne blew out an exasperated breath. "I don't need emotional closure. *I'm not grieving.* We weren't that close. I'm upset, uncomfortable with the conclusions being drawn. There are things that don't add up, and I want to find out more. But I need your help. I want to go talk to Cory's wife, and I'd like you there as a sounding board, someone with your expertise." She stopped suddenly. "Look. I promise you, if that goes nowhere, I'll drop it, pay your fee, and that's the end of it." She twisted in her seat. "And in case you're wondering—I see that look in your eye—my sobriety is going just fine. Thank you very much, Dr. Rhodes. So, how about it?"

"All right. I guess that can't hurt. But before we do that, let me see what I can find out on my end. I have a... connection with the police."

Roxanne smiled. "I bet you do. That hot detective you were on television with that night."

Jill restrained herself from an eye roll. Roxanne wasn't the first person to remind her of Detective Nick Webb's entry into her life, along with the romantic insinuations. Just because he was good-looking, around her age, and apparently single, no one could resist pairing the two of them together. She ignored Roxanne's last comment. "I'll get something set up with him."

17

Detective Nick Webb wasn't exactly busy when his cell rang. He'd been doing research on a case that was nearing a conclusion. That meant dragging in the suspect from day one, a drug-pushing punk he'd already arrested once before, who'd been identified by a witness as the perpetrator of the murder of a rival gang member. Webb was collecting evidence against the self-named BTK, a/k/a Darius King. In true gangster wannabe fashion, he'd taken the same moniker as a famous serial killer to sound more lethal.

Webb had almost enough to make Darius crack. Once he did, Nick could turn him over to the narcotics division with a penciled-in plea deal, and they could go to work on his nefarious gang's other activities. That would put the top of the gang's leadership in the bullseye.

When he saw the caller ID, his heart skipped a tiny beat, but he tried not to read too much into the fact that she was calling him after nothing but silence for several weeks. She'd been a third-party consultant on a murder case of his a few weeks back. Jill's help on the case had proved invaluable, though hazardous, as she managed to put herself in harm's way. Luckily, he'd been there to prevent her demise at the hands of the real killer.

"Nick Webb," he said, with a trace of formality.

"Detective Webb," she said, and he was far too glad to hear her voice. "I have a... friend who is concerned about someone who recently died. I'm wondering if you can tell us more about it. She's an attorney, and she could eventually get all the records, but we'd like to shortcut the usual channels if we can. If you can help." She sounded a bit hesitant.

He thought about how to respond. *It's good to hear from you.*

But that would sound far too warm and personal. *And you are…?* Ridiculous. She'd never believe he'd forgotten her. Instead, he went with, "I'm doing great, how about you? And it's Nick, just in case you forgot." *Sarcasm. Wow. Way to go.*

"Um, I'm good. Thanks for asking. Sorry, I guess I'm rushing around too much. I know you prefer Nick."

The tension left his shoulders, and in its place was embarrassment. "Sorry, too. It's been a long day, but that's no excuse. It's good to hear from you. How can I help?"

She quickly explained what she wanted, and he agreed to help. They made plans to talk later. As he hung up, he wondered if they could meet in person. Maybe he'd make that a stipulation in the exchange. A slow smile lifted his mouth.

A wadded-up piece of paper hit him on the back of the head, and he swiveled around to find his partner, Rick Stone, giving him a smirk. "What the hell was that for?"

Stone shrugged. "You tell me. I haven't seen that kind of look on your face since… well, never. Whoever she is, she must be hot." He mocked fanning himself and knocked over his coffee canister in the process. "Shit! Look what you made me do."

Nick swiveled away and clicked his keyboard, searching through his contacts. "You're full of exactly what you just said, brother," he threw over his shoulder. "Maybe she is hot," he added, thinking about Jill's hair, the way she carried herself, and her calming voice. "Jealous much?"

"Hey, buddy. I had a date last night that you wouldn't believe," Stone bragged, leaning back in the rolling office chair at his desk, forgetting about the bad hinge. "Whoa!" he yelped as he tumbled backward, barely catching himself before he fell. He scrambled to pull up his considerable weight, face turning purple as the other detectives in the room guffawed.

Rick was twice divorced—and trying to make a go of it again in the dating world—a father to two grown boys and the best partner Nick had ever had. Though his rough way of handling people, his girth, slightly disheveled appearance, and offhand remarks might turn most people off, he was very good at his job. And an excellent partner. He was sharp, driven, and tenacious, with a long history of solving cases. He'd mentored Nick in his early years as a Dallas homicide detective.

Ignoring the snickers, Stone strolled over to Nick, peering over his shoulder at the computer screen. "What are you working on, anyway? I thought we were going after BTK. It's about time we pulled his sorry ass in here and worked him over."

"We are. I'm just doing a quick favor for... a friend." Nick found what he was looking for but turned around to his partner. "Did you get the search warrant?" BTK lived with his mother in a run-down house in south Dallas, but he spent most of his time at his girlfriend's. Their plan was to use the search warrant at his girlfriend's first, hoping to find the murder weapon and pick him up after that. Evidence in hand would give them more leverage for the interview.

"On it," Stone said and moved away.

That was good because Nick didn't want his partner watching while he composed the email. Rick hadn't exactly been warm and friendly to Jill during the case, despite the fact that she'd turned out to be integral in solving it. No need to stir him up again.

He hit send and sat back. He was curious to find out why Jill needed a copy of a death certificate. On a guy who'd drowned.

CHAPTER THREE

Jill pushed the door open and called out to her sister. "Hello?"

Instead of Jade, Jill was surprised to hear a little girl's voice. "Aunt Jill!" Small shoes slapped against the hardwood floors, and soon her waist was enveloped by the arms of a six-year-old girl who bore almost the identical features of her mother. Carly's upturned face beamed.

"Hey, pumpkin. What are you doing home?" She kissed her niece on the top of her head, hugging her in return.

"Teacher something, I don't know. Let's go to my room! It's a surprise!" Carly tugged Jill's hand impatiently.

"Sure, sweetie. But first, let me speak to your mom." Jill found her sister in her ultramodern, chef's kitchen, chopping up vegetables on the huge island in the center of the open space. "Hey," she said, hugging the woman who'd grown up alongside her. Jade's dark hair, though a bit longer, was as lush as Jill's, and her gray eyes, height, and slender build mirrored her sister's. Even their voices were similar. If one of them answered the other's phone, only a couple of people could tell the difference.

But in other ways, the resemblance diminished sharply.

A talented, accomplished artist, Jade wandered at times into the mystical, espousing ungrounded theories about how life worked. She was less direct in contrast to Jill's bluntness. She deferred to her husband in a way that Jill could never imagine herself doing with a partner.

Jill marveled at their differences. But as always, she felt immediately relaxed in her presence. "What's up with Carly being home?" She picked up a cherry tomato and popped it into her mouth.

"Teacher conference day. Daniel's working as usual and probably not coming home until late, so we're on our own. Right, pumpkin?" She smiled at her daughter. "We've got plans later, right?"

Carly pouted. "Sure, Mommy."

"What's with the face? I thought you were excited about going to the museum."

Ignoring her mom, Carly ran her hands along the top of the island, stopping at Jill and tugging her hand again. "Let's go, Aunt Jill."

"Okay. Be back in a minute," Jill told her sister, letting Carly pull her out of the kitchen and down the hall.

Carly was a budding artist herself. The hallway of the house was filled with framed drawings and watercolor paintings spanning from around age three. She loved art shows and most museums.

A few minutes later, after being introduced to the newest additions to her niece's little family of dolls and stuffed animals, she asked, "What was that about, not wanting to go to the museum?"

"I don't know." Carly's eyes had dropped, and she moved restlessly. First, picking up one stuffed animal, then another, hugging it, then putting it down, only to pick up another. *Self-soothing behavior.*

"I like it better when it's just Mommy and me." She dropped the stuffed animal and trailed her hand along the princess bedspread, circling first one princess, then another. Then, starting over again. *Repetitive self-soothing.*

"And when it's not just you and Mommy?" Jill kept her voice calm.

"I don't know. I want to go watch TV." She moved out of her room in the abrupt way only a kid does, no longer interested in the conversation and ready to move on to the next thing, leaving Jill baffled. And concerned.

Back in the kitchen, Jill was surprised to catch Jade lifting a glass of chilled white wine to her lips. She sat on the barstool at the marble-topped island and watched Jade closely.

"What?" Jade's cheeks had pinked considerably since Jill had left the room. "Can't a girl have a glass of wine in the middle of the day without judgment?"

Confrontational. Defensive. Not like her at all. "Of course, you can. No judgment here."

Jade softened visibly, though her cheeks remained flushed. "Sorry. It's been a long week. Month, actually."

No one said anything for a moment because words weren't needed. Jill got up and moved around the island, pulling her sister in for a quick hug. Something they rarely did, both preferring dialog over physical intimacy.

As she held her sister close, her thoughts spun back to that day, not long ago. The frantic call from Jade had almost stopped Jill's heart. *Something's wrong with the baby! I'm bleeding. A lot. And it hurts so much!*

And later, crawling up into Jade's hospital bed, holding her while she sobbed. Daniel, Jade's husband, sitting in a nearby chair, head in his hands, uncharacteristically silent.

Jade's voice brought her back to the present. She'd momentarily put her head on Jill's shoulder, then straightened up, brushing away a tear. "I'm okay. I'm good." She went back to chopping vegetables, adding them to the salad bowl nearby. "Other people, however, as you know, *doctor,* aren't doing as well. Any good stories you can share, some trainwrecks you're healing?" She chopped a bit faster. "Actually, forget my lame attempt at humor. I do have something I want to ask you."

"You know I can't talk about my patients, even if I don't use their names."

"I know, I know. Um, I wondered, from your *expertise,*" she said, exaggerating the word a bit, "do people in your field think it's best to tell someone about an affair or not? I mean, if you knew a friend was being cheated on, would you tell her? Or him? Or would you advise one of your patients to do that?" Jade's eyes were focused on the cutting board, but she raised them briefly to Jill's. Then quickly dropped them again.

How could she have overlooked this? Jade had asked almost the same question a few weeks earlier, but their conversation had ended abruptly. With the murder case and all that had happened with it, including her own brief hospitalization, she'd completely forgotten to take up that thread with her sister. "What's going on here? Hey, Sis, look at me. Is there something wrong?"

Jade laid down the knife, picked up her glass of wine, and took more than a sip. "Nothing. It's a friend of mine, someone who's going through a tough time in her marriage." Still no eye contact. Jade moved to the refrigerator, opened it, and searched for something. *Classic evasion behavior.* When telling a lie and not being someone who lies well, the default is to avoid eye contact and engage in distracting behavior.

Jade wasn't a liar. She didn't have a habit of dissembling. She was pretty much an open book. And typically, she was sunny and positive, but today, Jill saw the signs of something entirely different. "A friend?" she asked slowly.

"Yes. Someone I met at the studio." Jade shared a studio with several artists who met regularly to work and socialize. "She's married to someone who... well, she says he works all the time, and it's getting worse. She complains about how much time he's away, that she hardly ever sees him. But my question is about telling someone. I... saw something I wasn't supposed to see. It was her husband, and he was with someone else. Another woman." She looked up at Jill at that point. "I don't know what to do."

Maybe it *was* a friend, after all. "Did you recognize the woman? Are you sure it was someone he was cheating with, not a business associate, a friend, a family member?"

"I'm sure," Jade said. "He was holding her hand, acting in a very intimate way. This woman and I have grown close. I don't feel right keeping it to myself, the fact that her husband is cheating, but I also don't want to break up a marriage." She poured salad dressing over the vegetables and tossed everything together, then set out two plates. They served themselves and began eating.

"Well, you have a couple of choices. One, you tell her. But then what if she doesn't believe you? Denial can be a powerful force. Also, there are people who would rather not know their partner is cheating on them. They would prefer to remain in the dark and wait for the affair to fall apart. Someone like that will resent you for shining a bright light on their family dysfunction." She'd had clients like that, usually women, but sometimes men. *Better to avoid confrontation, hope for the best, and bank on the fact that you're the one to whom the cheater returned each day.*

She briefly thought of Tim, her client from earlier in the day.

25

Did his wife know about the affair? Was she in denial, hoping it wasn't real, a passing fling?

She continued with Jade, watching her face as she spoke. "Two, you don't tell her, stay out of their business, and hope it works out for them. But what if she finds out later you knew but didn't tell her? That can create resentment, too."

"So, what you're telling me is I'm going to lose either way. She'll hate me if I tell her, and she'll hate me if I don't." Jade put down her fork and took a large gulp of wine.

Jill spoke gently. "I don't think this is really about a friend. We're talking about you, aren't we?" She waited a moment, having pushed in a way that could easily backfire. "Is Daniel cheating on you?"

Jade's husband, Dr. Daniel Webber, was a renowned surgeon. Jill enjoyed being around him. He was smart, well-spoken, and while he was a bit arrogant, their conversations were always stimulating. He piqued her curiosity and challenged her. Of course, he often reminded her that she wasn't a *real* doctor. Only a *psychologist*, and like many medical professionals she'd encountered in her career, he clearly viewed her field as though it sat on the level of tarot card readers and psychics. As long as they kept the wine flowing, it was mostly good-natured.

Jade shook her head. "No. Absolutely not. This is a friend. I thought you could help me figure out what to do, but now you're creating ridiculous theories. Just forget I brought it up." She stood, went around the island, and began cleaning up. This time, when she picked up her wine glass, her hand shook slightly.

"Jade, I'm so sorry. I didn't mean anything by it—"

"Yes, you did. You always know better than anyone else, especially when it comes to me and my life. You think you can tell me how I feel, what's going on with me. *What I should or shouldn't do.* You never really liked Daniel, anyway." She set down the wine glass just a little too hard, and silence filled the space between them.

Jill was at a loss for words.

Carly stomped into the room, saving them both from the awkwardness that had crept into the room. "Mommy! Let's go. I want some chicken nuggets. You promised if I went to the museum, we could get chicken nuggets. And tater tots, too."

Jade turned to her daughter with an indulgent smile. "Yes, I did. Go get your sweater and say goodbye to your aunt!" she called after her. But Carly, motivated by chicken nuggets, was already down the hallway, moving at warp speed.

"It's okay. I better go, anyway. I have patients this afternoon." Jill rose, crossed the space between them, and hugged her sister briefly. Whatever had just happened would be sorted out later. There'd never been anything that had remained between them for any length of time.

It was an unwritten rule of law that had existed since they were little girls. Ever since the day they'd been reunited after the only real separation they'd ever endured.

It was only later, as Jill sat back after reading her notes for her upcoming client's last session, that she remembered Carly's odd statement. *I like it better when it's just Mommy and me.*

Had her sister been meeting someone at the museum? With her daughter in tow?

But Jade was an open book. Artistic and free-spirited, with a healthy dash of common sense. Never secretive.

So, she shrugged it off.

CHAPTER FOUR

"What are we doing here, Roxanne?" Jill shut off the engine and turned to her former client. "I don't think it's right to just barrel in there with theories that may be entirely untrue. She just lost her husband."

Jill's workday was over, and she wanted to be home now, curled up with a good book and a glass of wine. That thought brought Jade back to mind and their lunch earlier in the day, along with lingering feelings of regret. And confusion about their conversation.

Jill hadn't yet obtained any results from Nick. Moving forward without that felt slightly uncomfortable, but Roxanne had insisted, and that tugged at her desire to be helpful. Plus, she had the luxury of time now. Tomorrow was a full day in her practice.

Roxanne took her hand off the door. "You're right. We need a game plan. I'm certain the death certificate is going to say Cory died from drowning. Maybe that's true, but I'm not sure."

"If not that, what do you think killed him?"

"I don't know. I just know something's not right about this.

He was young, his whole life ahead of him. Sure, he was a jerk at times, but still..." She stopped, lost in thought and remembrances.

"How well did you know Cory?" Jill asked.

"Not that well. Not personally at all, really."

Odd. Normally, when someone became concerned about the death of another person, it was because their relationship was close enough to warrant the concern. But sometimes people meddled in others' lives for reasons other than a bond between them.

"So, what is the 'game plan'?" Jill asked.

"I want one thing. I want to convince Erica, Cory's wife, to have an autopsy done." She turned her blue eyes on Jill. "I want you to use your super-shrink powers to help me do that."

Jill sighed. "Roxanne, I don't think it's ethical for me to try to push her into anything. That's not what I do—"

"You don't? Weren't you the one who manipulated me into recovery by bringing up my daughters?" Roxanne pointed out. But her mouth curved upward.

"Good point. And I stand by my therapeutic methodologies. Especially if they work."

Now they smiled at each other, and something unexpected passed between them. A certain kinship and wave of warmth. They were two professional women with demanding lives. They were around the same age. Roxanne was a former client, but only for two sessions. *Could she be a future friend?*

They exited the car.

Jill decided to let the encounter with Cory's wife unfold organically. But within limits. First, there would be compassion, and second, there would be a quick exit if the grieving widow wasn't up for the conversation.

After pushing the smart doorbell, they waited, but not for

long. They heard someone approach the door. There was a pause, and then, it opened slowly. A man in a tee shirt and shredded jeans, maybe mid-forties, short hair sticking up as though he'd just run his fingers through it, and feet bare, stood there. "Can I help you?" he asked tentatively.

A voice called from nearby. "Travis? Let me get the door, honey." And now they faced Cory Holloman's widow. Her ash blond hair was pulled back, and she was dressed casually in gray sweatpants that hung loosely on her frame, no makeup.

"Roxanne? What are you doing here?" She looked puzzled and spacey. *Was she drugged?* If so, likely a benzodiazepine, a prescription sedative often given to people when facing a severe personal crisis.

"Erica, I'm sorry to come by without calling, but it's important. Can we come in?"

She nodded and opened the door wider. "Yes, but only for a little bit. I was resting."

As they made their way into the house, the man called Travis slipped away without a word. Erica said nothing to him as he went, and he said nothing to her.

"Can I get you something?" she asked, her words a bit slow and her eyes slightly unfocused.

"No, that's not necessary," Jill said. "I'm Jill Rhodes, and I'm here with Roxanne as a sort of consultant. We're so grateful for your time, and we won't take long." She gave Roxanne a pointed look behind Erica's back. Roxanne gave her a stubborn look in return.

They sat in a living room that was light and bright, nicely decorated. But there was a vague sense of shadows, an emotional residue, perhaps, hanging in the air. Jill shook it off and focused on Erica.

"What can I do for you?" Erica asked, wearily tucking a stray lock of hair behind her ear. Her manners perhaps dictated that she should offer to be helpful despite her own deficits at the moment. This was Dallas, Texas, after all, a city full of people who largely prided themselves on friendliness, helpfulness, and being of service.

"Erica, I'm so sorry for your loss. How are you holding up?" Roxanne asked, pausing momentarily. "The funeral is in a couple of days, right?"

"I'm okay so far. Yes, it's on Friday." Erica's eyes began to fill. "You're going to be there, aren't you? I was hoping you might say a few words about Cory since you worked together." She let the tears fall, not bothering to wipe them away.

"I will. You can count on me," Roxanne told her, touching her hand briefly. "Look, Erica, this is awkward, but the reason we're here is because I feel like there's something wrong with how Cory died."

"Something wrong? What are you talking about? Of course, it's wrong. He was way too young to die. I never thought... I got home and went to sleep, and I didn't know he was already there, just... He often went out with friends. I didn't give it another thought... But he didn't that night. He... *I don't know what he did.* I don't know how this happened. I can't believe I was at a *spa* while my husband was drowning!" Her guilt and self-blame now on full display. "Oh, God." She broke down, sobbing.

This was a mistake. Jill turned to Roxanne and spoke softly but firmly. "I think we should go."

But Roxanne had that stubborn look on her face. Ignoring Jill, she spoke to Erica. "Again, I'm so sorry for your loss, Erica. But there's something you may have forgotten. Or maybe Cory didn't ever think to tell you. *He was a competitive swimmer in*

31

college. It makes no sense at all that he would go for a midnight swim in his own pool, which I'm sure he used regularly. And somehow *drown*."

Jill's eyes snapped to Roxanne's. *A competitive swimmer?* Why hadn't that come up in their initial conversation?

Erica looked up, tears still streaming. "What did you say? A *competitive* swimmer? He never told me... of course, he used the pool. Pretty much every day. He said he needed the exercise, and he liked the water, so he usually got up early and swam for about a half hour. But he never told me he was competitive..." Shock registered on her face. "And how...exactly... did you know this?"

"Bragging rights," said Roxanne reluctantly. "A bunch of us attorneys were at the bar one night having a little fun, and some of the guys started talking about high school and college sports. It was one-upmanship, and Cory made sure we knew how many swimming medals he'd won, along with the fact that he got an athletic scholarship. But then he developed asthma, probably caused by excess chlorine exposure, and had to stop swimming competitively."

"We have a saltwater pool. He insisted on it, but he never told me why."

Roxanne and Jill sat quietly, letting her absorb all the new information.

"I don't know why I didn't think of it sooner. I didn't know he was competitive, but I knew he swam in the pool daily and that he was a good enough swimmer. Why didn't I question it?" Now, her self-blame had new ammunition. "What kind of wife finds her husband drowned and just takes it for granted it was an accident?"

Jill stepped in. "No one ever wants to think someone they love was deliberately harmed in some way. You did what most people would do. You called the police. They, and the medical examiner, drew their own conclusions." Which gave her the mental note to follow up with Nick later about the death certificate.

"But what should I do?" Erica asked them.

Roxanne was ready. "I think the next step is to get an autopsy done. Maybe I'm wrong. Maybe something happened that caused him to drown completely by accident. But I keep having this sense that it's more."

"An autopsy? But the funeral is coming up, and he… isn't it too late for that? He's already at the funeral home. I sent his best suit…"

"Good point," Jill said to Roxanne. "If he's been embalmed, I don't think they can do an autopsy."

"I think they can," Roxanne said. "I worked on a case once where the family pushed for an autopsy on their elderly father after he was already embalmed. The medical examiner had ruled it natural causes because he was old. They didn't want to believe it because he'd seemed so healthy, but it turned out to be true, unfortunately. All that working out and healthy eating hadn't prevented him from a heart attack." She shook her head a bit. "Anyway, I believe we can get it done for Cory. With your consent."

Erica wiped her eyes on a sweatshirt sleeve. "Yes, of course. I dread finding out, but then again, I can't stop thinking about him drowning, and if it was something else, maybe a heart attack or something else…" Her voice trailed off.

But there would be no escape from the guilt. The only thing worse than losing a partner was the slim possibility that you might have prevented it but weren't there to do it.

Roxanne and Jill rose and promised to follow up with Erica, conveying their condolences once more. At the door, Jill paused.

"Erica, I'm curious. Who is the guy that let us in the door?" It was intrusive and she knew it, but she couldn't stop herself.

Erica smiled sadly. "That's Travis, Cory's brother. He...needs help, and since their parents are both deceased and now Cory is gone... all he has is me. I'm not sure what I'm going to do."

"Was he here while you were away that night?" Roxanne asked.

"Yes. I think so. But I'm a bit tired, so if you'll excuse me—" She gently closed the door before they could ask anything further.

As they drove away, Jill reflected. *Special needs?* Travis looked perfectly healthy, but she knew looks could be deceiving. The body can be intact while hiding a psychological interior that doesn't adequately provide for coping well with life.

CHAPTER FIVE

DAY TWO

Lauren knocked on Jill's partially open door. Jill had just finished her case notes for the morning and was thinking about calling Jade for dinner later. Ethan, her maybe fiancé, was planning on going out with business associates for the evening. Again. She found her own apathy about that a bit disturbing, but she wasn't willing to take a deeper look at what that might mean.

"Hey," Lauren said. "It's that hot detective. Nick, something." She arched her eyebrow and fanned herself.

"Show him in," Jill instructed, ignoring the innuendos.

"Check that. But later, you owe me some juicy updates."

"There won't be any—" but Lauren was gone, and in her place stood Detective Nick Webb. She felt her neck begin to flush, so she turned, tucking files away and praying for the rosy color to abate. "Nick. Thanks for coming by."

He tucked his long form into one of the chairs in front of her desk and smiled. "Glad to. I think you got the death certificate

35

for Cory Holloman I sent over by email. As you thought, his death certificate says he died of natural causes, drowning. But I did a little more checking. First, I found out the initial ruling was done by a coroner. It was the middle of the night, so that was who was on duty."

"What does that mean? For the ruling," she asked.

"A coroner isn't the same as a medical examiner and may not be medically trained. Most likely, he did a cursory investigation and drew a quick conclusion, which leads me to the other thing. I talked to one of the cops who took the 9-1-1 call and showed up on the scene." He rubbed his chin. "From what I heard, the wife told the cops Cory drank and imbibed various legal and illegal substances on a regular basis. He quoted her as saying, 'I'm not surprised,' or words to that effect. He also mentioned she didn't seem particularly broken up over her husband's death."

Jill frowned. "That can't be right." Jill frowned. "We saw her just yesterday, and she was distraught."

Nick shrugged. "Just repeating what the cop told me. It could be his faulty impression. He's a rookie and maybe not yet that great at reading people. Also, I asked if he wrote down that quote on the spot or if he wrote it later from memory. It was the latter." His gray-green eyes studied her. "What are you doing involved in this, anyway?"

She bristled a bit. "That's between me and my client. But I can tell you she thinks there's something not right about death by drowning. Cory was a champion swimmer in high school, so much so he was awarded an athletic scholarship. But later had to stop swimming due to health issues. Anyway, my client has convinced Cory's widow to get an autopsy done."

"An autopsy? Interesting," he said. "What does your... *client*... think it will reveal?"

"That's a question for her. I can't say any more at this point. But thanks for doing the extra legwork." She stood, prompting him to rise with her. He paused.

"Um, Jill. Want to grab a drink sometime?"

Jill froze. Multiple conflicting inner voices momentarily stole her ability to respond. Then she collected herself. "Thanks for the offer, but evenings, I'm usually with my fiancé, Ethan." She couldn't bring herself to look him directly in the eye for reasons she didn't quite understand.

"I see," he said carefully.

She looked up. "You do?"

He continued gazing into her eyes, and something about the way he watched her created a softening of her bones. She said nothing for a moment, allowing the sensation to slowly ebb away. "What do you see?"

He didn't hesitate. "I see a beautiful, intelligent woman who isn't sure about the guy she's with. But she's loyal to a fault and won't let herself think about that. 'No' on the drink means she has boundaries, doesn't allow herself to do anything that could be deemed inappropriate or disloyal."

She felt mildly gut-punched. Her mind and heart wrestled with Nick's words, rejecting them as soon as she considered them. Outraged at them while they easily settled into her system. She knew she'd consider his words for a long time, turning them over and over, searching for how much truth had just been laid bare.

She'd unwittingly invited this man to see her in a way she allowed very few people to do, and it shook her. *Intimacy*. Or, as her mentor had taught her, '*into-me-see*.' This was why she rarely invited others in. A mistake in this case, for sure. "You don't really know me," she said softly.

"Not yet," he said, smiling as he turned to go.

Jill's phone vibrated with an incoming text, and she grabbed it gratefully, stabbing at the screen. "Sorry, I have to get this," she said, not even looking up at Nick.

"Sure," he said as he strolled to the door, but she called him back.

"Wait!"

He turned, curiosity raising his brows. And maybe something else.

"I just got a text from Roxanne, my client," she said, then hit herself in the forehead. "Can't believe I just said her name."

"Cone of silence," Nick assured her. "What is it?"

"The autopsy results came back, along with a toxicology report. It looks like Cory was poisoned before he drowned. The revised medical examiner's report now says the ruling is no longer natural causes and is still under investigation." She turned to her laptop and opened her email. "She's sending the full report over now." After a moment, she motioned to Nick.

Together, they read the new report from the office of the Medical Examiner, scanning to get to the conclusions.

Following a comprehensive investigation and autopsy, it has been determined that the cause of death in this case was a combination of drowning in a swimming pool and selenium poisoning.

The subject was discovered submerged in a swimming pool, and the initial assessment suggested that drowning was the sole cause of death. The lungs were filled with water, confirming that the subject was alive when he went into the pool and subsequently drowned.

However, further analysis and examination revealed high

levels of selenium in the subject's bloodstream, indicating selenium poisoning as a contributing and/or causal factor.

Selenium, when ingested in high doses, causes a variety of effects. The subject may have experienced severe gastrointestinal upset, with cramping and abdominal pain. The subject may have experienced neurological symptoms such as dizziness, tremors, or muscle twitching. The subject may have experienced respiratory symptoms, including difficulty breathing, coughing, and even respiratory failure. These symptoms, cumulatively, likely contributed to death by drowning.

It is currently unclear how the subject was exposed to selenium. However, it is possible that the subject accidentally or deliberately ingested or inhaled the substance before entering the swimming pool, which could have contributed to his inability to swim and ultimately led to drowning.

In conclusion, the cause of death in this case was a combination of drowning in a swimming pool and selenium poisoning. The exact circumstances surrounding the subject's exposure to selenium are unknown, and the case is still under investigation.

Jill turned to Nick, her eyes wide. "*He was poisoned.* Roxanne was right. This was no accident."

Nick straightened slowly. "Why do I get a funny feeling hearing you say that? You do know you're not a homicide detective, right? Let's review. The last time you got involved in a suspicious death—a murder—you almost got yourself killed. Oh, and let's review further. Someone in this room actually *is* a homicide detective. Oh, wait. That's me." He gave her a hard stare. "I think you should leave this alone."

His words landed with the weight of truth even as her defenses rose. "Let's review one more thing, Detective Webb. This woman has retained me to help her, and I'm not going to abandon her." She cringed inside. Roxanne was a colleague of Cory's, not the grieving widow. But Jill wasn't ready to let this go. "I never said I was going to do any investigating, anyway. I'm a psychologist. I help people deal with difficult issues, and that's what I'm going to do for Roxanne."

"As long as that's where it ends," he said.

Oddly, his tone didn't completely offend her. It was paternal, no doubt. A bit controlling, yes. But it was also strangely filled with something that felt like genuine concern.

"Whatever I do, it's at my own discretion," she said with finality.

"*So stubborn.* I'm never going to win an argument with you, am I?"

And the implication landed somewhere in her solar plexus, rather pleasantly, to her great surprise. *They'd have more discussions in the future.* Okay, maybe arguments.

But the fact remained, he planned on being in her life in some way.

CHAPTER SIX

Nick Webb and Rick Stone stood outside the door of the apartment. The doorbell had proven useless, and after pushing it several times, Stone banged on the door. The door frame's paint was chipped, and the stairwell they'd climbed was strewn with dead leaves and bits of trash. "Nice place," Stone observed as they walked up earlier. "Guess he's not doing very well with his *business.*"

"Still too low in the pecking order," Nick said.

They heard a baby cry inside and shared a look. Stone said, "Huh."

The door slowly opened. A girl with blonde hair streaked blue and green stood there. Her eyes held a hint of fear. She propped an infant on one hip, holding a pacifier in her other hand. The baby's eyes dripped with tears. The baby girl, judging by the pink outfit she wore, shoved her two middle fingers in her mouth and tucked her face into her mother's shoulder.

Nick spoke. "Destiny Soto?" At her nod, he continued. "I'm Detective Nick Webb, and this is my partner, Detective Rick Stone. Is your boyfriend home? Darius King." Everything would change if they'd misjudged BTK's current whereabouts. They'd watched him enter his favorite seedy bar in Deep Ellum, where they'd seen him spend hours every afternoon for the last three days.

"No. What is this about? Did something happen to him?" She spoke with the kind of acceptance that pointed to the inevitability of knowing that someone at some point would show up on her doorstep to inform her of his untimely, but almost certainly violent, death.

The two detectives looked at each other. "Not that we know of, ma'am. But he has been implicated in a serious crime. I'm afraid we'll have to come in and take a look around," said Nick.

She shoved hair out of her eyes. "Wait. You can't come in here unless I let you in, right?" She began closing the door.

Nick pulled out the search warrant and stuck it through the rapidly closing door opening. "We have a search warrant. You don't have a choice but to let us in."

She grabbed the warrant and stared at it, eyes widening as she scanned it. She raised her eyes to theirs. "Please don't scare the baby." She opened the door and let them in. She placed her daughter inside a playpen on the floor, tucking a blanket over the now sleeping form.

"I'll take the bedroom," Rick told his partner. He headed to the hallway off of the tiny living room.

Nick searched the living room, turning over sofa cushions, opening cabinet drawers. He moved to the kitchen and continued. After a few minutes, he stood still in frustration. *Might as well take a chance.* Moving back into the tiny living room, where BTK's girlfriend Destiny stood, he approached her. "Listen. We're looking for a weapon. If you help us find it, it will go a long way to maybe keeping you from being charged as an accessory." He winced inside. Technically, they had no reason to believe the girlfriend had had anything to do with the murder.

Her eyes widened. "What? Wait. I don't know what you're talking about. I don't know anything about any *weapon*..."

He pinned her with a look. "Right now, you have a chance to avoid prison and take care of your baby. But if they charge you, they'll put the baby in foster care." He turned as if to walk away. "Hey Stone! Let's get back-up and tear this place apart."

"Wait! No, please don't." Her eyes darted around the room. Nick watched where her eyes went and, more specifically, where they didn't go. If you knew there was something incriminating around, and you were afraid the person in front of you might find it to your detriment, your mind couldn't help but think about it. *What it was. Where it was. How close to it the person stood.* To compensate, the guilty party would purposely avoid looking at the location of the contraband.

And she was desperately avoiding the kitchen area. "I wonder what's in the freezer?" Nick said, moving toward the tiny galley kitchen.

"Nothing!

Bingo!

"But I might know where he keeps his... his gun," she said desperately.

Nick registered her dead giveaway. *Drugs, most likely, probably in the freezer.* But he wasn't here for that. "Okay. I'll bite. Even though you just told me you don't know anything about it."

"You have to promise me that's it. I'll give you the gun, and you'll leave. Promise?"

Nick sighed. "I can't promise you anything after this, but yes, right now, we'll take the gun and leave."

She weighed her options. "Okay," she relented. Walking over

to a baby stroller, she turned it on its side. Taped on the underside was a gun. From where Nick stood, it appeared to be a 9mm, most likely a Glock or Beretta. Just what they were hoping to find.

She reached out her hand, but Nick stopped her.

"No, don't touch it!" he cautioned. "Stone. I've got it," he called to his partner. Just as he bent to pick it up, the front door flew open.

"What the fuck?! Hey, man, what are you doin' here with my girl?" BTK, wearing a bright red cap turned backward and a yellow tee shirt, stood glaring, his heavily tattooed hand reaching for something.

This was a recipe for disaster. "Police! Freeze, asshole," Stone said, rushing into the room, pulling his service weapon, and pointing it at BTK.

But BTK's hand was empty as he brought it around and began raising it. *Must have left it in his vehicle*, thought Nick.

"Drop it!" squeaked Destiny. *Oh shit*, thought Nick as he turned. In the melee, he'd forgotten to secure the gun. And now she stood holding it shakily, pointing it at Nick's partner.

There was little worse than a person unfamiliar with a weapon aiming it at another person, adrenaline surging through the body, a toxic combination of panic and possibly anger. Even if not intending to do harm, a terrified person could easily fire the weapon.

Nick and his partner exchanged a brief look.

Stone held up his other hand placatingly. "Now, now. No need for that. I'm gonna put it down, nice and slow." He began slowly lowering his gun hand while continuing to speak softly to Destiny. "Just like this, see? I'm gonna put it on the floor, very carefully, because we don't want it to accidentally discharge. The baby is right over there, and we don't want her to get hurt, do we?" He carefully turned his head and slid his eyes over to the baby, who now stirred restlessly and began making whimpering sounds.

She couldn't help herself. Destiny's eyes followed Stone's glance. "It's okay, baby. Mama's here," she cooed, but you could hear the panic in her voice. Her eyes darted back and forth between the baby and Stone. But the strain of trying to look fierce to Rick Stone while also soothing her now crying baby was too much. Her arms began lowering the weapon.

Nick had been watching BTK edge back toward the door. But first things first. While Destiny remained distracted, he stepped up calmly behind her, reached around, and took the barrel of the gun in his right hand, twisting it sharply. She yelped in pain and released the gun. Nick quickly checked the safety, which was still on. He pocketed the weapon, turning back toward BTK. "Darius—" But he was gone.

"I've got the girl, go," Rick said.

While Stone subdued Destiny, Nick went after BTK. He stood on the landing for a brief moment, scanning the area. It didn't take him long before he spotted a flash of yellow and red hitting the bottom landing of the stairs and bolting to the right of the building. He took off running after BTK, cursing his loafers.

As he hit the building corner, Nick looked for him again. Another flash of yellow ahead around another corner. Every time he thought he was about to catch up, BTK gained another ten yards on him, twisting and turning through the neighborhood of apartment buildings. Home turf advantage.

Nick flew around yet another corner, into an alleyway between buildings, and saw nothing. There was no flash of yellow or red. No sign of BTK. Not even a sound in the distance of shoes hitting the pavement. Frustrated, he stopped and huffed, trying to get his breath back.

Resigned, he turned to go back and froze. At the mouth of the alleyway stood BTK and two others, both of whom wore athletic jerseys and towered over BTK as well as Nick.

"And what do we have here?" Sneered BTK. He sauntered toward Nick, his friends acting as his back-up, and as he did, he pulled a switchblade and popped it open. "What exactly were you doin' in *my* place, with *my* woman and *my* baby? First off, throw me that gun you stole from me."

"You are making a huge mistake," Nick said evenly, knowing his own mistake. He'd pursued a violent suspect with no back-up. He slowly drew BTK's gun from his pocket and dropped it on the ground near his own feet.

"Kick it over here, asshole!" shouted BTK.

Nick kicked it behind himself, far away from BTK.

Darius let loose with more obscenities. "You gonna pay for that, asshole!" He crouched and began waving the knife back and forth in front of himself as he slowly advanced.

Nick spread his hands. "Darius, you know I'm a cop." This wasn't their first run-in. "If you don't drop that weapon and back off, you won't see the inside of that apartment or your little family for a very long time," he said firmly.

The other two men exchanged worried glances. Nick could see a vague family resemblance to BTK. Most likely, they were his relatives. Cousins, maybe. Not gang members.

He stared at the one on the left of BTK. "You two don't want to be mixed up in trouble with Darius. You think you're doing him a solid, but what you're really doing is getting ready to occupy a prison cell next to his. Is that what you want?"

The two guys glanced at each other, swapping a silent message. "Yo, Darius. We don't want no trouble from the cops."

But BTK stood his ground, and at that, his two 'friends' backed up and slipped away, leaving him on his own. A string of obscenities flew out of his mouth, and he spit on the ground. When he looked up, he faced the wrong end of Nick's service weapon.

"Drop. The. Knife."

But he flew at Nick instead, and Nick silently cursed him. He had no desire to shoot the guy. He only wanted to take him in and turn him over to narcotics after charging him with murder. They needed him as an informant first. The rival gang member he'd killed was gone and not coming back. Whether or not they got justice for him was secondary, as cold as that felt.

Everything slowed down for Nick as the knife drew closer, powered by a hopped-up guy, definitely from anger, possibly from drugs, intent on doing him bodily harm. His training told him to aim for center mass and do everything in his power to completely stop the guy, even if it meant death.

But that wouldn't do.

Luckily, Nick was a good shot and didn't need to hit center mass. He lowered his weapon and fired. BTK screamed in agony and went down, the knife flying away. He writhed on the ground and grabbed his lower leg, which now spurted blood. If Nick held any sensitivity about the language being directed at him, he'd have been blown back by now. But he didn't. "Shut up," he told BTK. "You're going to live."

Nick quickly removed his tie and made a tourniquet, fighting BTK the whole time as he wrapped it around his leg and pulled it tight. But he succeeded in slowing the blood from the guy's now likely shattered tibia. He rolled BTK on his side and cuffed his hands behind his back, enduring promises for his own death and that of everyone he knew.

He stood and pulled out his cell, calling 9-1-1. Then, his partner.

Hours later, back at the station, Nick faced Captain Ed Thomas. Thomas was a strong, firm leader. He was fair and disciplined and did things most often by the book.

He ran a hand over his mostly bald head. "What the hell, Detective Webb. It was supposed to be a simple search and seizure. Now I've got a young *mother* in custody, her *kid* with family services, and it seems she isn't exactly no one. She's the daughter of a guy with lots of money. Thanks to him, she's getting out on bail, having shed no light on BTK or any of his activities or friends. Not to mention the fact that it's her word against yours and your partner's that she drew a gun. According to her attorney, she's the victim here."

Nick sighed inwardly. "I get it. But she's not my concern."

"Well, she's *my* concern. I don't need another victim-of-the-bad-cops lawsuit on my hands. She's claiming all kinds of emotional harm, PTSD, you name it. I'm told that if we don't drop this, she's going on the air tonight. Holding the baby, her dad's attorney at her side, who, by the way, is an absolute barracuda of a defense counsel in designer shoes. Crying foul, no doubt, on the entire department."

"So, drop the charges," Nick said impatiently. This whole case had blown up. BTK was laid up in the hospital following extensive surgery on his leg. He wasn't talking about anything. Getting ready to file suit against the department with his own grievances, most likely. Probably with his girlfriend's attorney.

All Nick had was a weapon he'd seized, which it turned out—no surprise—wasn't registered to Darius, and with numerous fingerprints—BTK's, Destiny's, Nick's, and who knew? His hopes of using the weapon to lean on Darius and get his cooperation were dashed. The witness who'd originally pointed the finger at BTK had been mysteriously stricken with selective amnesia and had no recollection of their prior conversation.

Nick didn't care about Destiny. Pursuing charges against her—assault on a police officer because of the brandished gun—wasn't important.

"Believe me, they will be dropped. I've already talked to the D.A., and the consensus is that she's not going to be charged. She apparently got pregnant and moved out of the family home with Darius. But she's back home now, and as long as there are no charges, life goes on. Teenage rebellion over, a grandchild to raise. Meanwhile, what is the status of the murder charge against Darius King?"

Nick de-briefed him on the case, a rapidly melting snow pile.

"Look, I don't need to tell you, this is a distraction you don't need," Captain Thomas declared. You've got other cases to get back to, so it's time to move on from BTK."

That was no surprise to Nick. He hadn't been that hot on the case from the get-go, anyway. It was essentially a favor for one of his colleagues in narcotics. Get BTK on the murder charges so they could turn him and go after his bosses.

Oh, well.

As for other cases, Nick had only a couple of them at the moment, both random shootings in bad neighborhoods. The kind that would likely never get solved. He needed something new. He needed something with some hair on it, something to get his blood rushing. Something unusual and different, a puzzle worth solving.

"Actually Captain...I do have something. It showed up on my radar recently, and I don't think anyone is actively working on it. There's this guy, a prominent attorney, who was found dead in the family home swimming pool. Coroner who showed up ruled it accidental death due to drowning. However, one of the victim's law partners pushed for an autopsy after the fact. The toxicology report came back with an inconclusive ruling, with evidence of poisoning. It was odd because the poison is actually a supplement people take. But in large quantities, it can cause death."

Stretching the truth, Nick continued. "It could be murder. His law partner believes it could be."

"His law partner," Thomas said. "Just how exactly did you get wind of this?" Captain Thomas' caterpillar eyebrows edged upward.

"Um, actually, it was someone else. Remember the psychologist who helped with the investigation of the teenage girl's murder a few weeks ago? Dr. Jill Rhodes. She asked for my... opinion... on the death certificate. And told me about the partner's suspicions."

Captain Thomas leaned back in his chair. "I don't like it, Nick. This sounds like a lot of guesswork by people who are not qualified to give any real opinion. What would you do with it? You can't just go dig around without a reason to do it. Did the medical examiner toss the case to us?" He pushed back from the desk and stood.

Nick stood as well. "I'll find out. If so, I want the case." He gave Thomas a hard look.

Thomas grimaced. "I'll give you a couple of days on it only *if* the M.E. tosses us the case. If you don't find anything substantial, then you're going back to your other cases. That's final."

Nick pivoted and left, smiling out of Thomas' view.

CHAPTER SEVEN

Jill and Roxanne were back at Cory's house. Before going in, they discussed their strategy.

"I say we go in with shock and awe. Give Erica the toxicology results, watch her reaction. Push her to tell us more about her relationship with Cory. Someone poisoned him, and maybe it was her. Or that strange-acting brother of his," Roxanne finished.

Jill thought for a moment. "I don't think that will help. She'll instantly be on the defensive and might clam up." She put her keys in her bag and turned to give Roxanne her focus. "Can you follow my lead for a few minutes? If we go in light, she may open up on her own. We could learn a lot just by giving her the space to unburden herself."

Roxanne looked like she might burst with restrained energy already. "For a few minutes, but if I see something, I'm going to say something."

That would be as good as it would get with Roxanne's unbridled, passionate nature. Maybe she should have conducted this visit on her own. Too late now, though. Then, a thought occurred to her. It might be possible to use Roxanne's passion to gain more information from Erica. It was risky but could be worth it.

A few minutes later, they sat in the Holloman living room while Erica fetched glasses of water. Sitting down, she presented a stoic expression this time, devoid of the grief she'd been awash with the last time they'd seen her. Jill decided to open with that. "How are you doing, Erica?"

Erica, looking straight ahead at nothing, answered, "I'm better. It's one day at a time, you know? Two days ago, I couldn't get out of bed. Today, I felt like cleaning out the garage. Cory kept things there, things I don't need, and it hurts to look at them. His bike, along with all his riding stuff—helmets, gloves, water bottles, knee pads. Lights, two or three fancy tachometers, things like that. He really liked to collect all that stuff, more than he could ever use. You can never have enough accessories for a hobby, I guess."

Great opening topic. "Did you ride together? Share that hobby or others?" Jill probed gently.

Erica huffed. "Me? No. I don't have an athletic bone in my body."

Switching subjects, Jill asked, "How did you and Cory meet?"

"Online. Our first date was at a bar. We closed the place down. It was an instant connection. He was my soulmate," she said, and now, her chin wobbled while she swiped at her eyes. "We were inseparable."

"How long did you date before you got married?"

"Six months. His mom was rather shocked," she added, and her eyes shone a bit. "She's a Park Cities lady all the way. Cory was supposed to get married at the Presbyterian Church, huge wedding, reception at the country club. But we didn't want all that."

Jill's eyes strayed to Erica's left hand, where an extremely large diamond sat. Three or four carats, easy.

Erica caught her staring. "Cory was very sweet about the proposal and felt the need to give me a ring that, for me, was a bit too much." She fingered it. "But since it was so romantic, I—" She stopped and sniffled.

"And your wedding?" Jill asked.

"We eloped. Went to Vegas. We both wanted the spontaneity of it. The little wedding chapel, making up our vows on the spot." Her eyes strayed as she re-lived the moment. "We always said we would throw a big party later, but—" She stopped, her eyes clouded.

Out of the corner of her eye, Jill saw Cory's brother. He'd already slipped past them, probably heading for the kitchen. "Is that Travis? How's he doing?"

"He's grieving in his own way."

Roxanne spoke up. "Let's ask Travis in for this next part, Erica. We do have some news to share with you about the autopsy."

Jill flinched inwardly. Now that the bomb was dropped, she'd have to move to her other strategy.

"I don't know. It's better if I handle it with him. He can be a little... unpredictable." Erica spoke firmly.

Jill noted a rise in tension. Maybe that was okay for now. "I'm afraid we can't tell you without Cory's brother in the room. It's necessary for his next of kin to be here, if available. And he is."

Erica turned her eyes to Jill, who wondered. *Was that doubt? Fear? Hostility?* "You can tell me whatever it is. I'm taking care of Travis, and I know what's best for him," Erica said.

But Travis walked into the room at that moment, curiosity etching his features. "Is it something about Cory? I want to hear it, too." He lingered near the doorway with uncertainty despite his words.

"It's okay, Travis. You don't have to be here, and I can tell you all about it later," Erica said soothingly. But she couldn't hide the underlying tension. It laced her voice and was reflected in her hunched shoulders, the whiteness of her knuckles as she fisted her hands in her lap.

Travis and Erica locked eyes, and something passed between them. He appeared to wobble, to hesitate.

Why would he hesitate to come into the room like that? Was he afraid of Erica?

The doorbell rang and everyone started just a bit.

Erica rose to answer it, and Travis took the opportunity to slip away again. Roxanne rose and followed him out of the room, stating a need to use the powder room.

A thin cover story, thought Jill. But that thought vanished as she caught the eye of the person Erica now escorted into the living room. *Nick.*

"Dr. Rhodes," he said. "What are you doing here?" His grey-green eyes pierced her.

"Detective Webb," she answered, rising. "I could ask you the same thing."

Erica stood looking puzzled. "You two know each other?"

"Yes," they answered simultaneously as they continued to stare at each other.

"Well, let's sit down and figure out why you're both here." Erica had broken the moment, so they all sat.

"Detective Webb called earlier and said he had something to share about Cory and the autopsy. Before he could get here, you two showed up," Erica explained. "Now, someone needs to tell me what this is about."

Jill chose to hold her silence while Nick explained the results of the revised Coroner's report on Cory's death.

Erica's face paled. "But that's impossible. He *drowned*. That's what they told me. I found him in the *pool*." She sounded desperate.

"He did, or at least, according to the coroner, he did. But since he was poisoned, it's difficult to determine if it was the selenium or some combination of that plus drowning that led to his death. But at the levels they found, it's clear the selenium was deadly to him. That leaves only two choices: one, he deliberately ingested it. Two, someone administered it to him." Nick stopped at that point.

"No. There's no way he would kill himself. He had me. We had a good life together. We were *happy*. At least, most of the time, we were." Her eyes slid away just a bit.

Jill jumped in. "Most of the time?"

Erica fidgeted. "Every couple has issues. *People* have issues," she amended. Erica looked up at Roxanne as she re-entered the room and took a seat. "You know what I mean, right?"

"Wait. What are we talking about?"

Jill updated her quickly, made a quick introduction between Nick and Roxanne, then directed her question at both women. "What kind of issues did Cory have?"

Erica looked pointedly at Roxanne, who sighed. "Cory had a problem with alcohol," she said.

Erica said nothing.

Roxanne said nothing more.

Nick's eyes narrowed. "What kind of a drinking problem, and what does that have to do with his death?"

Roxanne looked at Erica again.

"I don't know. But we were working things out on that... issue.

It's just that he'd started up again lately after making another effort to stop. It's like something was on his mind, something he was stressed out about. More than the usual stress of work, of his caseload." Erica looked back at Roxanne.

Roxanne shrugged. "I don't really know a lot about his caseload. We weren't working together that much."

Nick looked exasperated. "All that aside, I have more questions." He turned to Erica and spoke bluntly, usurping Jill's plan for shock and awe. "Just how bad were the issues between you and your husband, Mrs. Holloman? It obviously angered you that he drank so much. What else were you fighting about?"

It was the standard assumptive question, designed to throw the person off balance, get them to say things from an emotionally triggered state. Nick had Erica in his crosshairs, but Jill wasn't at all convinced.

"We weren't fighting!" Erica's nostrils flared. "Yes, he was drinking again, but no, we weren't fighting about it. And there weren't any other issues, no more than any married couple—"

Quickly, before she had a chance to reset, Nick continued, "Tell me about your financial situation."

Erica glared at Nick. "I don't have to answer any more questions, especially about our *finances*. I think it's time for all of you to leave," she said, rising.

Jill intervened. "Let's all calm down. Erica, I think we just want to figure out who would want to hurt your husband. Why someone would poison him. I know you want those answers, too. We're not here to point the finger at you. But you know him better than anyone. Could we just ask a few more questions? Then we'll leave."

Erica's chest rose and fell quickly, but she sat back down. "What do you want to know?"

"Who would want to hurt Cory? Can you think of anyone who was angry with him?"

Erica shook her head at first. "No. He only had a few friends, but as far as I knew, no one I would call an enemy." But then she looked up sharply. "Wait. He told me a few weeks ago that one of his cases had... I think he used the word 'resurrected.' I thought that was odd, but he wouldn't say much more." She rolled her eyes. "Attorney/ client privilege and all that."

Roxanne leaned in. "Erica, can you remember anything else Cory said about the case? Anything at all could be helpful."

"Not really. Except... he said, 'I probably deserve whatever happens.' I thought he was being his usual dramatic self. You know, his courtroom persona. He used to practice his opening and closing remarks in the bathroom mirror, and he sounded like he was onstage." She looked prideful. "He was really good, wasn't he?" she said almost wistfully.

Nick took over. "Mrs. Holloman, one more question. If someone—a former client, for instance—wanted to hurt Cory, how would they manage to poison him? It had to have been ingested here." His skepticism was clear to Jill, but she noted that he restrained it, perhaps to avoid setting off Erica all over again.

"I don't know how. We're here all the time when people are around. It's not like someone could break into our home and somehow poison my husband, and we wouldn't know it. That's crazy."

"How about Travis? Does he invite people over? If someone showed up and you and Cory weren't here, would he let them in?" Nick asked.

"He wouldn't do that." She looked firm. Or was it defensive?

"Doesn't he live here?" Nick asked.

"Yes, but it was supposed to be temporary. He understood

NINA ATWOOD

it wasn't his house, so he wouldn't bring people here. We were in the process of finding a small condo nearby so we could look after him. Now..." She looked away.

"What about a housekeeper?" Nick asked.

"No. She cleans on Saturday mornings, and we're almost always here. Besides, she adored Cory. She was his family's housekeeper, was with them for many years. Before his mother passed away. She came to work for us after that."

Nick continued along the same line of inquiry but drew blanks. "Ms. Holloman, my team will have to look through your home and try to find the source of the delivery of the poison."

Erica stiffened. "I don't see why."

Nick's eyes were blank. "It's standard procedure in a suspected homicide."

"Well, I'm not comfortable with that," she said firmly.

"You don't have a choice. You can let us do it voluntarily, or we'll bring back a search warrant. And I have to warn you, if there are any signs of evidence being removed, it won't go well."

Roxanne intervened. "It's better if you just let them do their job, Erica," she said.

Erica hesitated, then resignation registered. "Can you do it now?"

"I'd like to take a quick look around," Nick said, rising. "But I'll have to bring back the forensics team if I find anything at all that looks related to—" He didn't finish the thought and stepped out of the room.

The tension kept everyone pinned to their seats while Nick explored the house. Soon, he reappeared. "This isn't productive, so I'm going to bring back the team. For now, I'd like you to leave the refrigerator and the pantry untouched."

Finally, they all rose to leave.

"If you think of anything else meanwhile, let me know," Nick told Erica, handing her his card. His eyes strayed. "Wait. Is that a liquor cabinet?"

"Yes, but it's usually empty," said Erica. She went over to the wet bar at the other end of the living room.

As she reached down, Nick told her to stop. "Wait. Don't touch anything. Just tell us what it is."

She straightened, and now her face bore a terrified expression. "Clients sometimes gave him gifts. Even spirits, since Cory didn't want people in his work life to know he was trying to quit." She pointed at a bottle of bourbon. But she looked puzzled. "I'm not sure how it got here because he stopped bringing things like this home—too much temptation." She looked up at Nick anxiously. "Do you really think it could have poison in it?"

"Let's not jump to conclusions," Nick said. "I'll take it in for testing." He was soon gone, evidence in hand.

After Nick's departure, Jill indicated they should leave. Roxanne, though, looked unsettled. "Let's pretend he didn't bring the bottle of bourbon home. How else would it get here?"

"Could it have been delivered?" Jill asked. She sometimes sent gifts by having them drop-shipped to the person's home.

"I don't know. If it was, I would be the person to receive it since I work out of the house a lot," Erica said.

At Roxanne's urging, Erica pulled out her cell and found the front doorbell video feed. After a bit of scrolling, she found it. An overnight courier handing over a box with the Spirits logo on the side. *To Cory.*

"When was that?" Roxanne asked, and they all noted the time and date stamp.

It was the day Cory died.

CHAPTER EIGHT

DAY THREE

"First off, what are you two doing? This is an official investigation at this point. The coroner's office handed it to us this morning." Nick ran his hand over his head. "I don't mean to sound ungrateful—you raised a yellow flag, and because of that, there was an autopsy. Otherwise, we'd maybe never have known your partner was murdered. *Possibly* murdered, although that's not certain."

Yesterday's meeting at Erica's had ended with the discovery of the bourbon bottle, after which they'd gone their separate ways. Jill had slept restlessly, turning over in her head the discoveries they'd made so far. The bourbon—would it show evidence of Cory's poisoning? Travis, an unknown factor in Cory's life. Erica, grief-stricken and possibly in denial about her husband's death. *Or, his murder.*

At least she'd managed to reach Ethan and set up time together for later that day.

"The last I checked, Detective Webb, I am a free agent. As such, I can visit my colleague's widow anytime I wish. And the last I checked, there's no reason I can't talk about whatever I want. With her." Roxanne glared at Nick. "I hired Dr. Rhodes to help me with... my own issues with Cory's death. And she can do whatever she wants in that capacity."

"Ever heard of obstruction of justice?" Webb said, his eyes flashing a warning at Roxanne. "If your activities get in the way, if you do anything with evidence, or influence any witnesses to hide the truth—"

"You can stop right there, Detective Webb. I don't like being threatened." Roxanne drew another breath, clearly about to blast Nick.

Jill had had enough. "Would you two stop it? This isn't getting us anywhere. I'd like to point out just one very salient fact." She paused. Both heads turned to her expectantly.

"And—?" Roxanne said.

"We all want the same thing." She turned to Roxanne. "You want to make sure that if Cory was murdered, there is justice for him. You have your reasons for wanting that, and I'm not questioning it. I want to help you do that if I can. I admit, at first, I was skeptical, but now I'm interested in helping—for your sake and for Cory's wife. And you," she said, turning to Nick, "just want to do your job to accomplish the same thing." She sat back. "I say we work together."

Nick was first to surrender, raising her estimation of him a notch. "You're right. If Cory Holloman was murdered, I want to see justice done. I'm sure you want the same thing, Ms. Fairchild." He gave Roxanne a disarming look.

Roxanne hmphed. But she nodded. "Okay, I'm in."

"Great. Now, what have we learned so far?" Jill queried.

Nick spoke first. "We know he died from some combination of poison and drowning. Once my team gets the bourbon tested, we'll know for sure if Cory ingested the poison in his own home. But there's still a lot we don't know."

He ticked off the items on the list with his fingers. "We don't know if there's money involved that may have been a motive for his wife to kill him. We don't know if there is a past client or someone else angry enough to kill him. We don't know anything about the brother, this Travis guy. Lastly, if he was poisoned, we don't know if he did it to himself or if someone else did it to him." He sat back. "Matter of fact, we don't even know if this is really a murder case yet."

They spent the next few minutes reviewing the conversation with Erica, including the revelation that Cory had indicated that someone might do something to him and that he might deserve whatever fate awaited him.

"All of this is hearsay so far," Nick pointed out. "We don't have any outside corroboration of Erica's story about her husband. She could be pulling us by the nose. I'm going to start by looking into their finances."

"Good. I'm going to head to the office and look into some of his cases. I can think of a couple of them with some people who might be angry. Really angry, as a matter of fact."

"I can help review those cases with you," said Nick.

But Roxanne was already shaking her head vehemently. "*No.* Attorney/ client privilege applies here, detective. Absolutely not!"

"You know I can get a subpoena," Nick said.

Jill sighed as the tension rose sharply. "Hold on. How about Roxanne and I look at the files together and make an assessment first. If that's okay," she said to Roxanne, who nodded. "We can bring the most likely ones to you later once we redact things that are privileged. There should be a lot of information that's of record anyway."

"I'm comfortable with that," Roxanne said. "Dr. Rhodes can sign confidentiality waivers, and we can bring limited evidence to you, detective. I'm afraid that's the best I can do at this point."

"Can you hold off on a subpoena for a while and let us do that?" Jill asked, figuring that if Nick wanted to, he could probably get a judge to give him access to all of Cory's cases. But maybe not. "Actually, since we don't yet know if the bourbon was poisoned, there's no person of interest, right Nick?"

At his reluctant nod, she continued. "There's really no reason for you to get a subpoena at this point, right?"

Nick tilted his head begrudgingly. "Okay. I get the point. You two do your thing, and I'll do mine." He stood. "We'll talk later." With that, he made his exit.

"Gee, touchy much?" Roxanne said sarcastically.

"I think he suffers from the same disease you and I do," Jill said.

"And what is that?"

Jill shrugged. "He wants control. He feels like he's losing some of it, so he doesn't want to stick around and have that point rubbed in his face."

Roxanne smiled. "Point taken. I myself do love having control. Speaking of that, let's go. I'm anxious to find out if Cory has an old client carrying a massive grudge."

"I'll meet you at your office later," Jill said. "I have a couple of things to take care of first."

Jill strode into her office, greeting Lauren, who stopped her before she could continue to her inner sanctum.

"Wait. There's something you might want to know. You remember that client who came in a few days ago? Tim something—"

"Yes, I remember. What about him?"

"He called and wanted an appointment."

"He already has an appointment set up."

"He wanted another one, now. Today."

"I can't take him right now, but Dr. Kelly can. You know he covers my emergencies when I can't."

"I know, duh," said Lauren cheekily. "I offered that, but he wouldn't take it. He hung up before I could find out if he was, you know, suicidal or something. Or tell him to call 9-1-1. Should we call him back?"

Jill sighed. "I'll call him back. Hold any calls that come in while I'm here." She turned, and when she got to her office, she closed the door. She looked up Tim's number and called. *Voice mail.* She left a message telling him to call back if he needed to come in now and that her partner would see him. She also instructed him to call 9-1-1 or go straight to the emergency room if he was in crisis.

Jill sat back, thinking about Erica and Cory Holloman. They were relatively young, both in their 30s, no children yet. They had loads of life ahead of them. It sounded like they were in love, although not without their problems. What could have happened that had led to his untimely death? Possibly his murder?

Then she thought of Cory's brother, Travis, the mostly silent person who'd likely been deeply affected by the loss. What did he know? That reminded her. She pulled out her cell and typed a message to Roxanne.

What did you find out from Travis, Cory's brother?

After three dots sat there for a few seconds, she got an answer. *Nothing... he totally clammed up.*

Jill sat back, not surprised. Roxanne had an aggressive way of approaching people, and Travis seemed like someone with social issues. On the spectrum? ADD? Possibly a personality disorder prohibiting him from normal interactions. Whatever the case, it was unlikely that Roxanne would have been able to pierce the veil of his issues enough to get him to open up.

Her cell dinged. *Hurry up... I think I found something. Someone who had a mad hate...*

Roxanne's impatient note would have to wait a bit longer. She texted a reply and punched the next number.

Jill leaned back from Ethan's embrace. His mouth traced her neck, but she gently pushed him away. "This is not the time."

He leaned in for another kiss, then pulled back, frowning. He moved away, into her kitchen, opening the 'fridge. "Got any beer?"

"It's kind of early, isn't it?" she pointed out with futility.

"So?" She heard the clink of bottles. "*Yes.* Here we go," he added, popping the top off of a bottle.

"Look, Ethan, I've got to get back to work. Come over here for a minute," she said, moving to the sofa.

He strolled over, taking a large gulp, then another, and wiped his mouth with the back of his hand. "What's up, babe?"

"I just want to talk for a minute. I've been putting you off about our engagement, and I need to clear the air."

Just a few short weeks earlier, she'd spontaneously proposed to Ethan. After he'd drunkenly proposed to her a few days before that, and she'd turned him down. Her proposal had come immediately on the heels of the last case she'd worked on. She'd been exhausted, a bit traumatized, and not herself, she'd realized later.

Now, the supposed engagement sat like the proverbial elephant in the room. Was it real? She didn't know. There was no ring, there was no date set, and she was uncertain. She loved Ethan, of that she had no doubt. *But was he the person she wanted to spend the rest of her life with?* Even asking herself that question created a swirl of conflicting emotions.

Against her will, she thought of Nick Webb and those intense gray-green eyes.

God, Jill. She shook off the reflections about Nick.

"It's just that the more I think about it, the more I realize we're not ready to get married."

"*We're* not ready? You mean *you're* not ready." His voice was flat, and she recognized the beginnings of an emotional escalation.

He took another gulp of beer, set the bottle down hard, and shook his head. "Shit, Jill. What the hell is really going on? First, you turn me down. Granted, it wasn't the best proposal in the world, but still. Then, *you* proposed to *me*, and now you're saying you're not ready to get married. What was that all about, anyway? Are you just yanking my chain?" He stood and began pacing. "You know what? I'm sick of this back and forth. I'm not your man-doll. You can't treat me like this and think I'm gonna stick around for it."

"Calm down, Ethan. I'm trying to talk about this with you. Most couples discuss marriage before they commit to getting married." Actually, most didn't, preferring to wrap themselves around the romanticism of the engagement and the wedding plans. Real conversations—about life, what they truly wanted together, children, religion, money, sex—be damned. But she'd put it out there because it was important to her. "I guess I'm saying *I* want to talk about it more before we... put a ring on it, make plans. There are things we've never talked about. Money, for instance. We have no idea of each other's financial status. Don't you think we should?"

"Are you for real? I asked you to marry me, you asked me after turning me down, and now you want to talk about our *balance sheets*. God, what a buzzkill, Jill. Is there even a heart in there?" He pointed at her chest. "Or are you all about the constant shrinking, the cold analysis, of everything?"

Jill flushed with something she couldn't identify. This felt so familiar, and not in a good way. She wanted to talk, to converse quietly about the things that mattered to them. Together, as a couple. But Ethan's resistance blocked her attempts almost every time. And now, on the all-important topic of marriage, she felt pushed out, stonewalled.

Her cell phone rang, and she quickly answered. "Hello. Yes, yes. Okay, I'll be right there." Roxanne couldn't be put off any longer.

Ethan glared at her as she stood and approached him. But he turned and stalked to the door. Before he could leave, she told him she would be too late that evening to get together.

"And why is that?"

"I'm working on a... special case."

"A *special case*. With that detective guy? Of course. Well, that's just great, Jill. See you around." And with that, he was gone, slamming the door behind him.

Jill's head spun with the dizziness of their interchange. What had started out as an attempt to have a dialog about the most important decision of their lives together so far had imploded. At first, it seemed to be Ethan's usual defensiveness, which she knew how to navigate.

But something else was going on. She knew it, could feel it. The smudges under his eyes from lack of sleep or something else. The way he'd constantly glanced at his phone as if he was waiting for something to happen. And most telling of all, the hollowed-out look in his eyes at the mention of her desire for deeper conversations.

CHAPTER NINE

Later that afternoon

Roxanne sat in front of Richard Driscoll, the managing partner of their law practice. He was an imposing but calm presence, whether in the courtroom or here, handling the occasional conflict between partners. Not to mention the complaints registered by their staff and junior attorneys. He also kept a stern eye on the top line and bottom line of the business, ensuring its longevity as a financially solvent firm.

Without him, their small band of legal eagles might have disbanded long ago. Instead, they were tight as a team. They resembled bickering siblings who, at the end of the day, couldn't do without each other and were loyal to a fault. Everyone leaned on Richard, and now, she needed him.

The puzzle of Cory was keeping her awake at night. There was one side of him—the side of Cory she'd known for years. Smart and relentless as a litigator. Selfish, self-centered, and narcissistic. He was interested only in his own personal benefit and, at times, a jerk.

Months ago, he'd cornered her in the copy room and made a completely unwelcome sexual pass at her. Looking back later, through the lens of her own sobriety, she recognized the bloodshot eyes, the lack of empathy, and the telltale odor. *A fellow addict.* She'd reacted instinctively to his advances, giving him a bloody nose, for which she'd received more hostility from him around the office. After that, he'd done his best to undermine her until something had shifted.

But was there another side to a colleague who was more complicated than she'd thought? In recent weeks, his demeanor had changed from narcissistic and arrogant to something resembling helpful. He'd mostly avoided her, and when he couldn't, he seemed almost embarrassed. Astonishingly, he'd begun exhibiting something resembling humility around the office. There was whispering at the water cooler. *Was he sick? Did he have terminal cancer?* But he kept his own counsel, never revealing the source of the changes.

Then, he and Roxanne were forced to travel together on a case. And everything changed after that, again.

Now, she needed to understand what had happened to him. It appeared he was murdered, and if so, by whom? Why?

Most importantly, what was she going to do about it?

"We need to talk about Cory," she told Richard. She quickly laid out the facts as she knew them so far.

"That is disturbing news. Cory had his issues, but he certainly didn't deserve to die so young. But murder?" He shook his head sadly. But he didn't look convinced.

"Right. I need to let you know that I'm working on finding out what happened to him, Richard."

"You're—*working* on it? Isn't this a matter for the police, Roxanne? This is a law practice, not a detective agency. We have clients who need your focus."

"I realize that, but I think I can put more focus on it and find answers more quickly than the police. And yes, they do have the case. But they are also slammed with more murder cases than they can possibly handle. You and I both know most of them slip through the cracks. I don't want that to happen with Cory's case." She reigned in her passion to make the last point carefully. "I'm not willing to let this go, Richard."

Driscoll sat back; his forehead creased. "I guess I'm at a loss here, Roxanne. You and Cory weren't exactly best friends. At times, I had to keep you from all-out war." He waved a hand in the air. "Yes, we're a tight group, and sometimes we argue. But you and Cory... although things seemed cooler lately. But of all people I'd expect to see doing this, it wouldn't be you."

How could she explain her relationship with Cory? Her interest in solving his death? It didn't even make sense to her.

Maybe she didn't have to explain it. "I know it doesn't make sense, not to you and not even to me. I just feel strongly that someone has to advocate for Cory."

"What about his wife?"

"She's overwhelmed with grief at the moment. I'm not sure she's thinking clearly."

"And you're not exactly overwhelmed with grief," Richard mused. "Which, again, makes this curious."

"I realize that, but—"

Richard held up a hand. "Roxanne, you've got to think about more than Cory. It hasn't been that long since you—"

"I'm well aware of the number of days of my sobriety, Richard," Roxanne said, crossing her arms. "None of this has anything to do with that." *Why did everyone treat her as though she stood perpetually on the edge of a cliff? As if the mere suggestion of anything stressful would send her plunging over to her death?*

"Yes, well, the point is, you're still not out of the woods, and I know you hate me saying that. As you know, I've run these traps before with other partners, and I'm familiar with the path. The first year is the rockiest, and any extra stress increases the chances of a relapse." He sat back. "The more I hear you talk about Cory and his possible... murder, the more I hear you getting obsessed with it. And we both know how that can affect you."

"Richard. I'm *fine*. I go to meetings almost daily. I talk to my sponsor regularly. I haven't felt even a twinge of temptation since... I don't know when." *Except for the dream, the night Cory died, when she'd tasted the cold gin.* "I swear, it's *exhausting* to have everyone up in my business all the time, taking my emotional temperature like I'm about to *die* from recovery."

Someone tapped on Richard's door, and he called out for them to enter.

In walked Dr. Jill Rhodes. "Claire said to come on back. Am I interrupting something?"

"Richard Driscoll, this is Dr. Jill Rhodes. Jill, this is our managing partner." Roxanne snapped off the introductions as she rose and strode to Jill.

"Nice to meet you," Driscoll said, shaking Jill's hand. He looked expectantly at Roxanne.

"Dr. Rhodes is a psychologist who is acting as a consultant on Cory's case. Don't worry, I'm paying her out of my own pocket." Roxanne took Jill's arm, guiding her out of the door. "I think I've made myself clear here. Oh—by the way, I'm using my PTO for the next couple of days."

72

"You know you have to request PTO, Roxanne, and I've never seen—"

But she was already out the door leading Jill down the hall to her office.

A couple of hours later, Roxanne put down the file she was reading and looked up at Jill. "I think this one is worth looking at."

Exhausted and about to throw in the towel, Jill bit. "Okay. What do you have there?"

Quickly, Roxanne laid out the basics. "Cory and I worked on this case not long ago. We disagreed strongly about continuing, and I lost that fight. A family-owned business run by the son of the founder. Small town, so the family is the main employer, very prominent and well-respected. A female employee came forward with a sexual harassment complaint against the son, the acting CEO. The more we dug around, the more it appeared to be a pattern, that he might be a predator." Her eyes were steely. "We were defending this guy, and I wanted to get out of it, refer him to someone else. But we got, still get, almost a million in corporate legal fees from the client."

"Correct me if I'm wrong, but don't you have an obligation to provide the best representation for your clients, even if you think they're guilty?" Jill thought of her cheating client that morning. While she couldn't possibly agree with his morals, she believed she could help him, especially since he was clearly unhappy with his own behavior.

"Yes, but I couldn't stand the thought of that girl—sitting there in the courtroom, weeping. I'd already seen her once in a deposition, and she was a wreck from what happened." She sighed. "It was that case that showed me I'm limited as a criminal attorney. I can handle white collar cases, on either side, but things like this... especially after what happened to Hayley."

Roxanne had pursued a deeply personal quest to find out what had really happened to her high school best friend, Hayley, murdered at the age of seventeen. That case had left its permanent scars.

"Anyway, one of the things my sponsor tells me is that I have to work on things I believe in, clients I believe in. I don't compartmentalize well, to put it mildly. If I have to work on something that triggers a lot of internal conflict, I jeopardize my sobriety."

"I know how important that is to you," Jill said and touched Roxanne's hand briefly. "What happened with the case?"

"So, anyway, Cory fought hard to keep the case, but even if he hadn't, Richard, our Managing Partner, would have. Fortunately, I didn't have to continue working on it. Then I went to the sidelines anyway to pursue what happened to Hayley. Later, I found out that we succeeded in defending that scumbag. He got off the hook and didn't have to pay her anything for the pain and agony he undoubtedly caused. The company offered to keep her in her job as a show of—something." Roxanne's voice was laced with disgust. "Well, really, to make the company look good. You know, *we keep our whistleblowers here, no repercussions.* That kind of thing."

"So, the client has no reason to be angry with Cory; in fact, he would be grateful, right?"

"Right. But the woman in question was undeniably hurt by the loss."

"How would you describe her? From what you recall from the deposition."

Roxanne paused thoughtfully. "She struck me as wounded or depressed, maybe as a result of what happened to her. But maybe in general. She wasn't exactly a strong woman. I would say she looked rather beaten down, maybe by life. Maybe by what happened to her."

"What gave you that impression? How she spoke? Her demeanor?"

"You know what? We video-recorded her deposition. I think I can find it." She picked up her water glass and drained it. "But first, let's get some food."

A few minutes later, while they ate Chinese food out of cartons, they watched Cory in action with his witness. And as they watched, Jill's heart sank with dismay, then pity, and later, disgust. *It would be a miracle if someone didn't wind up going for blood after that. If it had been me, I might have thought about killing the guy.*

CHAPTER TEN

The deposition

The plaintiff sat demurely, dressed casually. She avoided eye contact with the camera, preferring to gaze downward. Occasionally, she pulled her long bangs out of her eyes and adjusted her glasses. The camera operator zoomed in on her features at the beginning as if to document her supreme discomfort with the proceedings.

She was pretty, in a girl-next-door way, though she seemed totally unaware of her looks. Instead, she appeared embarrassed to be seen. When she raised her hand to push aside her bangs, Jill could see her unpolished nails appeared bitten to the quick. Also, the slight tremor. She sipped water frequently, and swallowing did not seem easy.

Nail-biting. Anxiety. Shyness, perhaps painfully so.

Caused by whatever she'd been through? Or maybe the fact that she was preparing to lie.

A male voice addressed the woman. "Please state your name and address for the record."

She did, but her voice was almost inaudible. "Melanie Albin."

"Please speak up, Ms. Albin." The defendant's legal counsel. *Cory.*

She cleared her throat and spoke louder, supplying her name and address.

Cory then asked opening questions to establish her employment—when she began working at the company, how much she was paid, the job title she held. Then, "And what is the nature of the work you performed at the company?"

"As I said, my role was executive assistant. I did all the things you would expect in that role—setting up meetings, managing the calendar, booking airline tickets and hotel rooms for travel, organizing documents, and supplying them when needed. Creating PowerPoint decks, taking calls, answering emails."

"And for whom did you act as executive assistant?"

She looked up, then, and spoke the name of the founder's son. "Matt, I mean, Mr. Sullivan." Her face turned rosy, and she looked down.

There was a pause, and then Cory asked, "When was the first time you had sex with Matthew Sullivan?"

"Objection!" The plaintiff's attorney, a male, intervened.

"This isn't a trial. It's a deposition, so we can ask anything we want," retorted Cory.

"She doesn't have to answer salacious questions like that," he declared indignantly.

Melanie Albin glanced sideways. Apparently, her attorney signaled that she could continue.

"Ms. Albin, you have stipulated that you had sex with Mr. Sullivan on the evening of March twenty-third."

Melanie looked up sharply. "It wasn't *having sex*, it was *rape*." Her face turned pale, and she looked down.

"You have alleged rape. Where were the two of you when this alleged event took place?"

"My apartment."

"Did you invite Mr. Sullivan into your home?"

"Yes, but it was supposed to be a stopover to get some documents—"

"Stick with answering the questions, please, Ms. Albin," said Cory sternly. It sounded as though he shuffled a few papers. *Stalling to gather ammunition?* "So, you asked him into your home. Did you offer him a drink?"

"Yes," Melanie whispered.

"You offered him a drink. Alcohol? Wine?"

"Wine."

"Red or white? One glass or two?"

Melanie's attorney interrupted. "What difference does that make?"

"The amount of wine she served him matters. It goes to the scene—the seduction that—"

"That's crazy!" Melanie's legal counsel defended her angrily. "She offered a glass of wine. So what? Move on!"

Cory continued. "So, you gave him wine, more than a glass. You 'hung out' in your living room with your boss, sipping wine together. You have said that he forced you to have sex. When this alleged rape happened, afterward—did you at that time go to the hospital emergency room and request a rape kit? Did you call the police? What exactly did you do after you allegedly were raped?"

Keeping her eyes gazing downward, she answered, but it wasn't discernible.

"Please speak up and look at the camera so that your

testimony is clear," Cory spoke in the tone of voice a teacher might use with a misbehaving middle schooler. *Biting, sarcastic, meant to establish authority, with the threat of forthcoming punishment.*

Melanie flinched but answered. "I said, I took a shower."

"You *took* a *shower*. You *washed away* any so-called evidence. Is that right?" Now, the tone was one of complete disbelief. "Can you tell us why, after supposedly being raped, you did not go to the hospital? Why did you not call the police and report it? And why you took a shower so that there would be no evidence?" Cory's tone now conveyed cold, harsh judgment. Condemnation.

Still staring down, Melanie wiped her eyes with her hand.

"Ms. Albin? We're waiting," said Cory impatiently.

"I was afraid."

"You were afraid. Of what, exactly?"

"The Sullivans know everyone in town. They're a prominent family. I didn't think the police would believe me, and I was afraid someone at the hospital would tell one of them. I—I didn't want to lose my job, at least not until I could find something else. I have a little boy," she said, that last part almost pleading for understanding.

"Losing your job, at least being afraid you would, that was more important than reporting a *rape*?"

Melanie sniffled. No answer.

"Speak up, Ms. Albin!" This time, Cory raised his voice.

"No, it wasn't more important. I just—I was afraid, it was late at night, and I just wanted... I just wanted..." Melanie's voice was ragged now.

"You just wanted what?"

"I wanted to wash off the way I felt!"

"And how did you feel?" Cory asked in a softer voice, baiting her.

"I felt dirty!"

"Is it possible that you felt dirty because you'd had sex with your boss? Your *married* boss? Did you feel dirty because you'd just *seduced your employer* and committed adultery?"

"Don't answer that!" Melanie's attorney intervened. Now, he directed his words to Cory. "This is ridiculous! You're supposed to be asking questions about her employment and the nature of the lawsuit. Not these salacious, inflammatory questions!"

"These questions are crucial because they reveal the nature of this frivolous lawsuit. Your client accused mine of rape. Her story falls completely apart because, according to her, instead of going to law enforcement, which is what any real victim would do, she said nothing. It defies belief. *If* there was any sex, it was because she invited her boss into her home and seduced him. Then, when she was placed on a performance improvement plan, she decided to sue for sexual harassment so she could get a nice payday before they could fire her. That's what this is about!"

"If you're going to accuse her of adultery, you've as much as admitted sexual harassment at a minimum! She was raped, but even if your client won't admit it, you just proved she was harassed when you accused her of adultery!"

"I proved nothing of the kind," Cory scoffed. "What I did was take your client's story and get her to admit that the basis of her lawsuit is nonexistent. *She's a liar.* She probably did have sex that night, but it wasn't with my client. He was home with his wife."

"Oh, and I suppose his *alibi* is his wife?" Melanie's lawyer's voice was booming at this point.

Cory shouted back. The argument continued, voices escalating on both sides.

The relentless camera remained focused on Melanie, who now sat crying softly, her shoulders shaking. She looked up then and spoke. "Please, stop. I want to stop. Please, turn it off," she implored whoever was behind the camera.

But the camera continued to run, and the deposition continued.

Her social habits were exposed. *Yes, she sometimes went out with girlfriends and drank. Yes, she sometimes met men at bars, and yes, she'd gone home a time or two with men she met at a bar.*

Her initial feelings toward Matt Sullivan came out. *Yes, she'd found him attractive. No,* spoken vehemently, *she would never have had sex voluntarily with him. She did NOT date married men.*

But she *had* dated a married man years ago, and when that came out, she turned to her attorney and begged him to drop the case entirely, terrified that her former lover's name would go into public records. Or that he would be called to depose.

Finally, the carnage ended, the witness left shattered.

CHAPTER ELEVEN

"Tell me why we care about Cory, Roxanne," Jill asked after they both sat in silence, trying to shake off the devastatingly emotional impact of the deposition. "I mean, I do understand the legal mandate to defend his client, but that was—it was *brutal.*" She paused, but the curiosity was still there. "What ultimately happened?"

"It never went to trial. The victim's attorney tried to negotiate a settlement with the company, but Cory took advantage of her emotional state after the deposition. He turned down the settlement offer and pushed for trial, but the victim wasn't willing to go any further. They dropped the suit."

"What is your theory at this point? Why did you pull out this case, and how do you think it's connected with Cory's death?"

"Before I answer that, tell me, Jill, what is your impression of Melanie after watching the deposition?"

Jill poked at the fried rice in a carton with chopsticks. She set down the food. "Her affect was that of someone who was traumatized not only by the event, the rape, but by having to re-live it in front of two men, plus whoever was behind the camera.

Her emotions struck me as real, not faked. If she'd been faking, I would have expected to see her push forward, continue the lawsuit. She would have had nothing to lose except legal fees, I suppose. Unless it was a contingency case."

Speculating on someone's guilt or innocence, truthfulness or not, was tricky in this instance. It wasn't easy at any point in her work. Individuals sat in front of her, with no family members or friends to add context, and described their problems. Always from their own point of view. They could be perfectly truthful but fail to convey their problems accurately due to their own biases and filters that clouded their ability to see themselves and others clearly.

Bias aside, the even bigger challenge was the tendency of all human beings to dissemble to some extent. Everyone had secrets, though, for most people, they consisted of the day-to-day 'white lies' that enabled them to manage relationships with less stress.

Then there were the things that felt too embarrassing, secrets that were best kept shrouded in the past, that were far too sensitive to risk exposure. Childhood losses and traumas that would be painful to re-live, that evoked deep feelings of shame when recalled. Adult life traumas that had been carefully guarded. Therapy offered people the chance to unburden themselves of those kinds of withheld stories. Often, Jill had the opportunity to help people feel less isolated, to feel less alone, as she assured them that their closely guarded secret wasn't that unusual.

These were the kind of secrets that required work to maintain, the kind that were wrapped around significant consequences, like the one held by her client Tim. Confidences that were typically shared with professionals like herself or with clergy. Sometimes with a close friend. If they were shared. But secrets revealed often led to exposure, which might be the point. Exposed and unburdened might be a relief.

Or a terrible regret.

Watching Melanie be deposed, it was unlikely she was lying and faking her emotions for one very obvious reason. She'd ultimately dropped the suit, not because she risked exposure as a liar, since it was a 'he-said, she-said' kind of case. Impossible to prove who was lying, especially lacking outside corroboration such as a video or a witness present in Melanie's house or physical evidence. Rather, she'd dropped it because it was too emotionally scarring on top of the event itself. Too traumatizing.

This was the primary reason that rape victims rarely went to law enforcement or, when they did, often backed out later. It was too difficult to have to tell the story over and over again, to testify in court and endure cross-examination. Worse, the risk of being accused of seduction in some form was too high, whether by virtue of clothing worn, or the fact that the encounter began at a bar, or on a date.

Or by inviting a trusted person into the home.

"She came across as authentic to me. I believed her," said Jill. "Your turn. Why do you believe this is relevant to whatever happened to Cory?"

"One more question first. Do you see anything about Melanie that would make you think she could kill Cory?"

"The problem is we see her in one context only in this video. It's a deposition, a high-pressure, high-stakes situation, and one in which there is maximum exposure. There's video being taken. Everyone is watching her closely. I can't see her suddenly erupting into a murderous rage or lunging at someone."

"But people do often confess their crimes under police interrogation. And I'm not talking about the kinds of interrogations that last for twenty hours, and people are deprived of food and water. I'm talking cases where the perpetrator is questioned for maybe a couple of hours and just can't seem to stop talking, eventually spilling the beans." Roxanne emphasized her point with a chopstick in the air.

"Right. Anyway, my point is, we don't know who Melanie really is just from this video. We don't know what happened after she recovered from the obvious devastation. Did she move on with her life? Or did she harbor anger that festered and turned to rage? And if so, could she have gone after Cory later? I'm saying, yes, it's possible."

It was possible, yes. Not probable. Plus, if Melanie had murderous tendencies, it seemed she might go after her rapist, not the attorney who raked her over the coals in a deposition. Wasn't what her employer did to her the far bigger wound?

Again, it was too little to go on, the video deposition. Who was Melanie, really? What was her life like now, after the case that was aborted? What was her connection later, if any, to Cory?

"I do have another question, Roxanne, and I know this may sound insensitive. I don't mean it that way. But I'm still wondering, what is it that makes you want to pursue this search for what happened to Cory? I keep getting the feeling there's more to the story for you, things you haven't shared. It's hard for me to help if I don't know everything." Even as she asked the question, Jill knew it was unlikely she'd get a straight answer.

Roxanne was brilliant, but she was also mercurial. Her personality could never be summed up with a simple assessment. She was complex, so much so that she undoubtedly left those who were close to her exhausted at times. She was the proverbial onion that therapists speak of—the kind of person who will reveal themselves in layers over time, cautiously, carefully, and sometimes, explosively.

Roxanne stood and began cleaning the conference room table. No answer to Jill's question.

Jill's phone buzzed. She glanced at the screen. *Jade.* She let it go to voicemail. She also noted the time and gasped. "I've got to get going, Roxanne. I'm late for another commitment." She stood to go, but Roxanne stopped her.

"Wait. Let's plan for tomorrow. I want to go see Melanie first. I want you to assess her in person, and I have questions for her as well." She paused. "And there's someone else. I have a suspicion that she isn't the only one who might have had a murderous rage toward Cory."

CHAPTER TWELVE

Hey, it's me. Um, I was hoping you'd answer. I really need to talk. It's nothing big. Well, actually, it's kind of big. But anyway... There was a small, nervous laugh. *Anyway, Daniel's away at a conference. At least, I think he is. But anyway... never mind. It's okay. You're probably working late again. You probably have plans tonight. I'll get in touch with you tomorrow. Oh, and Jill? I love you. No matter what happens, remember that. And remember what I told you six years ago. That is always true. Forever. Wow, that sounds dramatic, doesn't it? Please ignore this message. I'm definitely feeling extra blue since... you know, since what. Okay! That's really it. Let's get together tomorrow night. Or the next night. Whenever you're free. Daniel's gone all week. Bye for real this time, Sis!*

Jill listened to the voicemail from her sister again. She sounded like herself but not quite herself. Definitely traces of sadness, *'feeling blue'?* Well, who wouldn't at a time like this? She'd lost a baby just a few weeks ago. A baby that she and her husband, Daniel, had tried to have for years.

And the reference to six years ago. What did that even mean?

Something tickled at the back of her brain, but she couldn't quite grasp it. She was supposed to remember that reference. Should remember it. But she didn't. Not now, anyway.

"Hello?" Nick's voice called out from Jill's reception area. She walked out, greeted him, and led him to her office. He was dressed casually. She tried not to look at the pulse in his neck or focus on the way he sat—comfortable in his own skin, long legs splayed. Thoughtful eyes watching her.

He glanced at his watch. "Working late tonight?"

"A little. I spent most of the day on Roxanne's case, but I managed to fit in two clients. Thanks for meeting me here. I'm sure you have other things you'd rather do with your evenings—"

He gave her a slow smile. "It's no problem. Not tonight, anyway."

"I thought I should update you on what we've found so far. We have reviewed more than half of Cory's cases. We found one that could be linked to Cory's murder. There was a plaintiff in a sexual harassment case. We watched the video of her deposition. Cory was... well, he was brutal with her." She spent a few minutes filling in some of the details.

Nick remained neutral as he listened. "So, you think this woman was so angry, so revengeful, that she poisoned a bottle of bourbon, gave it to Cory, and killed him?"

"I didn't say that." Nick's skepticism, while appropriate, irked her. "But Roxanne thinks there's something there. I'm neutral. I'm not convinced this woman has the personality structure to nurse the level of rage it would take to plan and commit this kind of murder months later. Not an explosive rage, either, but the kind that can simmer, gradually growing into the desire to act." Her eyes searched over Nick's head for a moment. "Also, my observation of her in the deposition was that she gradually fell apart. She didn't have that toughness that some people have, the ability to take a stand, to face down anyone who threatens them. The more Cory questioned her, the more she crumbled. She became more and more distraught."

"Did you believe her story? Was she raped?"

"There's no way to know for sure, but yes, I found her to be very credible. But it's still hard to imagine her enraged. She was so… sad."

"But if she was victimized, wouldn't that take a lot out of her? I've seen a lot of victims of assault on the witness stand over the years, and a fair number of them aren't able to withstand cross-examination." He hesitated. "We try to prepare them for testimony, but it's hard to know in advance who will stay strong and who… won't."

"What about revenge? How many cases have you had that involved victims who later became perpetrators? Who got revenge by killing the person who'd hurt them? Especially women."

"None. It probably happens, but I haven't seen it."

"I'm not surprised," she said. "Most of the time, people fantasize about revenge but don't act on it. When someone hurts you, devastates you in some way, there's an overwhelming sense of injustice. The scales that are normally balanced in the relationship have gone on a massive tilt. One person has gained the upper hand in an intolerable way, and the other feels their power has been stripped away." Jill felt heat gather in her neck and face. She knew what it felt like to lose all power and, later, to carry the burn of injustice.

"Are you okay?" Nick peered at her. "How about some water." He got up, went to her credenza, and poured water.

She took it gratefully and sipped, trying desperately to alleviate the dryness that gripped her mouth and throat. "Anyway," she cleared her throat, trying to continue. Felt the heat rise more, now with embarrassment.

Nick pretended not to notice. "You know what? I'm starving. How about we go grab a bite to eat while we talk?" He stood and found her jacket, offered it to her. "I'll drive."

Jill took another sip of pinot grigio, allowing her body to gradually relax. She'd picked at her salad while Nick ate his burger. Her eyes strayed to her cell, on the seat in the booth next to her. Still no answer from Jade in response to her earlier text. *Hey, sis, sorry I didn't get back to you—text me when you can talk.*

"So, Doc, back to the topic. We were talking about fantasies and revenge," Nick said, a bit of a spark in his eyes, a tiny smile.

Sense of humor. She rolled her eyes. "Right. Actually, I wanted to know—did you get results on the tox screen of the bourbon?"

"Doesn't happen that fast. I'll push again tomorrow, see if I can get a rush on the results. Back to revenge—what's that old saying? Revenge is—"

"A dish best served cold," she finished for him. "And in this case, yes, there was a significant interval between the deposition and Cory's death. But it's a long journey from wishing ill on a person to making it happen. Most people indulge in fantasizing about something bad happening to the person who hurt them, at least for a while. Some people longer than others." Her thoughts strayed to a client, a woman whose fiancé had dumped her three days before their wedding for another woman. The client had spent months in therapy nursing fantasies of how she might destroy the happy couple's life.

After months of revenge talk, Jill had introduced the notion of a different kind of revenge. *Sometimes, the best revenge is living a great life. Maybe supply evidence that what he did was just a speed bump that had little impact on your life.* After that, her client began carefully constructing a new kind of revenge. She went to a spa for ten days, signed up for personal growth classes, focused on taking great care of herself, and on rekindling her social life. Her goal? To show up glowing with happiness and health at the annual charity gala they'd both attended for many years.

Of course, along the way, as she'd developed her newly redefined 'revenge' plan, she'd rediscovered herself. By the time she'd seen him at the gala, it no longer mattered what he thought or if he had any regret about leaving her. By then, she saw him as the guy who'd been too weak to just be honest about their relationship. She'd greeted him warmly while secretly feeling grateful that she wasn't with him.

"Jill? Where did you go?"

"Sorry." *Bad habit, going off somewhere in her head.*

"No need," said Nick, giving her his slow smile. "I was just thinking about what you said. That there's a big difference between imagining hurting someone and actually doing it. My world is filled with people who don't even bother with the 'imagining' step. They just go right into action, and whatever weapon is handy, they use that." He wiped his mouth with a napkin. "But if someone does want to get back at someone who hurt them, what is the motive? What's different about that person vs. the one who just thinks about it?"

Justice and injustice. Power and the loss thereof. Gradual erosion of your moral compass because you can't get past what happened, what was done to you. Calcification of empathy because you received none at a critical juncture.

And what enabled recovery? What was the cure for the deep ache of having been terribly wronged? Especially if the person who wronged you was the person who was supposed to love you, protect you.

There was possibly one motivator for revenge that stood out amongst the others. One that might drive someone into action, while other motivators merely sparked fantasies of retribution.

She shared a few theories with Nick. "Frustration, humiliation, and insult. I'm imagining how Melanie, the plaintiff in Cory's case, may have felt following the deposition. Powerless, as she realized she was in for a bigger fight than she'd imagined at the beginning of the lawsuit. If she transferred her feelings to Cory, where they'd previously been focused on her employer, who she alleged raped her, I could see something beginning to build in her that maybe wasn't there before."

"Transferred her feelings?" Nick asked. "A little less psychobabble, please." His eyes sparkled with humor as he spoke.

She didn't take it personally. "Transference: the process by which someone who has feelings toward a significant person in their life begins to feel it about someone else, whether positively or negatively. It happens in my work a lot. Patients can see me as the 'good parent' they never had, which prompts bonding, a necessary dynamic for therapy to be successful. It's also what happens when couples see each other as possessing all the most annoying characteristics of their parents." She smiled.

"Also," she tapped the side of her wine glass, "she may have flipped from victim to perpetrator because the deposition triggered another side of her psyche. Before that, she'd felt victimized and maybe weak, and her attorney became her rescuer. After the deposition, maybe she realized she wasn't going to be rescued."

"No hero anymore may have left her feeling too vulnerable," mused Nick. He was familiar with the hero dynamic, as a couple of his relationships in the past had proven. Women sometimes thought he should be more than he actually was, a regular guy who happened to solve crimes for a living. "But what does all this mean?"

She took another sip of wine. "She'd have to rescue herself. And since she couldn't do it through the legal system, she would have to take matters into her own hands. It would also be very symbolic. She killed Cory, a representative of the justice system that failed her. And she got justice for herself."

Jill excused herself to go to the ladies' room, and while she was there, Roxanne called with startling news.

They'd found a file in Cory's desk. Not a client file. The contents of this file were a dozen or so handwritten notes.

You will pay for what you did.

You will suffer like you made me suffer.

You're dead already. It's just a matter of time.

And the most chilling of all.

Look behind you. I'm there. But you'll never see me coming.

She decided not to tell Nick about it. Not yet.

CHAPTER THIRTEEN

After finishing up with Nick the night before, Jill had gone home and collapsed, sleeping restlessly. Early this morning, she'd spent time with Lauren re-arranging her schedule, moving her healthier clients out for a couple of weeks and others to late afternoon times. That allowed more space to spend time with Roxanne on the case, which now gripped her in an unexpected way.

She wasn't sure who she was really trying to help. *Roxanne?* The truth was she could handle most of it herself. *Cory?* More likely, his widow Erica, who was appropriately devastated and possibly just beginning to realize she needed justice for her husband. *Nick?* He seemed tolerant of her involvement in the case, but he certainly didn't need her.

As she waited, she glanced again at the long text from her sister that had finally pinged, apologizing for not responding and promising to update her later.

From Ethan, nothing. But she hadn't reached out to him, either.

She startled at the tap on her window, then let Roxanne in her car. "How did you get this set up?" Jill asked her. They were parked in front of a rather large brick home in Frisco, a large suburb of Dallas. She studied the exterior, noting the manicured lawn and landscaping, the imposing size of the two-storied, traditional structure. Looking up and down the street, she noted a variety of versions of the same kind of homes. Very high-end suburban, no doubt a family enclave of couples in the heyday of raising kids. At least one well-paid professional breadwinner in each household.

"I told her I had questions about her case. She wanted to know if she needed her attorney present, and I told her no. Surprisingly, she bought it." Roxanne shrugged. She briefly updated Jill on the research she'd done prior to the meeting.

Jill reminded her of their strategy and coached Roxanne about her part. *This could be anything from uncomfortable to downright chaotic.* Maybe they should have asked Nick along. No, that would have probably inhibited any chance of getting Melanie to open up. While 'protect and serve' was something Jill believed in, she also recognized that there was a fair level of paranoia with regard to law enforcement in today's world, some of it justified.

A few minutes later, they sat in a comfortable family room. One whole side of the room was covered in toys, though corralled from the main area. Melanie sat somewhat uncomfortably, her belly protruding. She looked days away from giving birth. Her hair was pulled back into a ponytail, but she still had long bangs, which she periodically brushed to the side. Her hand steady, this time.

Roxanne led. "Thanks for meeting with us."

Melanie interrupted her. "I don't understand—what is this about? My case was over a long time ago. And, um, the baby is asleep, but when he wakes up, I'll have to take care of him."

"We understand. I do have some news, and it is connected to your case. Cory Holloman died recently. Actually, his death is suspicious, and because of that, we're looking at some of his old cases. Cory was the—"

"I remember who he is," Melanie said stiffly, her face hardening. "I remember him quite vividly." She sat back and crossed her arms.

Jill stepped in. "Ms. Albin—"

"It's Mrs. Howard, now," she retorted.

With a trace of pride? Roxanne and Jill exchanged a brief glance.

"Mrs. Howard. First of all, I'm so sorry about what you went through that led to your case. I watched the deposition. I'm sure that was very difficult for you, and I truly empathize—"

"*You have no idea.*" A fire now seemed lit. "First, my employer did the worst thing a man can do to a woman. Then I got raked over the coals in the deposition, blamed for what he did because I invited him into my home. I didn't exactly have much of a choice that night. What was I supposed to do? Tell my *boss*, 'No, you can't come in while I find my bag and get those papers for you?'" She shook her head in disgust. "It comes down to this. I was *blamed* for what he did to me!"

"And that isn't right. Not at all," began Jill.

"I'm not going to re-live it with you. My therapist told me to stop doing that; it was traumatizing me all over again. I don't know why you're here, but I can't afford to get upset like this," Melanie said, uncrossing her legs. She held both hands across the front of her belly. *Protecting the most vulnerable.* She looked like she was about to usher them out.

The demure, downtrodden witness of a couple of years ago was nowhere to be found. In her place was a much stronger, much more confident woman. *There can be recovery after trauma, and life can go on.* Married now, one baby and another on the way.

Her son from a previous relationship probably a teenager now. *A lot of care for and focus on others, one of the best cures for pain.*

Also, anger, now freely expressed, not held back. Victims often turned their anger toward the perpetrator inward toward themselves. The result: *low self-esteem, eating disorders, substance abuse, depression, anxiety, suicidal ideation.* It was a long list. This was especially true for women, genetically and societally predisposed to repress anger.

With Melanie, was this justifiable, understandable anger? Or was it anger that had boiled over into rage?

She wouldn't know unless she could get her to open up. "I'm so sorry, Mrs. Howard. Please, we just have a couple of questions, and we'll be out of here. I promise." Jill's voice was pitched low and soft, her breathing measured. "It's not about what happened to you. It's about Mr. Holloman."

Melanie sat back, arms still crossed. But the defiant look slowly drained away, and in its place was resignation. "Okay—but make it quick."

Roxanne glanced at Jill and began. "As Dr. Rhodes said, Cory Holloman died recently. We're wondering if you had any further contact with him—after the deposition and the dismissal of the case."

Jill watched Melanie closely.

"No, of course not. My... attorney handled everything after the deposition."

"And can you tell us why you dropped the case?" Roxanne asked delicately, as Jill had advised her to do. "Maybe you can tell us what happened with your employer after the deposition for some background information."

"I was told that I shouldn't quit the job, to continue going to work and see if there was retribution for the lawsuit. Then, we could go back again with a whistleblower case. So, I did for a while. I needed the income, and there wasn't a lot of opportunity since it was such a small town. But it was awful. All my so-called work 'friends' would barely talk to me. My boss acted like nothing ever happened; just shoveled as much work on me as he possibly could. He didn't do anything that would give me a new basis for legal action, but after a few months, I couldn't take it anymore."

"So, you quit? How did you support yourself after that?" Roxanne's eyes strayed to the large room in which they sat.

Melanie shifted a bit. "By then, my husband and I were talking about marriage. He encouraged me to quit, and we moved in together."

Roxanne shifted back to the earlier question. "Can you tell us more about why you dropped the case? And if you've had any second thoughts about that. Regrets. Wish you'd gone forward, taken a big, old bite out of your former boss."

"Yeah, sometimes I do. If it was my daughter, I would push her to prosecute, to go to the police immediately." She rubbed her belly with her left hand. "But I didn't have anyone to lean on back then. I was afraid, so I didn't act when I should have. By the time I did the deposition, I was in bad shape. Even though I had my attorney, I just didn't want to go through it all again in court." She continued rubbing her belly gently. "Do I have regrets? A ton of them. I wish I'd moved away from there so I wouldn't have felt like I had to stay in that job. I knew the first few weeks he wasn't a good guy. I felt uncomfortable around him anytime it was just the two of us." Her expression fell. "Yeah, I really regret staying there."

"Your gut was telling you something," Jill offered. She saw it all the time. Hindsight often afforded people the chance to validate their gut, the remembrance of those internal warning signals that they had ignored. Some learned from it, and knew to trust those instincts in the future.

Others received the same lessons repeatedly.

"So, you dropped the case because you didn't feel like you could withstand the judicial process," Roxanne offered. "Was that because of the way Mr. Holloman questioned you? You must have been angry about that later."

"He was awful to me! Look, I don't want to get into it again, but let's just say I'm not exactly crying over his grave." She looked shocked at her own words. "I mean, I don't wish to say bad things about the dead. But if you're asking me if I had a red-hot hatred for him after that deposition, yes, I did."

Roxanne pounced. "Enough hatred to go after him personally?" She pulled a file out of her bag, opened it, and laid out several handwritten notes. "Did you write these notes and send them to Cory Holloman?"

Melanie picked up one of the notes, studied it curiously. "That's not my handwriting," she declared. "I would never do anything like that."

Odd. She didn't immediately say she hadn't *written* the notes. She said it wasn't her *handwriting*. Jill opened her mouth to ask the next obvious question, but Roxanne got there first.

"Whose handwriting is it, Ms. Howard, if it's not yours? Is it your husband's? We know you're married to your attorney now, to Will Howard. That's your husband, right? He represented you in the lawsuit, and he was there during the deposition. He tried to defend you."

Melanie's face flushed. "Yes, I married my attorney. What a cliché, right? But he's been the best thing that ever happened to me, and I'm happy now. He's the reason I've moved on from the past." Her defensiveness was rising again.

"Maybe," said Roxanne. "Or maybe he was so angry about the way Mr. Holloman treated you, your husband went after him. He nursed the anger; it turned to rage, and he planned a way to get back at him." She stopped for a moment, letting the accusation hang in the air. "Or maybe you both went after him."

"How *dare* you—" Melanie began, her voice rising in volume with each word, her face flushing deep red.

"*Roxanne*," Jill said tersely. She turned to Melanie. "I'm sorry, Ms. Howard. If you'll excuse us for a moment, I'd like to speak to my colleague in private." She stood.

Roxanne followed her to the foyer of the house, fuming. "What the hell, Jill? I was on a roll, and we were about to get to the bottom of this!"

"I didn't realize we were going to play good cop/bad cop with her," Jill shot back. "The most important thing is we need to get her to open up, and she's not going to do that if you keep pushing her so hard." She took a breath. "Look, let's both calm down and get back in there. Try to keep this on track a little longer."

But when they turned to go back into the room, Melanie stood holding her cell phone in her hand. "Get out." And she pointed her cell phone at them. "I'm recording you now. My husband says if you don't leave, you'll be subject to criminal prosecution."

They turned and left, saying nothing until they were in the car.

Jill sat still, but Roxanne broke the silence. "That went well, don't you think?" She gave Jill a wry smile.

Humor as a deflection. "Not really, no."

"I guess I forgot I wasn't in court. No witness on the stand."

"Except," Jill said. "There is one thing."

"Really? One whole thing?"

"We found out she's capable of anger, and we know she did have a red-hot fury toward Cory. Two things. We also know she's married to the guy who defended her. I'd say they both have plenty of motive."

"We knew that already," Roxanne said, clearly exasperated.

"Let me see those notes again," Jill said, an idea popping in. She looked at them slowly, carefully. "There's something odd about these notes. See this one?" She pointed to the one that said, 'Look behind you. I'm there. But you'll never see me coming.'

"So?" Roxanne shrugged and tossed all the notes back into the file. "What did we learn in there that's new? That we can use?"

"I'm not sure. There's something about the notes." Jill thrummed the wheel with her fingers, the oddness of the notes and what they could mean eluding her. "But I don't think Melanie did it. She has so much to live for now. I have a really hard time seeing her risking her new life to get back at Cory. She's got two children and one on the way. A comfortable life with a husband who loves her. With that much hope for the future, I can't see the anger turning into rage and murder."

"*Hope*," Roxanne echoed sarcastically. "Isn't that just sugar-coating for the soul? People hang onto hope in the most impossible circumstances, don't they? It tastes so good, but it's not good for you." She rummaged in her bag, pulled out her cell, continuing to talk, mostly to herself. "Give me a cold, hard dose of reality any day. *That* I can deal with." She looked up at Jill and grinned. "Now I can. Not so much in the old days, right?"

"In my world, hope is the one thing that keeps people going, especially those who have plenty of reasons to give up. If I can help them find hope, they can recover from almost anything." Even to herself, she sounded a little bit like a fairy godmother waving her magic wand.

But hope had saved her at one point.

"Yeah, well, time to go to the place where there's definitely no more hope," Roxanne said.

CHAPTER FOURTEEN

As they stepped inside the chapel, the warm glow of sunlight filtering through the stained-glass windows embraced them. The walls were adorned with intricate carvings and elegant decorations, creating an atmosphere of serenity and reverence. Softly flickering candles cast gentle shadows across the room, lending a peaceful ambiance to the space.

At the front of the chapel, an ornate altar was draped in a rich velvet cloth, its delicate lace trimmings catching the light. Rows of polished wooden pews stretched to the back, each one adorned with a small cushion of plush velvet, offering comfort to the mourners who were scattered about.

The sweet fragrance of fresh flowers filled the air, their vibrant colors creating a striking contrast against the muted tones of the chapel's interior. Soft strains of classical music filled the chapel, their mournful notes echoing off the high ceilings, stirring emotions no doubt for some. As they sat, Jill could feel the weight of the occasion settle upon her, the air heavy with grief and sadness.

In the center of the altar, a beautifully carved, polished

casket rested, surrounded by a sea of flowers and wreaths. A photograph of Cory, smiling and carefree, rested on a large easel nearby, a reminder of happier times. A solemn-faced minister stood nearby, ready to lead the mourners in prayer and offer comfort to those in need.

"Funny, I don't remember ever hearing anything from Cory about going to church, let alone belonging to one," Roxanne whispered to Jill as they passed down the aisle. At one point, Roxanne gave a tiny wave to a blond woman who wiggled her fingers in response. They settled close to the back.

Erica sat in one of the two front pews. She was dressed entirely in black, including a small hat with a veil over her face. Jill couldn't see her face, but her head was bowed as though she was sitting quietly in prayer. Travis sat a couple of feet away from her, his gaze straight ahead, not moving.

How incredibly sad to lose a husband so young. To not have the comfort or distraction of children to carry her forward. To have to determine the welfare of her husband's brother, a dependent though not truly related.

It was a small chapel, a separate structure from the main sanctuary of a large church in Preston Hollow, one of the wealthiest neighborhoods in the city of Dallas. As she gazed around, Jill couldn't help thinking it would be a beautiful venue for a small wedding.

And as Jill sat there, surrounded by the beauty and serenity of the sanctuary, she couldn't help but feel a sense of awe and wonder at the fragility of life and the power of love and community in times of loss.

The music stopped. Silence now filled the room except for the occasional creak from the wooden pews as people shifted in their seats.

Jill scanned the room as they waited for the service to begin. A number of men in suits, accompanied by women, most likely their spouses. A small contingent of younger people sitting in groups, heads down, but not in prayer. Unless you considered it prayer—the worship of a tiny screen. Occasionally, they pointed out things on their screens to one another.

"Partner. Partner. Associate. Bunch of junior associates." Roxanne whispered and pointed surreptitiously. "That is Claire, our legal assistant, sitting up front. The one I waved at. A few people I don't know, but pretty much everyone here is from work." She nodded her head toward a pew to their left and behind them. "Except for her. Don't have a clue who she is."

Jill looked to her left but not directly at the subject of Roxanne's remark.

The thirtysomething woman sat by herself. Her head was bowed, her eyes downcast, her face a mask. She looked at no one. Made no eye contact.

Not surprisingly, Melanie and her husband, Will, were not present. *Were there other clients present?* Jill wondered.

The minister stepped up to the podium and stood quietly for a moment.

He began in a somber, sonorous voice. "Dear family and friends. We gather today to celebrate the life and mourn the passing of Cory, a beloved husband, son, brother, friend, and member of our community. We come together in grief and in love to honor the memory of a young man who was taken from us far too soon.

"It is with heavy hearts that we gather here today to say goodbye to a life that was cut short. We mourn not only the loss of Cory but also the unrealized potential of what could have

105

been. We feel the weight of sorrow and pain that comes with losing someone so young, with so much left to give.

"In times like these, it is difficult to find the right words to express the depth of our emotions. We may find ourselves questioning why such a tragedy had to occur and struggling to make sense of the pain and sadness that we feel. But even in the midst of our grief, we are reminded of the hope and comfort that can be found in our faith. We believe that Cory has found eternal rest in the loving arms of God and that he is now free from the suffering and pain of this world."

As the minister droned on, Jill's mind wandered. *Was it true?* Did faith provide comfort during times of suffering and pain? Many of her friends believed that it did. But faith was rarely the topic with her clients. For them, suffering overrode any faith that they may have held prior to their tragedy, sometimes to the point that faith was abandoned. *How could a loving God allow such things to happen to them?* She struggled to answer those questions herself, let alone for her clients. Her standard response: *This sounds like something to discuss with your priest, minister, or Rabbi.*

It was a cop-out, in a way. But her belief was that her mandate was to be agnostic to the presence of or the absence of the faith of her clients.

What did she believe? *Faith is a belief in things we cannot prove.* That was as far as she'd gotten. Maybe as far as she would ever get.

And what did Ethan believe? Stunned momentarily, she realized she had no idea. That thought shone a spotlight on the second of two major areas of life they'd never explored as a couple. The two hottest topics to air and align together. *Money and faith.*

Her attention returned to the minister as he finished the service with a prayer. "As we honor Cory's memory today, let us also find strength in the love and support of one another. Let us draw comfort from the knowledge that we are not alone in our grief and that we are surrounded by a community that cares deeply for us. May the love and light of God shine upon us all during this difficult time. Amen."

After that, Roxanne led the very small selection of colleagues who made their way to the podium and spoke about Cory. "He was a gifted litigator, and he was my friend," she ended.

Others spoke about Cory, but their words were few, their discomfort apparent. Jill couldn't help but wonder if Cory's spirit hovered nearby, shaking his head at the disparity of warmth and affection from those in his professional life. She felt a sudden tug on her arm.

"Let's boogie out of here," Roxanne whispered urgently to Jill. "I have an idea."

They slid out of the pew and headed out the back.

Outside, Roxanne insisted they stand near the entrance to the chapel. She seemed to be waiting for someone. After numerous people had gone by, she pointed and whispered to Jill.

The woman who'd sat in the back, the one Roxanne hadn't recognized, approached. She seemed distracted, in a hurry to leave, but Roxanne stepped in her way. "Excuse me."

The woman stopped and focused on Roxanne. Lines of worry and pain etched into her forehead, giving her an air of weariness. Her full lips were pressed tightly together. Her blond hair was pulled back into a simple ponytail, and her face was free of makeup, yet she still radiated a natural beauty that came from within.

As she looked up, her eyes met Jill's, who could see something reflected in them. *Was it grief and sorrow? Or something else?*

"Yes?" she said, clearly puzzled.

"I'm afraid we've lost our information, and we're not sure where to go for the graveside service. Can we walk with you?" Roxanne looked uncharacteristically puzzled.

"Well, I—" she glanced toward the parking lot filled with cars. "I wasn't sure if I—"

Roxanne introduced herself. "I'm Roxanne Fairchild. I worked with Cory; we were partners in the law firm. I'm afraid I can't remember you; please forgive me. You are?"

"Lindsay." She didn't offer a last name. "Um, nice to meet you."

"Likewise. This is Jill Rhodes, a friend. How did you know Cory? I'm sorry to be so nosy, but I thought I knew all of Cory's friends. It's such a tragedy. I still can't believe he's gone." Roxanne had now tucked her hand into Lindsay's arm and was pulling her along down a path that led to a tree-shaded area behind the chapel.

Lindsay seemed to struggle for words. "I—I'm just a friend." She stopped, and her mouth closed in a line. "But I think the graveside service is a couple of miles away, at the funeral home."

"A friend from where? It's funny, I don't think we've ever met. Were you at Cory's last birthday party? His wife, Erica," Roxanne pointed to the widow in the distance, "threw the most amazing shindig. Everyone from the firm, a bunch of Cory's college friends. I don't remember seeing you there."

"No, I... I'm not a college friend." Lindsay's face paled, and her eyes darted toward the receding parking lot in the now greater distance. "Um, the parking lot is that way."

"Oh, silly me! Of course, it is." Roxanne said with a laugh. She sounded ditzy, the exact opposite of who she was. "Now, you said your last name was?"

And as though she'd never meant to say it, but Roxanne

had prodded it out of her, she told them. "It's Thomas, Lindsay Thomas." She allowed herself to be pulled to the parking lot.

"Which car is yours?" Roxanne asked, shading her eyes from the sun as she surveyed the vehicles.

"It's okay. I know where it is. I... I'll see you there," Lindsay said, recovering herself. She pulled her arm away from Roxanne, though it took a tug to get out of the grip. She abruptly turned and began walking away rapidly. Soon, she was lost in the sea of automobiles, and it wasn't clear which one she got into.

Roxanne made as if to follow her again, but Jill pulled her back. "Let her go. We'll see her at the graveside. Too pushy, remember?"

But Roxanne shook her head. "We won't see her there. She's gone, and I think I know why."

CHAPTER FIFTEEN

On the way to their destination, Jill queried Roxanne. "What was that all about? Why do you think that woman left like that? You know something, don't you?"

Roxanne sighed. "No, I really don't. I'm going to find out, though. I have some ideas, but let's get back to that later. Right now, we need to show up for Erica."

The afternoon was filled with paying respects to Cory Holloman's widow. After the graveside service, they dutifully showed up at her home for the traditional after-funeral gathering. It was surreal.

The elegantly decorated home was filled with Cory's partners and associates, plus a couple of other people from the funeral— the minister being the only one Jill recognized. The living room had been transformed into a catered event space, with tables adorned with elegant floral arrangements and trays of hors d'oeuvres and drinks. The guests moved about the room, mingling with one another and engaging in idle chatter, their voices filling the air with a polite buzz.

The widow, Erica, stood near the entrance of the room,

greeting the guests as they arrived with a warm smile and a handshake. She seemed calm and composed, her demeanor reserved and distant.

Travis was nowhere in sight.

As the guests made their way around the room, they spoke in hushed tones, sharing small talk and exchanging pleasantries. Jill tried to tune in, to discern the level of grief, of intimacy, or any other indicators of the relationship these people had with the deceased. There was little mention of Cory, and those who did speak of him did so in vague terms as if they were talking about a stranger.

Despite the lack of connection to the deceased, there was still a sense of community and respect among the guests. They had come together to honor the memory of a life that had passed, even if that life was largely unknown to them. They were colleagues, partners, and associates in a law firm, so they were bonded in other ways, perhaps around the difficulty of their work.

Most of the guests seemed to be here for the food. As if it were any other afternoon party or pleasant event. As though they would go home and later gab about which hors d'oeuvres had been the best, which drinks they'd enjoyed, or the recipes they might ask for later.

Erica touched none of the food. She held no drink in her hand. She spoke to the hired wait staff, ensuring that her guests were offered a steady stream of delicious bites, their glasses filled, but she took nothing for herself.

As Jill and Roxanne stood near Erica, Jill noted the widow's demeanor. Her eyes were clear, no traces of tears or redness, and there were no indications that she was medicated. Her makeup was impeccable. Either she'd been dry-eyed since applying it earlier that day, or she'd touched it up between the service and now.

Her expression was stoic. She neither smiled at people nor did she engage in the kind of banter that grieving people sometimes hid behind. She only offered brief nods and sometimes allowed people to take her hand as they spoke to her.

Someone touched Jill's shoulder. *Nick.* "Hey," she said as she turned to him. "What are you doing here?"

"Seems to be our refrain, doesn't it?" But he gave her a smile, which undid the sense of rebuke she'd felt coming. "I wanted to give Ms. Holloman the toxicology results. Might as well include you two in that conversation."

"Is this the right time? We just came from the funeral," Roxanne interjected. "I mean, to talk to Erica. She has a lot to deal with. How about just telling us? You can de-brief her later."

"Nice try," Nick said to Roxanne. "But she's entitled to know since she's the one who gave permission for the autopsy. Not to mention, it's her husband. It wasn't an official investigation at that point, remember?"

"Fine," said Roxanne impatiently. They all agreed to wait until later.

As the event ended, the guests trickled out of the home, offering brief words of condolence to the widow before leaving. There was a sense of closure to the event as if the guests had fulfilled their duty to pay their respects, but there was little emotion or connection to the experience.

The book of Cory's life had closed quietly, with little to acknowledge the impact he'd had on others, whether positive or negative. *Had he made a meaningful contribution in his life?* Jill wondered.

After the last guest departed, they sat down with Erica. Nick shared the lab findings. "The lethal level of selenium found in the bottle of bourbon is consistent with acute selenium poisoning. They explained that selenium poisoning is rare, and it is unlikely that someone would consume enough selenium through their diet alone to reach a lethal level.

"The medical examiner then went over the possible sources of selenium in the alcohol. The likelihood that it was added to the bottle by the supplier who distilled it is pretty much nil. Likewise, the supply chain—on a truck, in a warehouse, or in the liquor store. The reason for these conclusions is twofold. One, targeting one person that way would be impossible. Two, contaminating anything in the food or beverage industry just doesn't happen anymore, thanks to heavy security at every step in the supply chain—video feeds everywhere."

Nick stopped, and Jill saw him watching Erica closely. "Bottom line, it had to have been intentionally added after purchase, with the goal of poisoning the intended victim. We don't know for sure if Cory *was* the intended victim, but it looks likely." He sat back, his eyes trained on Erica. "The medical examiner changed the cause of death to poisoning, which may have been the sole cause or may have contributed to the drowning. Either way, officially, it is now a homicide case."

Erica closed her eyes briefly. "Thank you for telling me. I'd like to understand what happens next, but I'm afraid I'm at my limit for today." She opened her eyes. "I think I need everyone to leave so I can rest. I'm sure you understand."

"There's more," Nick said. "The fingerprints on the bottle were Cory's, plus another set, but the other prints aren't a match to anyone in the system. We're going to need to interview you and Travis, plus get his fingerprints to eliminate him."

"Interview us? What for?" Erica was confused. Or defensive. Her eyes turned steely. "Do I need an attorney?" She turned to Roxanne and raised her eyebrows.

"No, you do not. But you can have legal counsel present if you want. Right now, our questions have to do with who had access to the bottle of bourbon as well as who may have given it to Cory. Assuming that's what happened," he added with a note of skepticism.

Was he implying that Erica was now a person of interest? Was he saying he suspected her of poisoning her husband? And why hadn't Jill wondered about those same things?

"As I told Ms. Fairchild and Dr. Rhodes before, the bourbon was most likely a gift from a client, delivered while I was out of town. Cory must have drunk it the night he died." Erica was firm, even though her story had a couple of presumed facts, tied with a bow of assumptions at the end.

Had it been a gift from a client? Or had someone else bought it and put it in the liquor cabinet to be later contaminated with a lethal substance?

"That's enough, Erica. I will go with you tomorrow to the police station for the interview," Roxanne said. "Meanwhile, don't say any more." She gave Nick a look.

Nick raised his hands. "I got the message. But just to clarify, we're trying to figure out who poisoned Cory, and that's what everyone wants. Also, we'll need the fingerprints of everyone at your law practice to rule them out. The bottle of bourbon," he added at Roxanne's puzzled look.

"There is zero chance you'll get the attorneys to agree to that," said Roxanne with finality.

Nick started to debate the point, but Erica interrupted. "If there's nothing more right now, it has been a long day," she said, ending the conversation. She rose and escorted them out.

Nick gave her his card as he left and said he'd be in touch.

Outside Erica's home, he stood with Roxanne and Jill. "What have you two been doing today?"

"This morning, we went to see—" Jill began.

Roxanne cut her off. "We went to the funeral and the graveside service. Not much else."

"Not much else, huh," Nick said. He turned to Jill. "Is that your story, too?"

"I—yes." Jill felt oddly compelled to back Roxanne in her prevarication. She could convince her later to share their findings with Nick.

"Right. So much for working together." Nick stalked away.

Jill watched his retreating back, already regretting her words.

"Care to explain? I thought we agreed to work with Detective Webb." Jill sipped her latte. If only she could put her feet up, but the coffee shop they'd chosen had no ottomans, unlike her cozy living room.

"I just didn't feel like sharing," Roxanne said flatly.

"Roxanne. That sounds like something a child would say. Come on."

Roxanne sighed. "Okay, I'll tell you what it is. I don't trust Nick Webb. Maybe it's because he's just too damn good-looking to be a real cop."

"Detective," Jill interjected, thinking Nick *was* too damn good-looking.

"Detective. Whatever. But how do we know he won't use whatever we find to take this case down the wrong pathway? I've done enough criminal defense work to see what you might not. Can't tell you the number of times we've found evidence the police either ignored or actively buried. Evidence that would have prevented our client from being indicted in the first place. Most likely, anyway."

"But don't you think it would be better if we were there when he interviews Erica and Travis? What reason would he have to include us now?" *What reason would he have to even talk to me now?*

Roxanne shook her iced latte and took a sip. "I'll follow up with Erica and make sure we're included in the interview. But you do have a point about Nick and the rest of the investigation." A sly grin slid across her face. "I guess you'll have to kiss and make up with him later. On our behalf. Get us back on his good side." She wiggled her eyebrows suggestively.

"Funny."

Roxanne raised her eyes to Jill, a serious expression creasing her brow. "Hey, I meant no offense." She took another sip while continuing to gaze at Jill. "How are things going with you personally? You have a special person? You're not my therapist, haven't been in a long time. It's okay to swap stories now, right?" She raised a quizzical brow.

"Yes, I have a... boyfriend." Jill briefly described Ethan and their relationship history, but not in great detail.

"So, he hasn't put a ring on it yet, huh?"

This was about to get way too complicated for Jill's comfort. "Not exactly. But I am curious about your thoughts on the woman at the funeral. You said you thought you knew why she disappeared so fast and why she didn't show up at the graveside service."

"Nice diversion. But about the mystery woman, I think it's obvious. She left and didn't go to the graveside service because she didn't want to be seen. Maybe she's afraid someone will recognize her. Same reason she sat in the back of the chapel and tried to slip away after the service."

That was the same thought that had occurred to Jill. "She seemed emotionally distraught, genuinely grieving. That would indicate that she's closely related to Cory. Do you know anything about his family of origin? Other than the brother who lives there. Maybe she's his sister." But that wouldn't explain her not wanting to be recognized. Why wouldn't a family member want to be seen?

But as soon as she thought it, she knew the answer. An astonishing percentage of families suffered from estrangement— relationships torn apart deliberately by one party or both. Who knew you better than the people who'd watched you grow up? Who understood better than family how to precisely insert the knife of rejection and ostracism, to permanently wound the heart?

And after such wounds were inflicted, what then? Even death might not be sufficient reason to re-establish contact. In this case, with the brother, Travis. Who may have been involved in whatever drove the sister out of contact.

But she was drawing far too many conclusions.

"I don't know anything about his family other than the brother we both met. But that's a great place to start tomorrow, don't you think?" Roxanne said as she stood. "I have got to get home to my husband and kids. You get to your client, and we'll touch base in the morning."

CHAPTER SIXTEEN

The building was quiet. Early evening was her most productive time for catching up on paperwork, the daytime hours being filled with people. Since it was mainly leased by small offices of professionals, Jill wasn't the only tenant who often worked late. Tonight, however, there was a surprising absence of others working late.

Jill opened the door to her reception area. *Unlocked.* Lauren must be sitting at her desk, no doubt studying for an upcoming exam. But as she made her way in, she was shocked to find that Lauren was not there.

The second shock was her client, Tim Hawkins, sitting on the edge of the sofa. With him was a woman she didn't recognize.

Tim rose quickly. "Dr. Rhodes, this is my wife, Leslie."

Where was Lauren? Her clients shouldn't be sitting here with no one present. But she recovered quickly and gave Tim's wife a warm smile. "Hello, it's nice to meet you. Please come in."

In her office, she took a moment to grab her smart notebook, and while she did, she noted the body language of her client and his wife. Tim's shoulders were rounded, and he had an oddly slack expression on his face. His wife, Leslie, sat rigidly, staring straight ahead. She wore jeans and a casually elegant blouse.

Had Jill been given the heads-up that Tim was bringing his wife, she'd have been better prepared. She could have asked him a few highly important questions first and ascertained the goal. Stated her policy on counseling both people in a couple—the benefits and the drawbacks. More importantly, that she would never counsel a couple where there was infidelity unless there was complete disclosure.

But since she'd had no advance warning, she'd have to go on instinct instead. "What are we talking about today?"

Tim looked quickly at his wife. She gave him a hard stare back.

Tim looked helplessly at Jill.

"I'm thinking you want to talk about the two of you. Where would you like to begin, Tim?"

"Um, yes, that's right. We're having some... issues." Tim swallowed.

"*Issues?* That's what you want to call it? You're a liar and a cheat, and all you can come up with is *we have issues? We* don't have issues! *You* have a girlfriend!" Leslie's eyes blazed.

"I swear to you, it was nothing. It was one time, on a business trip. I'm not cheating on you!" Tim's eyes were wide, and a thin sheen of sweat had popped out on his forehead.

"Do you really think you can gaslight me? You are apparently stupider than I ever thought possible. I have the credit card bills. I know exactly what you've been doing and for how long!" Leslie turned to Jill and spewed. "You knew my husband was cheating on me! Don't you have a duty to... to... do something? But you were *counseling* him! To do what? Leave me for the other woman?"

"Tim, I think you owe your wife the full truth at this point." Jill was on a slippery ethical slope, but she wasn't going to sit there and get blamed. "Let's all calm down and talk. This is an extremely upsetting situation with a lot at stake. But I'm sure you both love your children, and that doesn't change. Tim, go ahead." She looked at him expectantly.

Tim looked panic-stricken. He cleared his throat and tugged at his tie. He gasped. "I... I can't talk right now. I'm having trouble breathing." His face was flushed.

Inwardly, Jill rolled her eyes. Was this one real, or was he faking a panic attack to escape accountability? She instructed him to breathe slowly and use acupressure points. Out of the corner of her eye, she noted Leslie's ongoing glare. No gesture or expression of empathy for her husband's distress. No hand placed on his back or whispered words of comfort. Understandable.

"Go ahead. Choke on your own lies," Leslie threw at her husband. "You have broken all your vows to me, and you have broken our family." She leaned in and spoke in an eerie stage whisper. "I know who she is. I'm going to go see her. You can't stop me." She sat back and put her hand in her bag. "But I'll make sure she doesn't break up any other families."

Tim continued to struggle to breathe, his eyes practically popping out of his head. "No... you can't do that," he said hoarsely. His face was white.

Jill's scalp tingled. She watched in horror as Leslie's hand slowly withdrew a pistol from the bowels of her designer bag. Her expression was triumphant as she pointed it at Tim.

Jill began speaking low and rapidly. "Mrs. Hawkins, you have children who I know you do not want to see you on the ten o'clock news tonight. Please tell us what you want. I'm sure Tim is going to be very agreeable to whatever you want."

Leslie laughed crazily. "What I want? What I *want* is for him to grovel. At my feet. To beg my forgiveness."

Tim looked ready to pass out.

"Do it!" his wife screamed, waving the gun in his direction. "Now!"

Tim slid to the floor on his knees.

Nothing in Jill's academic experience had ever addressed a scenario like this. Nowhere on the road to her doctorate was she prepared for what to say to talk someone down from the threat of violence. *In her office.* Up close like this.

However, she had been confronted by a killer with a gun not that long ago. It had been at night, in the woods, over treacherous ground, and the killer had pointed the gun directly at her heart. She'd heard it go off and thought she was dead.

But she wasn't dead. Throughout most of that ordeal, she'd kept her rational mind intact, devised ways of fighting back, trying to extend the time to give herself the space to figure out how to survive. But she wouldn't be alive and sitting here now, had it not been for Nick.

This time, she was on her own. She took in a ragged breath and breathed out slowly as she spoke to Leslie. "I'm sure there are words you want him to say." She saw she had Leslie's attention, so she kept going. "There are specific things that he needs to acknowledge to you, right? He's lied to you, and now you want the truth, the full truth. Isn't that so?"

"Yes!" Leslie hurled invectives and took full advantage of her extensive vocabulary of scatological language, all targeting her husband.

Tim flinched. "I'm sorry! I'm so, so sorry! Please, baby, put the gun away." He began to cry.

"Tim, Leslie has things to say to you, and there are things she wants you to say. It's time to quit thinking of yourself and listen to her." Jill kept her voice modulated and worked to gain eye contact with Tim. This was a twisted version of standard marital therapy: *Listen. Share. Listen more. Show remorse. Empathize. Apologize.* Not much to go on, but it was the only thing she had at her disposal.

"Why did you do it?!" Leslie continued pointing the gun.

"I—I'm stupid, that's why. I'm so sorry—" Tim managed to squeak out the words.

"That's not the reason! Tell the truth!"

Jill intervened. "Tim, just say it like it is."

"Okay, but again, I'm so sorry, baby. I met this woman, and I was feeling lonely. She invited me to her room, and I went because I wanted something new, something to make me feel young again. And—"

"Finish it! Tell me about the sex," Leslie pushed.

"And, well, the sex was great." Tim's head was bowed, and his tears dripped on Jill's carpet as he spoke, his voice dropping to a whisper.

Leslie used her eerie stage whisper again. "And at any point, did you think about me? About how you were hurting me?"

"Of course, I did! I love you, baby."

"Liar! Tell the truth!"

"Please, can we stop this? I don't want to hurt you anymore," Tim begged.

Jill kept her eyes trained on the weapon. Since her encounter in the woods with a madman, she'd learned a few things. She'd taken a class or two. In one of them, she'd learned how to overcome the threat of an active shooter situation. It was counter-intuitive and went against the hard-wired primordial survival imperative, which in the present scenario would mean getting as far away from the gun as possible, as quickly as possible.

Instead, she knew she had to do the opposite. Despite the warning signals in her brain, she had to move toward the danger. Despite the thudding of her heart, she leaned in closer to Tim and Leslie, speaking low and giving him more instructions. "Go ahead and tell her the full truth, Tim. It's what she wants, what she deserves. She's been hurt, deeply hurt. She wouldn't be this angry if she didn't love you. But now you need to make her understand that you see her pain, that you feel terrible about causing it." Her words were aimed at Tim but meant for Leslie. *Would they hit the target?*

"You're right, baby. I didn't think about you, about how much I was hurting you. I was *selfish*. I know I've hurt you... I don't deserve you."

Leslie sat back a little, lowered the gun to her lap. Her chin wobbled. "You scum. You *filth*. You destroyed our life together! I hate you." And now a tear made its way down her face.

Jill heard a noise. *Oh, God.* The door from the hallway into the reception room had just opened and closed again.

"Hey!" Lauren's voice sang out. "I got us a snack since I figured you would be working late. There's a great little bistro that just opened up. Some of your favorites—I have... drumroll... garlic fries! Ta-da. Do you have any idea what time it is, though?" As she continued talking, her voice gradually rose in volume. She was rapidly making her way to Jill's inner office. "You're finished with your clients, right?"

Leslie's face hardened, and she raised the gun again, this time pointing it at the door. "Tell her to get out of here!"

But the door was already swinging open.

Jill swung into action. Contrary to the messages screaming

from her amygdala, she moved directly toward the danger—in the line of fire between Leslie and the doorway through which her beloved assistant, Lauren, was walking.

Lauren froze, her eyes scanning the scene in bewilderment. There was no time to convince her to run, to get out of there, not quickly enough to avoid Leslie's shot once fired.

"What's happening—" Lauren began, while at the same time, Tim tried to get off the floor.

Leslie gripped the gun with determination, her fingers tightening.

Jill moved her hands to the barrel of the gun, grabbed it from the underside with both hands and began pushing it up toward the ceiling. She prayed that there was no one in the office above hers, but she'd have to take that chance.

As the barrel of the gun moved 45 degrees upward, Leslie managed to squeeze the trigger once. Then again. Jill flinched each time, terrified.

Then Leslie screamed as Jill continued pushing the barrel further, twisting the woman's hand and fingers awkwardly. Then, the barrel was pointed at Leslie's chest, and, unable to maintain a grip at that angle, she let go.

Jill jerked the gun away and quickly shoved it across the floor and under her desk, far away from Leslie, who now did a surprising thing. But maybe not so surprising, considering what had just happened.

Because when Leslie had fired the gun, all Jill had heard was a loud click. And another.

"Gotcha," Leslie said to her husband, giving him an odd smile as she pointed her index finger at him and pretended her thumb was a trigger, which she snapped down. "You get to live. The gun wasn't loaded."

Lauren ran to Jill and wrapped her arms around her in a fierce hug. "Thank God you're okay!"

"We are all okay," Jill said, "but I'm afraid you're not, Mrs. Hawkins. What you just did is, I'm pretty sure, a felony. Lauren, call 9-1-1."

"Already done," Lauren said as she began speaking into her cell. "There's someone here with a gun threatening to shoot us. No—no one is injured. But hurry, please."

"No, wait! No one's hurt. We'll just leave. Please don't turn her in," Tim begged. He pulled his wife into an awkward embrace, which she allowed, but the thin line of her lips and expression of disgust told the full story. *A marriage in ruins, criminal charges ahead, their lives forever changed.*

Jill felt bad for Leslie and for Tim, as second thoughts flooded her consciousness. But the call had already been placed.

Much later, after statements had been taken and Leslie led away, Jill and Lauren sat and talked briefly. "What was that thing you did? You just went for the gun! If it had been loaded, you'd have been shot!" Lauren's eyes filled with tears.

Jill touched her hand, trying not to notice how her own hand was shaking. "Actually, I wouldn't have been shot. It happened really fast, and you couldn't see from where you were standing, but I had the gun pointed at the ceiling before she pulled the trigger. It's a technique I learned in a self-defense class. It turns out that if you can overcome your fear, you grab and twist the gun barrel upward rapidly. That does two things. Three, actually. First, it surprises the shooter—they don't expect their intended victims to make a move like that, the assumption being that *they* are in total control. Two, it aims the shot upward, so no one gets hurt, even if the gun goes off. And three, it twists the shooter's fingers painfully, so they're forced to let go, giving you control of the weapon."

"That is totally awesome. You're, like, a superhero now!" Lauren beamed.

Jill didn't feel like a superhero. Her heart had still not slowed to its normal pace. Her head buzzed with the adrenaline still surging through her system. It all felt so surreal that a part of her was in disbelief. "It's not heroic when you do the right thing, Lauren. I'm just relieved that no one was hurt." *Except emotionally.*

They locked the office and headed home, both utterly exhausted, not only from the day but from the plunging drop in adrenaline. They hugged goodbye more warmly than usual.

Jill's cell rang as she drove home. "Hello."

"Are you okay?" Nick's voice held a tone of urgency. "I was in my car, and I heard the call go out on the scanner. I recognized your office address. Did something happen in your building? Were you involved?"

"I'm fine. It was an unfortunate incident with a client and a gun."

"What?!"

"It's okay. It turned out the gun wasn't loaded. She just wanted to make a... point... to her husband."

Nick was silent. "I—how often do your clients show up with guns? I mean, I know you're dealing with people who aren't exactly well-balanced, maybe even—"

"I know. Never. I've never had anything like that happen before."

"Sit tight. I'm on my way there to make sure you get home okay."

"No need, really. I'm on my way home now."

He was silent for a moment. "Are you sure?"

"Yes. But thanks for checking on me."

"How about breakfast in the morning? I want to know what happened."

There was a brief, awkward silence. Then, they both spoke at once.

"Listen, Nick, I—"

"Jill, I—"

"You first," Nick said.

"I just want to say I'm sorry about not telling you everything earlier today. I don't mean to cut you out. I know we're all trying to get to the truth, and we'll get there faster if we work together." Jill breathed out in relief. "Your turn."

"Um, actually, that was what I wanted to say, too. I'm sorry I left like that."

"It's okay."

They made plans for the next morning.

As she pulled into her parking garage, Jill felt her neck flush with something she couldn't quite identify. Maybe it was the stress of the evening's events. Maybe it was common fatigue. *But the conversation with Nick had felt like they were a couple making up after their first fight.*

CHAPTER SEVENTEEN

DAY FIVE

"Have you ever thought about installing a panic button in your office?" Nick asked Jill as he buttered a piece of toast.

After sleeping restlessly again, Jill had gotten up early and gone for a run. Refreshed, she'd quickly dressed and met Nick at a diner not far from her condo. Coffee was her craving at the moment, and food not far behind. She hadn't eaten dinner the night before, so the omelet on her plate was rapidly disappearing. "Yes, but I didn't think it was necessary."

Nick's eyebrows raised slightly. "Uh-huh."

"It's controversial, you know. If I'm afraid of my clients, maybe I'm not treating them correctly. Or diagnosing correctly. I aim to only treat patients within my area of best skills. For more severe mental health issues, there's medication or hospitalization, so I send those kinds of patients to psychiatrists." She sipped her cappuccino. "This client showed no signs of violence, so I had no reason to be afraid."

Nick pointed. "You have some... on your mouth..."

She wiped away the foam.

"But in this case, the client brought in an unstable spouse," Nick pointed out. "I'm guessing that's not the only scenario in which you could be in the crosshairs of a violent, crazy person."

Jill shook her head. "My practice is mostly individual psychotherapy with people who are perfectly sane. They're dealing with depression, anxiety, or relationship issues. Couples and families. I'm not an emergency room."

"No, but a 9-1-1 call a little sooner than *after* the gun was fired would have been good. Even if it wasn't loaded." He shrugged. "What kind of a nut job does that, anyway? Have you diagnosed that woman?"

"I can't comment on that." Since most of it was now a public record, she'd given him the highlights of the previous night's events, leaving out the part where she'd wrestled the gun away from Leslie. No need in getting commentary on that—she was pretty sure she knew what Nick's stance would be. "Anyway, let's talk about the case. I'm meeting Roxanne after this, and I'd like to hear what you're focusing on."

"I can't comment on that since it's an open investigation," he said.

She started to protest, but then she noticed the lift of his mouth, the light in his eyes. *Teasing me.* "Funny."

She spent the next few minutes describing the visit to the plaintiff in Cory's case, Melanie. She also gave him an overview of the deposition they'd watched on video prior to the visit. "I think there could be something there," she finished. "Either her or her husband. It seems like both of them have reason to be angry toward Cory."

"Mad enough to kill?" he asked.

"I don't know. The difficulty with emotions is they're not predictive. You can be furious but do nothing about it. You can be angry one day and feel foolish about it the next. You can love someone but never tell them. Feelings don't necessarily lead to behavior." She sighed. "If the way people felt pointed accurately to what they might later do, my job would be much easier."

"So, are you saying this couple has every reason to kill, but we have no way of knowing if they actually did go after Cory?"

"It's not that cut and dried," she said. "Angry, yes. Still angry? Maybe not. Angry enough to act on it? Impossible to know." She studied Nick. "What's the next step for you?"

"I'm wondering where the bottle of bourbon came from."

"That reminds me. We found a video feed of the delivery of the bourbon on the day Cory died. The day his wife, Erica, was gone to an out-of-town spa."

Nick's mouth twisted a bit. "That's interesting. But it does give us something to look into. I don't suppose she still had the box with the label."

"No. She'd already thrown it out."

"Of course," Nick said sarcastically.

"You don't still think Erica had anything to do with Cory's death, do you? She was out of town at a spa. I'm sure that can be verified."

"Do you realize how often people kill their spouse, crying giant crocodile tears, even on television? And later, we find out that's the person who did the deed. It's *almost always* the spouse, Jill."

"I guess I knew that, but in this case, how would she have done it? She wasn't there. The bourbon was delivered to the house that day while she was gone."

"Right." Nick looked frustrated.

"Uh, there's one more thing we haven't told you," Jill said.

"Roxanne found a file in Cory's office. It contained numerous handwritten notes threatening him. Apparently, he'd been saving them over time."

Nick leaned forward. "And you're just now telling me this? Please also tell me no one handled the notes."

Jill felt a small wave of embarrassment. "Yes, we touched them to look at them."

"Great," Nick said. "No one thought about possible DNA or fingerprints?"

Jill was silent. She'd thought of those things, but Roxanne had already gone through the file, and she wasn't going to tell Nick that.

Nick cleared his throat. "Moving on. What's next for the dynamic shrink and legal duo?"

"I'm not sure yet. What's next for you?" She wasn't above holding back a little until she could get more from Nick.

"I'm getting financial records today, plus I'll see if there's any way to find out where the bourbon came from and who sent it. I think I'll pay a little visit to Melanie's husband, the attorney who represented her and later married her."

"How can you find where the bourbon came from? The package was thrown out, so we don't have a tracking number."

"There are ways. We know the day the package was delivered, and Holloman had to sign for it, so that means there's a record with the delivery company. Plus, these days, packages are regularly scanned and photographed by the USPS and other services."

"I'd like to go with you to visit Melanie's husband," Jill said.

Nick sat for a moment. "Maybe. Your turn. What's next for you and Roxanne?"

"Roxanne found another case of Cory's. Someone else on the

other side of the litigation table. She didn't tell me much yet, but apparently, there's a guy who believes Cory stole his daughter away from him."

"Stole his daughter?"

"Custody case. Apparently, Cory played dirty, and the dad lost."

"That sounds worthwhile. We'll go together. Melanie's husband, and then, the guy whose daughter was stolen."

Jill wiped her mouth, unsure. "I have to run that by Roxanne first."

"Fine. I'll have to run it by my partner first," Nick said stubbornly.

Stalemate. Jill hadn't exactly gotten along well with Nick's partner, Detective Stone, on the last case. As a matter of fact, he'd been downright hostile to her. She sighed. "How about we just go and sort things out with our... *partners* later?"

"Deal," he said.

"First, I have to take care of something else. How about I meet you at my office in a couple of hours?"

"Fine."

"Hey. Is he in?" Jill spoke to the receptionist at Ethan's company, a commercial real estate developer.

The receptionist widened her eyes. "Hi, Dr. Rhodes. Um, give me a minute, please." She turned away while picking up a landline phone, then spoke too low for Jill to hear. *Odd*.

Turning back, she spoke to Jill with an expression that begged forgiveness, her cheeks reddening. "I'm sorry, but he's not here."

"Okay. Do you know when he'll be back?" Impatience stirred,

but Jill had grown tired of not getting a response from Ethan and was ready to face him, business day or not.

"Uh—not exactly." Her face froze at that point.

"Is there anyone else around who can tell me?"

"Um—" Her mouth hung slightly open.

"Never mind. I'll just go back and talk to Sharon." Ethan's assistant didn't work solely for him, but she generally knew the whereabouts of the handful of sales guys she supported since she managed their calendars.

"Um, Dr. Rhodes—"

Jill marched down the hallway, the receptionist's meek voice calling out feebly behind her. She rounded a corner, and as she did, several people looked up sharply. A couple of people stood. She glanced behind, anticipating that someone important was trailing her, but no one was there. A woman's voice called to her, and she turned to find Sharon hurrying in her direction, concern etching her features.

"Jill. Please, come on in." She escorted Jill into a small vacant office and offered her a place to sit.

Jill declined the offer. "Sharon, thanks for seeing me, but I'm a little puzzled. Where is Ethan? And why is everyone staring at me?" A slight buzz traveled through her system.

"Please, sit down for a minute. I'll explain."

Jill sat on the edge of a chair. "What is it?"

Sharon sighed. "I'm so sorry to say this, but Ethan no longer works here. He... the company parted ways with him a few weeks ago."

Stunned, Jill couldn't think for a moment. *Ethan, fired from his job? Weeks ago?* But now, all the clues cascaded at once. The drinking, even more than usual. Leaving in the mornings at irregular times with excuses that didn't make sense. Dressed casually for the day with odd explanations for that. Commercial real estate work was like legal and financial services. Professionals 'dressed for success,' even in today's world of ever more casual business attire.

The defensiveness when she'd mentioned they might share financial information before setting a wedding date.

"What happened, Sharon?"

Sharon looked pained. "I can't talk about it. I'm sorry. H.R. regulations, confidentiality, and all that."

Whatever the reason, it wasn't good.

"Hypothetically speaking, the usual reasons people part ways with this company are?" Jill fished.

"Hypothetically speaking, it's performance related. Also, attitude and... personal issues. But I'm speaking in general," Sharon said, hesitating. "I take it he hasn't told you."

"I've been working a lot, even in the evenings. I don't think I've been there for him like I usually..." But Jill's words trailed off. *Covering for Ethan, again. A bad habit.* A tiny ache in her chest began to spread. How far apart had they grown? What else didn't she know about the life of the man she thought she wanted to marry?

Nick's words came to mind. *I see a beautiful, intelligent woman who isn't sure about the guy she's with. But she's loyal to a fault and won't let herself think about that.*

What else was she not letting herself think about? *Suppressing important personal insights. Denial.*

"I'm not going to ask you to divulge why he's no longer employed here. But I think you can tell me what his behavior was prior to parting ways with the company. Was he coming in late? Leaving early? Not showing up for client meetings? Did you notice him changing in any way?" Jill stopped herself. *Too many questions. Too anxious. Give her a chance to breathe.*

What Sharon revealed next was nothing like Jill expected. And it poured out of Sharon like she'd been holding it back for some time now. At the end of it, Sharon was in tears. And Jill was in shock.

CHAPTER EIGHTEEN

Nick walked into Jill's reception area. Her assistant, Lauren, greeted him with a huge smile. "Hey, Detective Webb. What's going on? Are you two in hot pursuit of some bad guys? I can't get her to tell me *anything*," she said, nodding toward Jill's inner office. She lowered her voice and whispered. "Just how bad are the bad guys this time?" Her brows raised in concern. "Do I need to be worried about her? By the way, did you hear about our little drama last night? This guy with the wife with the gun... and Jill just grabbed it away from her with this awesome Ninja move and just—"

Nick interrupted, not wanting to encourage Lauren. "No. And, yes. And I'm a little short on time, so if we could..." He gave his watch a meaningful glance.

"Yeah, sure. Let me just..." she picked up the phone.

"Wait!" he said abruptly. Lauren paused with the phone at her ear. "What did you say about a Ninja move?"

"It was amazing!" Lauren gushed. "I walked in, just bringing in dinner like we sometimes do. There's this great little bistro just down the street, and they have the most amazing garlic fries! I almost, like, tossed all of it in the air when I saw the gun pointed right at Jill! I just stood there, frozen, totally lost it, had nothing to say, nothing I could do, I just—"

"The *Ninja move?*" Nick wanted to shake her. *What the hell had Jill done?*

"Right. She just reached over, grabbed the gun," she said incredulously, "and it went off, like, two times, but it wasn't pointing at anyone, so no one got hurt. In a split second, Jill had the gun, and it was over. It was like something in the movies!" She stopped and peered at Nick. "Uh oh. You're, like, *mad* at her about this. Hey, the gun wasn't loaded, so it wasn't a big deal," she said, shrugging. "But the mad thing—I like that protective vibe you've got going on about her."

"Lauren."

They both turned to Jill.

What had she heard? he wondered.

"Nick. Please, come in," she said, but her expression told him nothing.

He followed her into her office. His eyes traveled over her hair, her shoulders, and further down to the way she walked. Her scent—*was that jasmine?* —wafted his way.

First things first. "What was that about you grabbing the gun the other night? Do you know how dangerous that is? You could have been killed! There are lots of ways to handle a confrontation with a person with a gun, but grabbing it isn't one unless you're highly trained. Honestly, Jill, you don't *seem* like a person who takes unnecessary risks, but—"

"The gun wasn't loaded." Her beautiful lips were drawn into a line. Her grey eyes sparked.

"But you didn't know that when you grabbed it," he said. He let out a breath. "I just—"

"Let's. Move. On."

He noted her crossed arms, the clear message in her eyes. *Back off.* "Okay. But later, we'll have a little talk about gun safety. Better yet," he said as an idea rose, "I'll take you for some training." He gave her a conciliatory look. "Gun range. Pointers offered by a professional. Okay?"

"Okay," she said, uncrossing her arms. She gave him a smile, and it went through him like a warm breeze. "Let's talk about what we're going to do next."

While it was nice on one level for Nick to express concern for her safety, it was also irritating. She'd been taking care of herself for as long as she could remember.

"Thank you for meeting with us, Mr. Howard," Jill said, sitting on one of the two chairs in front of the rather large desk. She and Nick had been shown into a standard legal office—case books filling the shelves, files stacked on the desk and credenza behind the desk, triple flat-screen computer monitors. On the credenza were photos of his wife, Melanie, and their children.

"Will." His tone was flat, his expression guarded. "I am in the middle of preparation for trial, and I'm afraid I don't have a lot of time." He was nice-looking but bore the evidence of a stressful, demanding career—expanding middle, tight expression, worry lines at the corner of his eyes. "You shouldn't have spoken to my wife," he added, and now it was clear why he'd agreed to meet with them—it was his chance to defend his wife, to make sure they would do no further harm.

Rather than try to defend their actions, Jill offered, "You're right. We meant no harm. We're trying to help someone else, and we realize how uncomfortable this may be for you."

"Yes. That sociopath, Cory Holloman, whom I understand is deceased. I can't say I'm sorry to see him go."

Interesting. "Why do you think he's sociopathic? Wasn't he just doing his job?" Jill winced inside as the question filled the air. *Cory's job... was that the main source of his problems?* Was it possible that while doing what he felt was right, others had suffered unnecessarily? Like Melanie, this man's wife.

But the bigger question was, who was Cory? Was he a caring human being who had done the best he could, both for his clients and for his family? Did he drink too much to overcome the angst of knowing he'd hurt other people to help his clients?

But sociopaths had no empathy. Right and wrong, the pain of other human beings, ethics, morals—those things didn't keep them awake at night. They didn't need to drink to excess or do drugs to relieve themselves of the burden of a conscience betrayed.

"He didn't need to do what he did to my wife. He could have offered a settlement. He chose to verbally assault her in the deposition. It left her an emotional wreck, and I couldn't talk her out of dropping the case." Howard's color had deepened as he spoke. "The only regret I have about his passing is now I can't..."

"Can't what?" Nick asked sharply.

Howard seemed to realize he'd said too much. "Why are you here?"

"We're here because we have reason to believe Cory Holloman was murdered," Nick responded.

Will showed no surprise. But of course, he wouldn't. They'd told Melanie that Cory's death was suspicious, and she would have repeated it to her husband by now.

"What does that have to do with me or my wife? Actually—

you know what?" His expression hardened. "I don't care about that. I have nothing to say. I think we're done here." He pushed back his chair.

"Before you kick us out, there's something you should know." Nick glanced at Jill before continuing. "We're looking into your wife's case again. As a potential criminal prosecution."

Will stared skeptically. "Are you putting me on?"

"You and I both know the statute of limitations hasn't run out on the rape case. There was never an investigation because she didn't report it at the time. But if she's willing to go to trial... we can open a case. These days, we can get convictions based on testimony, especially if we find other victims. You know, *hashtag me too.*"

It was a stretch, but Nick and Jill had agreed that if they dangled the chance to go after Melanie's assailant, it might get her husband to open up about Cory. Nick had agreed to use his influence with the D.A.'s office to get the case opened if the couple wanted it.

Will rubbed his chin thoughtfully. "At least she won't have to deal with Cory Holloman again. Could be some other bottom-feeding defense jerk, though. I'm not sure she would go for it, but I'll find out." He sighed. "Okay, you got me. What do you want to know?"

"A couple of questions. First, tell us where you and your wife were the night of Holloman's death. We're ruling out people who may have had a grudge. You know how this works."

"You're talking to me like I'm a suspect!"

"Which you will be unless you give us an alibi," Nick said evenly. "Where were you that night?"

"Home. Together."

Nick and Jill exchanged a look.

"Just how angry were you about what he did to your wife in the deposition?"

"I wanted to kill the guy," Will said. "But I'm an officer of the court, and I would never do it. As for my wife, she wouldn't hurt anyone. She catches and releases bugs at our house." His mouth twisted a bit. "We have three children. The last thing we would ever do is risk losing them! You're barking up the wrong tree."

"We're trying to help Cory's wife get a sense of closure," Jill said. "But the deposition was brutal," she said, meaning it. "I saw your wife gradually crumble the longer it went on. The way he brought up her personal life, the attack on her integrity..." she paused.

"He was an attack dog, and he deserved to be put down!" Will's face flushed. A tiny bit of spit formed in the corner of his mouth as he continued hurling ever more colorfully descriptive terms to describe Cory's character. He drew a breath and gradually calmed down. "Yeah, I thought about going after him, but I wouldn't do that. I didn't do it. Kind of wish I had, though." He stared at them defiantly.

Time to switch tactics. "You were both in the legal community here in Dallas. What can you tell us about Cory Holloman? Gossip in the courthouse corridors. Anything at all can help us," Jill queried. "Before your wife's case, were there other encounters you had? Things you heard about him."

"Sure. He had a reputation as a bulldog who would pursue cases relentlessly. He was a hard-nosed litigator, the worst of his breed. Judges respected him for the most part, but attorneys hated going up against him. He won almost all of his cases." He ran his hand over his head. "I didn't like it when I first saw his name as counsel for Melanie's employer."

"What about some of his cases, people he went up against.

Anyone you ever heard about that might have reason to be angry, or to hate him, want to hurt him?" Nick asked.

Will looked thoughtful. "One that I heard a lot about was a custody case. Apparently, the kid was born after the mom had broken up with the dad. He found out about it and sued for a genetic test, which turned out to be positive. He then had to sue for visitation because the mom wouldn't let him see his daughter. Cory was counsel for the mom and pulled some dirty tricks in court that caused the dad to lose."

"What kind of tricks?" Jill asked. This was the second time they'd heard about the custody case.

"Don't know. But I did hear something about how the dad threatened him in open court. I heard he yelled something like, 'You'd better watch your back, look behind you all the time because I'll be there.' Something like that. The Judge sent him to jail for contempt and fined him. I doubt he came out of that any happier."

Jill looked sharply at Nick. The notes. *Look behind you. I'm there. But you'll never see me coming.*

CHAPTER NINETEEN

As Jill walked into the dimly lit jazz wine bar, a sultry melody emanated from the gleaming brass instruments in the corner. Soft crimson light bathed the room, casting a warm, inviting glow on the exposed brick walls adorned with vintage wine posters and abstract paintings. The low hum of chatter mingled with the intoxicating scent of oak barrels, earthy undertones, and the faintest hint of cigar smoke.

The sound of a saxophone pierced the air, its deep, soulful notes weaving seamlessly with the rhythmic plucking of the double bass and the soft patter of brushes on the snare drum. Jill welcomed the sense of nostalgia and felt transported to a bygone era of speakeasies and sophisticated charm.

She'd never enjoyed contemporary music as much as she did that of the best jazz musicians of the early to mid-twentieth century. She loved Miles Davis, Thelonious Monk, and Billie Holiday. The crooners also captivated her; Bobby Darin's "Beyond the Sea" always carried her away to a place of fantasy, one in which romance was assured, never-ending, and comfortable. Elements missing from her own life.

She quickly nestled in a corner booth and ordered a glass of wine. A few minutes later, while enjoying the buttery notes of her chardonnay, she let her eyes close, swaying ever so slightly to the music, utterly absorbed in the experience.

After the meeting with Will Howard, Nick had agreed to meet later with her and Roxanne. Jill had seen a couple of her regular clients before making her way to their meetup spot, deliberately early. She'd hesitated for a moment, considering Roxanne's sobriety, still in its infancy, but after asking, was assured it wasn't an issue. She might be new to sobriety, but Roxanne was iron-willed and had adamantly insisted on this venue.

While she waited, personal issues tugged at Jill's attention. *Ethan.* Explanations were owed. He'd been deceiving her for some time about his employment. Most likely about his financial situation. Who knew what else?

She knew from her work that when people chose to deceive their partners, it was usually not on one topic alone. Often it was a complex web encompassing the main arenas of life: money, sex, and family. Work, too, especially if connected to threads of deception involving money.

Another woman? It was possible. He'd been behaving cryptically for some time. Her stomach sank, and she took a larger sip of wine. Her sister had asked her—hypothetically—if she'd want to know if her partner cheated on her. Though she'd denied it was about Daniel, could it have been about Ethan? Jade hadn't been ready to divulge the actual source of her question. But would Jade hide something that significant, something that impacted Jill's life? *Everyone lies...* an undeniable truth. For a myriad of reasons. But would Jade lie to her?

Something was definitely going on with her, something she hadn't felt comfortable sharing a couple of days ago. Carly, her precocious niece, had partially spilled the beans. There was someone Jade was meeting with her daughter in tow. Or had met at one time. Maybe many times. *I like it better when it's just mommy and me.* The implication that mother and daughter were regularly accompanied by someone else. Someone who was clearly not Jade's husband.

Maybe it was nothing. Children got impressions of adult activities but without the ability to fully comprehend the meaning of them. Perhaps Jade and Carly had run into someone at the art museum, and Jade had decided to linger, to continue walking the exhibit with this other person. Jade knew a lot of people in the art world in Dallas. It could be as simple as a chance encounter.

"This seat taken?" Nick's voice interrupted. He slid into the booth on the opposite side.

"What can I get for you?" Thomas, the bar's Maître D', and someone Jill knew well, approached as Nick sat. He was far more than a waiter, more than a host and greeter. He owned the bar, and he often catered to his favorite customers like Jill and Jade, who were regulars.

"Sam Adams, please," said Nick. After a couple of minutes of listening, Nick spoke. "Music here is smokin'. Come here often?"

"Sometimes," she said, impressed with his use of jazz terminology.

"Not often enough," said Thomas, smiling as he set down Nick's drink. He lingered. "How's it going, Dr. Jill? You're looking as ravishing as ever but maybe a bit tired. Working too much, as usual?"

Jill shrugged, suddenly uncomfortable with the attention of two attractive men at the same time. Thomas was quite a bit older, but he was an impressive person: kind, cultured, successful, and nice-looking. He always made her feel welcome, though he'd never hit on her. For years, he'd been married, but two years ago, his wife of over twenty years passed away from cancer. She'd recently felt a slight shift in their camaraderie. "I'm fine, Thomas. Thanks for asking."

He hesitated, his eyes straying to Nick. "I'm always glad to have new people find my little hole in the wall. Thomas Vaughn." He held out his hand for Nick to shake, who did, providing his name but leaving off his professional title. "Welcome. You're a friend of Jill's?"

"More than that," Nick answered. He appeared to be studying Thomas.

"He's a Dallas police detective," Roxanne provided, sliding into the booth on Jill's side. "Sparkling water with a twist of lime," she told Thomas, smiling. She also ordered an appetizer.

"Will do," said Thomas, smiling back at Roxanne. "Detective Webb." Nodding to Nick, he left the table, disappearing for the night.

"Where are we at this point?" Roxanne asked, unaware of the energy passing between Jill and Nick. "I have a couple of things, but you two first. You're the ones out there talking to people."

Nick answered first. "I wanted to get financial information on Cory and his wife, Erica. Just to rule out any suspicions about her. But there wasn't much I could get at this point, given there's no charge, person-of-interest status, or any other reason to get a court-ordered disclosure of their financial records. The things I can easily get are bankruptcy records, lawsuits, that kind of thing. Nothing there, as far as I can see. Their house, tax records."

Roxanne popped a piece of calamari in her mouth and chewed quickly before speaking. "I have some insight about that. Our firm did some work for Cory and Erica just a few months ago. First, it seems that Cory's mom passed away and left an inheritance in the form of a trust, naming Cory and his brother, Travis, as beneficiaries. The trustee, who manages the trust, is a third party, the bank's private wealth department where Cory's mom kept all her financial assets."

Nick leaned in, interested. "Does that mean Erica inherits Cory's portion of the trust?" he asked.

"Nope. It's an irrevocable trust, meaning that when she passed, the beneficiaries were set in stone: Cory and his brother. Upon either of their passing, the other brother becomes the sole beneficiary. Erica has no right to any of the money or the property. It seems the house was purchased by the trust and is held that way, not by Cory and Erica."

"How large is the trust?" Jill asked. "And how does it function? Does it generate income?"

"Yes, it can provide income at the discretion of the trustee. But who knows how much that amounts to. Could be small sums. Could be far more. But I was told it's substantial, whatever that means."

"Maybe we should talk to the trustee, find out how much," said Nick.

"Wouldn't work. Without a signed release from Travis, the trustee can't share anything about the trust."

"Let's put this in context," said Jill. "Erica owns nothing, or not much of anything, from her and Cory's life together. The house isn't hers, and she can't get any of the assets in the trust. She actually had a disincentive to kill Cory. Without him, she's financially out in the cold. At any minute, Travis can ask her to leave the house."

"She does have a job," Roxanne added. "Real estate agent. She's not going to be destitute, but she won't be mega-wealthy either, at least not from Cory's trust." She paused. "Could be she's highly successful in her own right and making lots of money. There's plenty of that to go around in the hot housing market we have in Dallas."

"Main reasons people kill each other," Nick said, ticking off his fingers. "One, sex. Someone gets in bed with someone else who they maybe shouldn't be in bed with. Someone else expresses their displeasure with a well-aimed deadly weapon." He gave Jill a pointed look. "Two, money. Somebody wants what belongs to someone else. Three, heat of the moment. Someone with no self-control lashes out at someone else. No more someone else."

"Do we have any evidence of either Erica or Cory cheating?" Roxanne queried.

"Nothing obvious from social media," supplied Nick. "Doesn't mean it didn't happen, just that they hid it well if it did."

Roxanne spoke up. "But in the case of Erica, again, where's the motive? Her bread was well-buttered with Cory. Seems like she'd want to hang on to all of that, take no risks of losing what she had."

"Another reason people kill each other. Revenge," said Nick with finality.

"Revenge for what?" Roxanne asked. "I think we're back to continuing to look into one of Cory's old cases coming back to bite him," she said. "What happened with Will Howard, Melanie's husband?"

Jill and Nick filled her in on the conversation they'd had with Will.

Roxanne shivered at the mention of the courtroom blowup, echoed in the cryptic notes they'd found in Cory's files. "Man, that's too similar to the notes to not mean something." She tipped her sparkling water and drank. "I think this case has revenge written all over it. Imagine being a father, denied normal visitation. My husband Henry would go ballistic if he couldn't see his girls."

"The notes." Jill tapped the side of her glass. "Why would someone send cryptic notes to Cory? That sounds more like a stalker, a stranger, than someone who knew him and who planned to kill him. I find that odd."

No one said anything.

Jill ruminated further. *Those who threaten tend not to act. It's the ones who don't provide any warning that we should be afraid of. 'You won't see me coming.' Not the words of the killer who wanted to strike without warning.*

Nick broke the silence. "It's a long way to go, from shouting something out in a courtroom to murder. Someone got the bottle of liquor, somehow injected the poison, had it delivered, and hoped Cory would drink it," Nick said. He shrugged. "There's a lot here that doesn't sound right, doesn't add up. Too many long shots someone took. Usually, revenge is more direct, more opportunistic."

"Right," agreed Roxanne. "Once, a guy who lost custody of his kids showed up at court with some serious firepower he intended to use on his ex. Luckily, he didn't realize he'd be caught at the security checkpoint."

"Unfortunately, I've seen too many women killed by their exes because they dared to leave," Nick shared unhappily.

The reminders hung over them, of the violence that continually dogged—and characterized—humanity.

Jill didn't bother to mention her client's wife, who'd come in waving a gun.

CHAPTER TWENTY

Jill rang the doorbell and waited. The distinct sounds of a television made their way into the hallway outside Ethan's condo. He was definitely home despite the absence of a reply to her texts. She rang the doorbell again, her impatience rising.

How could he do this?

It was one thing to lose a job and hide that fact for a while out of embarrassment. It was another thing to completely ghost the woman he'd said was the love of his life, had wanted to marry.

She raised her hand and started to bang on the door. Suddenly, it was pulled open by a complete stranger, a guy in sagging sweatpants and with wet hair framing his mostly bald pate. "What the hell are you ringing my doorbell for?" He swayed a tiny bit.

Her mouth hung open for a moment. Then, she tried to peer around the guy. "Where is Ethan?" Oddly, the inside of the condo didn't look familiar. She double-checked the number on the door.

The guy took a moment to look Jill up and down. "Don't know. But I can be Ethan if you want." He smirked and swung the door open wide, sweeping his hand clumsily inward. "I have beer."

Confusion swirled. "I'm looking for my fiancé, Ethan. He lives here! Who are you, and what are you doing here?"

"Uh, I hate to disappoint you, sweetheart, but there's no Ethan here. I moved in two weeks ago. I can show you the lease if you want." He smiled sloppily. "I think it's in the bedroom…"

Jill's common sense was at war with the reality before her. This was Ethan's condo. She wasn't inebriated and confused; in fact, she'd only had one glass of wine, and that was two hours ago. Unless the drunk guy in front of her was some kind of magician who'd made her fiancé disappear, Ethan had moved out, apparently a couple of weeks ago, without telling her.

Massive cognitive dissonance.

She turned and walked away.

"Hey! Don't leave! Jeez… what a douche… ring my doorbell and won't even come in and…" the guy's belligerent voice trailed behind her.

Ethan—job lost due to unpleasant circumstances. Moved out of his condo, no communication to her about the significant changes in his life. She felt painfully jolted. More than that. She felt suddenly displaced, unmoored. She and Ethan had their issues, but fundamentally, she thought they were okay. Just a few things to work through.

Her mind traveled to scenes from their courtship, and sadness tugged at her heart. Their first date—bowling, of all things. She'd bested him, but it turned out later he was a great bowler, so he'd no doubt let her beat him. They'd eaten hot dogs, and Ethan had reached over to wipe the mustard off of the corner of her mouth, and it hadn't been a come-on. He'd smiled sweetly at her, and she'd instantly felt a spreading warmth inside, a sense of having found someone safe. Someone who might actually be there for her.

But that was years ago, and now, she wasn't at all sure who Ethan was. Was he the wonderful, sweet guy she thought she'd found but going through a tough time? Did he need her to stand by him, overlook the deceptions? Or was he 'over her,' trying to find a way out, either because of his issues or despite them? Was someone else standing by him, offering him comfort?

Compassion warred with shock and fear. She'd never be able to sleep tonight without getting to the bottom of it. But how? He wasn't answering her texts or calls.

In her vehicle now, Jill sighed deeply. She had only one option left at this point, and it wasn't her first or best choice. It was risky, potentially even more stressful than going home and obsessing. But it was all she had.

"Jill! I wasn't expecting you tonight..." Deborah Palmer ushered Jill in. "Is something wrong? Are you okay?" Her voice was laced with concern, but there was something else.

Deborah stood with Jill in the foyer, not inviting her further into the house.

Ethan's mom was definitely put off at the moment. Normally, she welcomed Jill with open arms.

"I'm fine; it's just that I can't get ahold of Ethan. I don't want to alarm you unnecessarily, but can you tell me when you last spoke to him?" Jill moved further into the house.

"Um, I'm so sorry, Jill, but I was about to go to bed." Deborah edged in front of Jill, effectively blocking her from going any further. "I've had a long day, and I've been feeling a bit tired lately. I just can't handle a visit right now. But I talked to Ethan not long ago, maybe an hour or so," she said, trying to reassure Jill. "He's fine, and I'm sure he'll contact you as soon as he's... free."

She tried to usher Jill to the door, but Jill wouldn't budge.

"I'm sorry, too, Deborah. Please forgive me, but I'm tired of getting the runaround from Ethan." She moved past Deborah and went into the family room. *Was that one of his sweatshirts on the back of the sofa?* Feeling bizarrely intrusive, she marched down the hallway to the guest bedroom, Deborah calling after her to stop. She flung open the door and stood there, gazing at Ethan's things. The closet door was open, and inside hung his clothes, other personal items strewn on the bed and floor haphazardly. His laptop sat on the desk in the corner.

"Jill, honey—" Deborah caught up with her—"I'm sure he would have told you. He's just a little bit stressed out right now with the promotion. He and his landlord just didn't see eye to eye on the lease renewal, so he's crashing here for a few days while he finds a new place. Let's go sit down and have some tea. I'm sorry you found out he's staying here this way, but it's just a small glitch. You know how he is—he'd forget his head if it wasn't screwed on!" She forced a laugh, then tugged Jill's arm, pulling her toward the family room.

"What promotion? What are you talking about?" Jill asked, refusing to sit.

Deborah moved into the kitchen and started boiling water. "Oh, you know! He's gotten another promotion. Those people just love him. He's their top sales guy, after all. And he trains the new people because he's the best at what he does." She beamed with pride for her only son. Her only child. "He's doing so well. He said he's going to buy his next home, another condo, maybe, so he doesn't have to deal with landlords again. But I'm sure you know that!" Her smile faltered a bit at this point.

She fiddled with tea mugs and tea bags, her hands slightly shaking.

"Deborah. Stop doing that and come over here," Jill said.

"It's almost ready!" Deborah almost sang out the words. "I just love English Breakfast, don't you? Although at night I prefer mint. It helps settle my stomach," she said as she placed her hand over her girth. "How is work going for you, dear? Ethan says you work too much, but I know you really like what you do. But it must be stressful dealing with people like that," she added, nose wrinkling a bit in distaste. "You know, dear, you are so career-focused... but I know Ethan wants a family, and I hope you do, too." She rambled more about having grandchildren someday.

Jill's stood frozen, past breakups weighing heavily. Each one, an opportunity to marry and start a family. But every one of them had been wrong for her, and she'd suffered the emptiness afterward, the discouragement. How many women settled for the wrong partner? To stave off the march of time, the gradual shrinkage of her biological window for becoming a mom.

The thought of settling for the wrong person in order to have children stole into her mind. Was that what was happening with Ethan? Was she stalling, putting off the inevitable next breakup, hoping for a miracle? Hoping that somehow, he'd be the man she wanted to marry, to father her children.

Or was she irredeemably picky? Were her standards so high that no man could meet them? A handful of her female clients flashed in her mind. Attractive, successful, and took great care of themselves. Perpetually single because no one ever quite measured up. Jill walked over and stood in front of Deborah. "Let's go sit and talk," she said gently.

Deborah's eyes filled with tears. She turned away from Jill and pulled a tissue out of her pocket and wiped her eyes. "I don't know what's wrong with me. Allergies are so bad. I'm going to the doctor next week and get on something." She choked back a sob but let Jill guide her to the sofa.

"Ethan didn't get a promotion, Deborah. He was fired by his company. He hasn't been doing well at all, not at work."

Sharon's voice echoed in her ears. In the end, she'd spilled everything, unable to contain her own shock. *He's in debt, writing hot checks. We think he's into something, maybe gambling. Maybe something worse. We couldn't keep him here, too much risk. Plus, whatever is driving his financial issues has taken him off his game. He hasn't had a closing in months. I'm so sorry, Jill.*

Deborah shook her head. "No, that can't be right. He told me he got a big promotion. He's going to buy a house..." but she looked up at Jill. "But I'm sure you know that since you're making plans for where you'll live after the wedding." She stopped and blew her nose. "There is going to be a wedding, isn't there?"

What was the right way to break through someone's denial? Especially when her own had recently been blasted away. Deborah seemed so fragile at the moment, so vulnerable. She'd been widowed for some time. Ethan's father had died of some form of heart disease years earlier. She lived modestly on the pension he'd left for her as well her own work as a substitute teacher.

"I'm sorry, but we do have to face this, Deborah."

Deborah's nose was red and swollen, her eyes bloodshot. She shook her head again but weakly. She sighed heavily and looked up. "Yes, I suppose so."

Jill took her hand and squeezed it.

Where to start?

Jill wondered what was really going on with Ethan. Why was he lying and hiding the truth of his life? Embarrassment and shame? Something more? Her own denial reached up and began whispering soothing words. *It's not what it seems like. He's just going through a rough time. He needs his mom's support, your love. It's going to be okay; you just need to talk about it, figure out what's next. Help him figure out what he needs to do to get back on his feet.*

On and on it went in a rapid-fire loop. She tried to shake off the obsessive thoughts, and at that moment, she heard the door to the garage open and footsteps approaching.

"Hey, Mom," Ethan called out. "What's for dinner? I'm starving." He stopped in the kitchen, his eyes shifting from his mother to his fiancé. His thick, wavy hair was disheveled, and he looked as though he hadn't shaved in days. "Jill. *What are you doing here?*" His tone was accusatory, devoid of any affection.

All ideas of comforting words vanished. "I'd like to ask you the same thing," Jill said, standing. She glanced at Deborah and said no more.

Deborah quickly stood. "I'll give you two some privacy," she said as she slipped away.

"Seriously? You show up here and spy on me? *Grill my mom?*" Ethan had gone from curiosity at seeing Jill to full-blown defense. He took off his backpack and threw it on the kitchen floor, where it slid across the room and banged into the lower cabinets. "Shit!" he yelled, then he kicked the nearest cabinet. Twice.

"Stop it," Jill said, shocked to her core.

"Stop it? *Stop what?* What are you doing here, anyway? I can't believe how little you trust me. I was busy today. I'm in the middle of some things, you know, like most people are, like *you* are most of the time!" Hostility radiated from Ethan. "Why is it you can disappear for days at a time, not answering my texts, doing whatever you're doing with that detective guy, Nick What's-his-name, and it's all good. But I have one day of not jumping on your texts, and somehow, I'm the bad guy. Huh? Why is that?" Ethan stalked to the refrigerator and flung open the door. "Where is my goddamn beer?" He shoved a few bottles around noisily and pulled something out. He pulled off the cap and gulped, his back turned to Jill. Slowly, he turned around. "Well. I guess now you have all the evidence you need to call off our engagement." He laughed sarcastically. "Oh, that's right. We're not really engaged, are we?"

Jill couldn't move. She'd never before seen Ethan express anger like this. Irritation, yes. Passive aggression, yes. But he wasn't really capable of violence, was he?

Three levels of violence. *Verbal*—emotional assault through the use of well-chosen words that pierced the recipient in ways that could never be undone. *Physical objects*—throwing and breaking things in the environment, an act of intimidation that telegraphed danger and threat to the other person. And the highest level of violence—*physical harm to an animal or a person*.

Sometimes, people began with verbal and escalated over time to physical harm to others. Especially if they ignored the roadmap to assault, failed to get help to control their anger and rage.

A sense of two realities and doubt swept over her, leaving her almost breathless. The man she'd loved, the one she'd wanted to marry, was a shadow, barely discernible.

The man before her—insecure, angry, hostile, and potentially violent—was a stranger to her.

"I think you need some time to yourself," Jill told Ethan as she turned to leave.

But before she could open the front door, he was there, holding it shut, blocking her exit. "So now you're leaving? Just like that. What's the matter? Can't take the heat? What happened to all the things you've said to me about commitment and love?"

She felt his breath on her neck and closed her eyes. "We'll talk later, Ethan. I'm not leaving you... I'm not breaking up with you. I just think we need some space to cool off." She turned to him and looked up into his eyes, willing him to be less angry. *Placating him with the lie that they weren't breaking up.*

His face was so close, and now he softened, closing his eyes briefly. "Jill." He put his arms around her and sagged. "I'm sorry, honey. It's been an awful week." He held her close, his voice breaking.

Jill could feel Ethan's tears on her cheek. She put her arms loosely around him. "It's okay. We'll talk later."

She slipped away moments later, but not all of her made it out of the home. Something broken and painful left a trail behind her and echoed along a pathway to the past.

But the future was dark and cold.

Some things, especially those that battered the heart, couldn't be undone.

CHAPTER TWENTY-ONE

DAY SIX

The sun sat just below the horizon, casting a faint glow across the Katy Trail in Uptown Dallas. Nicely paved with lanes for runners as well as bikers, it wound through neighborhoods, behind homes, bordered by trees and foliage. Vibrant hues of pink and orange blended seamlessly into the deep purple and gray of the night sky as the sun continued to rise. A gentle breeze rustled the leaves of the surrounding trees, carrying with it the sweet aroma of blooming flowers. The air was crisp and invigorating, the perfect temperature for an early morning run.

Jill walked briskly along the trail. She wore a light jacket, leggings, and a pair of comfortable sneakers, her hair pulled back in a ponytail. Her eyes, a piercing gray, reflected the darker colors of the sky as she took in the beauty surrounding her.

As Jill walked, she inhaled deeply, letting the fresh air fill her lungs. She drank in the breathtaking nature around her. The melodic sounds of birdsong filled the air, creating a symphony of nature's music. A red cardinal flitted from one branch to another, its vibrant feathers a striking contrast against the verdant foliage. She accelerated her walk into a jog, passing by fellow early risers. They exchanged friendly smiles and nods, acknowledging the shared appreciation for the beauty of the day.

She picked up her pace, accelerating into a run that blurred the scenery she passed, as well as the people. Her cares and concerns fell away. Soon, there was nothing but the feeling of her heart thumping and her breath rapidly drawing in and out. The feel of her feet hitting the concrete.

After twenty or so minutes, Jill slowed her run to a jog, then later, to a fast walk. She'd covered the trail to a turnaround point and headed back. Finally, she slowed to a stroll, came upon a bench, and paused, sitting for a moment. She waited for her heart rate to slow and breathing to normalize.

As the sun continued its ascent and the city came alive, Jill knew it was time to face the day. Reluctantly, she glanced at her phone and registered the string of text messages. She sighed and stood. No respite from the issues that dogged her.

An hour later, Jill's head pounded, the benefits of her morning run having slipped away. She sipped coffee with one hand while managing the steering wheel with the other, praying for the caffeine to work its magic.

Ethan. He was in the middle of a life crisis brought on by career failure. Possibly by a series of financially disastrous decisions. Definitely exacerbated by the move-in with his mom. His messages this morning, one after the other, dripping with remorse. *I'm so sorry, baby. Please forgive me.* Multiple emojis.

Where was the emotional space?

It was so hard to refrain from responding, offering reassurance she didn't feel. To fix it. But what was she going to fix?

She was too familiar with the pull to go to work on a loved one, to apply her expertise to help them solve the big issues that plagued them, without being asked to do so. Her mom, Crystal, flashed in her mind. An ancient tug-of-war between them.

Jill: It's just a tiny pill. Take the medication, Mom, and do it consistently. I promise you'll feel better. And stay off the computer for a while. Stay away from all those websites.

Mom: You have no idea what it's like. I take those pills, and I gain weight. He barely looks at me now. Do you think he's going to want me when I weigh 25 pounds more?

Jill: He loves you, mom. He adores you! These are stories you tell yourself. It makes you feel insecure, but you're lucky. You have a wonderful husband, Mom. Have you tried meditation yet, like I told you? It's just ten minutes a day, and you can use this app. This one focuses on gratitude, and it's a proven way to fight depression.

An endless loop with no resolution.

She parked the car and met Nick and Roxanne, greeting them distractedly. They had a game plan, though, for this play, they'd have to wing it at a certain point.

A few minutes later, they sat with Erica. She was dressed for success—pearls, silk blouse, stylish dark jacket with skirt, with tanned bare legs, and heels. Her hair was impeccable, and her nails were done. The frazzled, grief-stricken widow had taken a back seat to the luxury home realtor. Erica glanced at her watch, and as she did so, the light caught a diamond-encrusted bezel. Her wedding ring finger was bare. The huge diamond ring sat on her right ring finger. "I just have a few minutes before I need to go meet some clients for a showing. What can I do for you?"

"Actually, it would be good to have Travis in this conversation," said Nick. "We've made a concession by not calling you into the station. But we have questions, and I'm afraid you're stuck with us until we get them answered."

She sat back and crossed her legs. "Go ahead."

Travis walked into view, headed toward the kitchen, and Erica called out. "Get these folks some water, hon."

He stopped, head down, and appeared to mumble something to himself. He nodded and disappeared, reappearing a few minutes later with a tray holding glasses of water. Cut crystal, Jill noted.

"We need you to stay for a few minutes," Erica told Travis.

With a wary look in his eyes, he nodded and sat. Close to the front edge of his seat. Hands folded carefully. "Okay."

Nick took out a small notepad. "Travis, can you tell us where you were the day your brother died. Starting with the morning and for the rest of the day and night."

Travis looked at Erica, who nodded. "Um, I was here most of the day. Then I went to my friend Ross's house." He looked again at Erica.

Was Travis asking for permission to speak?

"What time did you leave to go to your friend's house?" Nick asked.

Travis looked at Erica again, who nodded. "Um, I think around 4:00?"

"Describe everything you did before you got to Ross's. Then tell us what you did at your friend Ross's."

Travis looked panicked and swiveled to Erica. She glanced away. He licked his lips and wrung his hands. "Um, nothing. I don't remember doing anything here at the house except hanging out in my room. Then I went to Ross's house and—"

"Where does Ross live, and what's his number?" Nick asked, pen poised over paper.

Travis gave him the information.

"And?" Nick prompted.

Travis licked his lips again. "I went to Ross's, and we played video games."

Nick gave him an impatient look.

Erica spoke up. "Travis, hon, just tell the detective how long you stayed at Ross's, what you did there, and when you came home. That's what he wants to know."

Travis shifted and ran a hand over his head, looking relieved. "We played Fortnite. Battle Royale with a bunch of other players. Ross and I made a pledge to go to the finish, but we kept getting knocked out. After the first time, we got in a new game. And kept doing that. We played all night." He stopped and looked down. "I came back the next morning, and Cory was dead."

"Did you talk to Cory that day? Before you left the house?" Jill asked gently.

"Um, no. I was in my room."

"And where was Cory while you were in your room?"

"I don't know."

"Did you see when the delivery came in?" Nick asked. "It was a box containing a bottle of bourbon."

"I was in my room," Travis said. He continued looking at the floor between his feet.

That checked out since they'd all seen the video feed showing Cory accepting the package.

A thought occurred to Jill. "Travis, do you understand what happened to your brother?"

Travis looked up. "Of course, I do. I'm not stupid. He drowned in the swimming pool."

Interesting. Apparently, Erica hadn't told him about the poison.

"That's all for now, honey. You can go back to your room after you take care of the kitchen." Erica spoke firmly, glancing at them.

Travis slipped away.

"A real fount of information," Nick muttered.

"He doesn't know his brother was murdered," said Roxanne accusingly. "Why not?"

"He doesn't handle things well. I'll tell him when the time is right. I don't want him going off the deep end with one of his... episodes."

"How does postponing it help?" Roxanne asked. "Bad news is bad news, no matter how long you wait to tell someone. I say you rip off the bandage—"

"It's my decision to make." Erica interrupted. "Are we finished?"

"One more thing," Jill said. "What's going to happen to Travis? Have you made any decisions about your life going forward?"

"I made a commitment to take care of Travis if anything happened to Cory. I intend to keep that promise."

"But what about your life? Right now, you're still adjusting to what's happened. But down the road, it may be a real obstacle to someone new—your former husband's brother, living with you," Roxanne pressed, tagging onto Jill's question.

Jill interrupted before Erica could answer, seeing an opportunity. "Maybe you could tell us more about Travis. You mentioned... episodes. What exactly is the reason he needs care? I don't mean to be insensitive, and I realize some things are not readily apparent, but he seems okay. He seems functional."

"Well, he's not. He suffers from severe anxiety. Trying to hold down his last job almost put him in the hospital. He couldn't handle the pressure of having to get there on time. He'd set his phone with three alarms, and still, he stressed about it. He became physically ill as review time approached. He quit the day before that." She sighed. "He's had therapy but not much and won't go back. He won't take medication because he doesn't like the side effects."

"What you're describing is treatable, with techniques that help people with brain re-mapping," Jill said gently. "But without treatment, it doesn't get better. It gets worse. He's young. You're talking about decades of care for him."

"My husband just died, Dr. Rhodes. Was *killed*. All I can think of right now is the next few days. Work is a distraction that helps me get through the day. Coming home, taking care of the house, dinner with Travis, it all gives me focus." Her nostrils flared, but her body was still. "I'll have to tackle the future later. Much later, after I get things sorted out. After I start sleeping at night again. Quit having nightmares about Cory floating in that pool." A tear slipped down her cheek, and she brushed it away. "They say you have to take it one day at a time. But right now, it's one *hour* at a time."

"Thoughts, anyone?" Roxanne asked. She tore a steaming hot croissant in half and slathered it with butter. Taking a bite, she practically moaned with pleasure.

Jill sipped coffee while Nick dug into eggs with bacon and toast.

"Aren't you going to eat?" Nick asked Jill.

She shrugged, feeling the knot in her stomach.

"Here," Nick said, handing her a piece of his buttered toast. "I never could stand to watch women starve themselves."

"Oh, no, thank you. I'm just not really hungry right now," Jill said, not taking the toast.

Roxanne raised her eyebrows. "Wow, way to make assumptions about her eating habits. Maybe she's just not hungry; ever thought of that?"

"I was just trying to be polite," Nick said defensively. "No need to make a big deal out of it."

"Polite? You're basically telling her she should be eating just because you think it's what she should be doing," Roxanne said.

Nick put down his fork carefully. "That's not what I meant at all. I just thought she might want some *toast*."

"Oh, I'm sure you're just so concerned about her well-being, right?" There was an intense look in her blue eyes as she angrily shoved aside a stray lock of dark, wavy hair. "It's not like we're in the 1950s anymore. Men telling their little women what to do, how to eat. How to take care of themselves. Or not."

Nick sat back, saying nothing.

Roxanne looked close to tears. She pushed aside her plate and crossed her arms over her body. She looked away, her jaw working.

Jill and Nick exchanged glances. Jill asked softly, "What's going on?" She waited for an answer that didn't come. "What do you want right now, Roxanne?"

Roxanne turned back to face them. "Right now, what I want is to get up and run out of here. And keep running." She breathed in once, let it go. "But my sponsor says I need to deal with it when I have... issues."

"Issues," repeated Jill.

Roxanne took a deep breath. "This is not what I want to talk about right now, but what's going on is my husband Henry is not exactly happy with me. In spite of months of sobriety, meetings almost every day. One minute he's micro-managing me, wanting to know my every move, taking care of me to the point I can't stand it. The next, he's angry and resentful." She turned to Nick. "Sorry."

Nick nodded.

"And now, I've done it again," Roxanne said wryly. "My sponsor says addicts always have a way of making everything about us. Can we please just talk about the case?"

Nick and Jill glanced at each other. "Of course," said Jill.

"My first impression is that the brother, Travis, is a pathetic guy who feels guilty about his brother's death," Nick started. "He wasn't home when it happened. Playing video games all night. Who does that in their thirties? But still, it's odd that Erica hasn't told him Cory was poisoned."

"My thoughts, too. Why is she holding back that information? Sure, he's clearly a guy with a lot of issues, but it's not like he's falling apart. Anyway, did we accomplish anything in that little visit?" Roxanne asked. "What do you think?" she asked Jill.

A number of things didn't add up, but Jill wasn't ready to throw random puzzle pieces on the table. Not yet, anyway. "Let's talk about what we know. We found out that Cory was the only person in the house that night. Assuming Travis's story checks out, which I think it will, given how easy it is to do so. So, Cory was alone when he had that drink, the one that led to his death. I think we're back to the main issue. Who managed to deliver a poisoned bottle of bourbon, from which Cory drank."

"Agreed," Nick said. "Which brings me to the delivery. After canvassing the neighbors, we got video feed of the delivery truck. That gave us the name of the carrier. With that and Cory's name and address as the recipient, we found out the pickup location. Here's the address." He scrolled on his cell and held up the screen for Jill first, who shrugged.

Roxanne drew in a sharp breath. "I think I know who mailed this."

168

CHAPTER TWENTY-TWO

As they took their positions, Detective Nick Webb pulled out the sturdy office chair, the wheels squeaking slightly against the linoleum floor. He sat down and steepled his fingers, leaning forward to capture the suspect's gaze. His eyes were piercing and relentless at first.

The object of his scrutiny sat in a less comfortable chair across from Webb at the metal table that gleamed under the harsh fluorescent lighting. An invisible barrier of suspicion and pressure filled every corner of the small space. The scent of stale coffee and sweat added to the overall unpleasant nature of the conversation at hand.

As a signal to the opening act of the play, Detective Nick Webb's eyes softened. "Thanks for coming in, Mr. Bennett. As you know by now, we're looking into the death of Cory Holloman." Nick laid out the reason for the meeting calmly. "We understand he was the opposing attorney in a custody case involving you and your ex-girlfriend, over your daughter."

Rick Stone, his partner, sat blank-faced next to him.

Nick opened a folder and re-arranged papers to buy time. He

looked up. "Let's begin with the court case involving you and Cory Holloman. You lost normal visitation rights as well as custody of your daughter, thanks to Mr. Holloman."

"That's right," said Kevin Bennett, his eyes narrowing as he shifted in his seat.

"You are allowed visitation infrequently and only with a social worker present."

"Yes," said Bennett, his jaw clenching. A small vein on the side of his forehead appeared.

"I can't imagine what it must feel like to not be able to see your own kid," threw in Stone. He took out a packet, pulled out a pinch of something, and put it in his mouth, between his lower lip and gums. "My kids are everything to me," he said, his enunciation slightly impeded. "I believe I'd have a thought or two about seriously hurting anyone who took them away from me. Maybe *more* than hurting them." He picked up a water bottle and spit in it.

"Man, I've got to be honest with you; that habit of yours is disgusting," Nick said to his partner, frowning.

"You know what, this stuff really helps me relax. Especially when I gotta talk about losing kids, like this conversation. Gives me heartburn just to think about it. Tough break," he said, looking mournfully at Bennett. "Besides, it's not that bad. It's just tobacco," he added with a nod toward Nick. He spit into the water bottle again, which had begun to fill with brown liquid.

"Yeah, but it's the way you're using it. You're basically spitting toxic sludge all over the place. It's nasty," Nick said, shaking his head.

Stone grinned. "Well, at least I'm not smoking it, right? I'm not charring my lungs, giving myself cancer. Plus, you don't have to deal with the smell. That's got to count for something."

Nick rolled his eyes. "Maybe. But it's still harmful. You know that stuff can cause all sorts of health problems, like gum disease. And you *can* get cancer from chewing, so don't kid yourself."

Stone shrugged. "Everything can give you cancer these days. No way to avoid it, so I might as well enjoy life." He turned to Bennett. "As I was saying, losing your kid must have been the worst day of your life. What did you do that made the court take her away? Neglect? Abuse?"

Kevin Bennett slammed his hands on the table and stood. "What the hell? Why did you drag me in here—to watch your stupid, dog-and-pony show over *chewing tobacco?*" His neck had turned red, and the vein on his forehead throbbed. "I didn't lose my kid because of anything other than my Ex's heartlessness and her... her lawyer! Who—" His jaw clenched. "I don't want to speak ill of the dead." He turned to go as if he could simply walk out.

Perfect. The room was now at the right temperature.

"Calm down, Mr. Bennett. There's something I want you to see," said Webb, swiveling his smart pad around. He touched the screen and played a video. "See that? That's you in the elevator in Mr. Holloman's building. See the time and date stamp? That was long after your case ended and not long before Holloman's death."

Bennett peered at the screen, sitting down to get a closer look. His face paled. "Yeah, that's me. What about it? It's a big office building with lots of people in it," he added defensively.

"True. But there's more. See this one?" He touched the screen again, and another video played. "That's the security camera right inside Holloman's office waiting room. That's you again." He sat back and waited.

Kevin Bennett shifted in his seat. "So what? I was there, but what difference does that make? And what does this have to do with his—" he stopped, clamming up.

"Cory Holloman wasn't your attorney. He was on the other side. He was opposing counsel in the case that cost you everything that means the most—your *daughter*. What reason could you possibly have to go see him except to go after him? Maybe get revenge." Nick watched his subject closely.

"That's bullshit!" Bennett said. "I didn't do anything to him! When I walked out of there that night, he was alive and well. I don't know what kind of game you're playing, but—"

Stone interrupted before he could continue. "Should we show him the other thing?" he asked his partner.

Nick paused, putting on a thoughtful expression. "Yeah, I guess so." He fiddled with the tablet for a moment. Looked up at Bennett. "It's a law firm, you know. A big part of their practice is criminal defense."

"Scumbag lawyers defending the bottom feeders of society," Stone said philosophically. He spit in the bottle again.

Bennett looked ready to explode. "Man, I know it. Helping liars and scammers get away with—"

"Stealing kids? Like your ex did to you with your daughter?" Nick asked.

Bennett ground his teeth. "Yes," he hissed. "But I swear, I didn't do anything to him. All we did was talk."

"All you did was *talk*," mused Stone. "You know, it never fails to surprise me how people just don't realize how many eyes are on them these days. Right?" he said to his partner.

"Right," said Nick. "Like the ones criminal defense attorneys use in their offices. The lobby, the hallways, and the interior of their offices. Keeping an eye on all of their—"

"Bottom-feeding clients," Stone finished for him. "Who stupidly carry weapons without bothering to conceal them." He pointed at Bennett. "Like you."

Nick turned the tablet toward Bennett. "Here you are, walking down the hallway with Mr. Holloman. See that bulge?"

"Pretty sure it doesn't mean you're just happy to see him!" Stone laughed at his own joke.

Bennett looked and paled further. "So what? I have a license to carry. I did nothing illegal."

"What exactly did you talk about?" Nick asked.

Bennett started to open his mouth, then clamped it shut.

"You know, this goes a lot easier for you if you tell us what went on that night," Nick told him. "At this point, we're just checking out our leads, and this is one we need to clear."

"Are you charging me? I know my rights. If you're not charging me, I can leave," said Bennett, but his expression registered doubt. And anxiety.

"Who said anything about charging you? We're just trying to find out what happened that night. You went to see Mr. Holloman. You went after hours—8:25 pm, to be exact. You found him alone there, which wasn't a surprise as you no doubt chose that time for that reason. Are you with me so far?" asked Nick.

Bennett said nothing for a moment. "It was nothing. We did talk about the case, but it was just—" He swallowed and stopped.

"You were packing heat. We're interested, you see, in why you went to see Cory Holloman, at that hour, with a firearm," said Stone, his voice carrying the implied threat. *Speak up and answer our questions. Or else*.

But Kevin Bennett had had enough. He stood. "Again, I'm asking. Are you charging me with something?" He looked from one detective to the other. When neither responded, he said, "Fine. I'm out of here."

They let him move toward the door. Then, Stone stopped him. "There's one more thing, Mr. Bennett." He paused, waiting for Bennet to turn and look at him. "It seems you sent a bottle of spirits to Mr. Holloman. We know that for a fact and can prove it with evidence. It was contaminated with poison that it turns out caused the death of Cory Holloman." He stood and approached the man. "Kevin Bennett, you are charged with the murder of Cory Holloman. You have the right to an attorney—" and he finished reading Bennet his Miranda rights as Nick Webb handcuffed him.

CHAPTER TWENTY-THREE

As always, Jill felt as though she'd arrived home. Though it was a professional space, the soothing colors, the warm, natural light filtering through large windows, and the potted plants in the office of her partner comforted her almost as much as his home. But conversations such as tonight's were forbidden there, a place he held as sacrosanct. No talk of their practice, their patients, or anything to do with work was allowed in the Kelly home. Only great food, wine, and lively conversation.

Sometimes, personal sharing between Jill and Dr. Kelly. Picking through their histories, unraveling conundrums. Though they invited his wife, Donna, to join their discussions, she usually begged off. Preferring to play the role of host, bringing them trays of appetizers and refilling their drinks.

Dr. Preston Kelly sat across from Jill in the semi-circle of comfortable chairs and sofa, the low coffee table in the center holding a few of his scattered collection of books. There was the obvious stack of self-help tomes, but also books on philosophy.

He was beginning to round in the shoulders, and the amount of salt in his hair was no longer a sprinkling. But the warmth in his dark eyes had only deepened with time, the compassion grown even greater.

Jill's voice held a hint of weariness as she recounted the challenges she was facing, her voice carrying a note of vulnerability despite her best efforts. She unconsciously reached up a couple of times to briefly massage her neck.

Dr. Kelly listened attentively, nodding in understanding as she spoke. He offered his support and advice, sharing his own experiences with challenging cases from his years of practice. As they talked, the gentle ambiance of the counseling office enveloped them. As always, a safe space for Jill to express her feelings and concerns. Gradually, her tense shoulders relaxed, and her demeanor softened. The conversation flowed naturally as the two therapists found solace and reassurance in each other's company, their shared understanding helping to lighten the weight of the difficult cases they were both managing.

But tonight, Jill found herself hesitating. This wasn't her normal practice download. It was more, and it could burden her partner unnecessarily. But there wasn't anyone else with whom she could have this conversation, not in the way she needed to do it. As her doubts swirled, Preston Kelly watched her. She could feel it. There was no option to pretend or to hide out emotionally. He knew her too well, better than anyone, including Jade.

His expression held a mix of compassion and professional concern, and she braced herself for the shift. The truly tough conversation was ahead. They sat quietly for another moment as though to turn the page in the book. Finally, he spoke. "What's really on your mind?"

Jill drew in a breath, and her answer spilled out quickly. "Two things. One, I'd like to share my impressions about the investigative case I've been working on. I just want to put a period at the end of that sentence. Two—Well, it's more personal in nature."

"Haven't you left something out?" He studied her.

She looked at him, genuinely puzzled.

"It's not every day you have a client show up with his wife who's carrying a firearm. Which she used to threaten both yourself and her husband." His look had shifted to deeper concern.

Jill sighed. "Of course. I didn't bring up that... incident... because I don't really feel any emotional residual from it. The gun wasn't loaded, and no one was hurt. End of story."

"Right."

"No, really. I'm fine, as far as that's concerned," she insisted.

"Which makes you unique. Unless you're a Navy Seal and confront life-threatening danger on a regular basis, your system has no way to integrate an experience like that without processing it emotionally." He studied her carefully. "If you were a cop, you would be required to do a stint in therapy before going back to duty."

She knew that tone, and she knew that Dr. Kelly's extremely well-developed bullshit meter was on to her. She shifted in her seat. "Okay, maybe you're right, but I do have something else that is far more important. I promise you, if I start to have any backlash from the gun-toting wife, I will let you know, and I won't hold back."

"I'm here when you're ready on that one," he assured her. Playfully, he gave her the *I'm watching you* hand signals. Then he spoke with gravity. "But you and I both know this is nothing to brush off."

She nodded, then dove into the case.

Following the last meeting with Nick and Roxanne, the detective and his partner uncovered definitive evidence that

Kevin Bennett killed Cory Holloman. He'd apparently gone to Cory's office one night and threatened him. The bottle of bourbon was mailed from his office. It was enough for them to move forward with an arrest.

Jill reflected out loud on the motive. "It was apparently revenge, the rarer of motivations for murder, typically because a lot of time passes between the egregious incident and the victim mustering up the energy to take action."

"You don't sound settled about that," Preston reflected back.

"I'm not settled with it," she said. "Something doesn't feel right. I dug around in some neuroscience journals, and it seems that the antecedent to revenge is typically some form of rejection. Social rejection is one of the most devastating of emotional wounds, so much so that teenagers will commit suicide if they are bludgeoned enough on social media by their so-called friends."

"Then there are mass murderers," Preston added. "Many of them go back to the school where they experienced rejection, where they were bullied. Symbolically, they kill kids who represent the ones that victimized them earlier in life. Adult mass murderers often go to the workplace from which they were fired," Preston observed. "They may kill the actual people who they believe ousted them from the company, but failing that, it's whoever is there."

"All revenge-seeking behavior, triggered by rejection," Jill said. "Rejection feels like death, which explains why so many mass murderers are willing to die."

"Goes back thousands of years when we needed the tribe to stay alive. Our very survival depended on it," Preston added.

"Hard-wired," Jill continued the thread. "And we still depend on connection to others. Our most difficult cases are the people who are socially isolated yet seeking to overcome anxiety and depression." Even with all of her research, Jill remained unconvinced. "But if rejection is the main motivator, where is that in this case? In the case of Kevin Bennett, there wasn't any rejection. Cory wasn't a friend or a lover or anyone meaningful to him."

"Right. But people do get angry over other issues. Conflict that spins out of control. Wasn't there a case not long ago about two guys who got into a dispute about the tree that bordered their properties?" Preston noted. "One guy shot the other guy. But we don't hear stories like that very often. Unless it's drug or gang-related," he said.

"Look at you, noticing the crime sheets," Jill teased him. "Of course, we do hear stories of domestic violence escalating to the point of murder," she said soberly. "But the revenge thing keeps sticking in my brain for some reason."

Another thought occurred to her. "You know what the creepiest thing is? The neuroscience tells us that when people *suppress* the pain of the rejection, they go into retaliation. The more they suppress, the more it turns into revenge-seeking behavior, and ultimately, when they do enact revenge, it's the *reward* centers of the brain that are activated. They actually experience *pleasure* as they inflict physical pain, even death, on their victims."

"Revenge is sweet, after all," mused Preston. "I wonder what else the crime statistics would tell us. About revenge and other motivators for murder," he said thoughtfully. But his eyes crinkled. "Maybe that detective you've been working with can provide some insight."

She ignored the last comment. "I'm still doing some research, but meanwhile, I'm having a hard time lining up the method of the murder with the so-called motivation. Kevin Bennet was so angry he confronted Cory and made threats in open court. That's passion, an explosion of emotions so strong he couldn't self-regulate. Then, months later, he carries out a twisted plot to kill Cory out of revenge, but he leaves a trail of breadcrumbs leading directly back to himself. It doesn't make sense to me."

"The mind of the person seeking revenge might very well cook up an elaborate plot to kill someone," Preston said. "But to your point, why bother? He didn't cover up his trail, and it would seem that if he spent time cooking up the plot, he would also pay a little attention to basic forensics. You said the bourbon bottle had his fingerprints on it? And it was mailed from his office?"

"Right," said Jill. "The level of rage that it takes, the kind that simmers for months, would, in my mind, result in a violent outburst. Follow Cory home and attack him there. Or find him in the parking lot of his office one night and attack him."

"Poison as a choice is curious," said Preston.

"It is," concurred Jill. "We see it used in those extremely rare Munchausen by Proxy cases, mothers slowly poisoning their children so they can gain the attention of medical professionals. But this is completely different."

"And what about the victim, Cory?" Preston queried.

"Since I never met him and didn't know him, this is mostly speculation. But it appears that he was narcissistic. Perhaps it gave him the fuel to perform in court the way he did, often at great expense to the opposing side." She paused thoughtfully. "Cory was so narcissistic that he injured people emotionally, leaving rage in his wake. That, I believe, is what led to his murder. One of those people came for him."

"What about his ability to change? What if he did turn the corner in his life, become less selfish? Could he have evolved past that?"

"Possibly. But that doesn't mean the people around him automatically stopped hating him." She sighed. "I don't know for sure. I'm still such an amateur at this crime stuff, anyway."

"Which brings me to a question I've been wondering about. Why are you working on these criminal cases? Besides your obvious attraction to Detective Webb."

She bristled. "I'm not attracted to Detective Webb, and that wouldn't be my motivation if I were. I'm a big girl, and if I like a guy, I can do something about it without taking time off from my practice to pursue cases like this." She glanced at her watch. "You'd better get home before Donna starts texting you." She stood.

"Nice deflection, Dr. Rhodes." His expression softened. "You know, it wouldn't be a crime if you were attracted to Detective Webb. The heart wants whom it wants, despite the logic of our brains saying otherwise. We'll leave that one alone, but we haven't tackled issue number two." He nodded toward the sofa.

She sat again on the edge and took a breath. "This won't take long. It's Ethan. I think we're over. This time for good." Yet even as she spoke the words out loud, she wasn't sure if they were true.

PART TWO

CHAPTER TWENTY-FOUR

Cory Holloman banged away at the keyboard, pausing briefly to take a sip of the now cold coffee. Occasionally, the hollow, cackling call of alcohol permeated his brain and body, accompanied by a slight shiver. But each time, he fought off the urges. He focused intently on the brief he was writing, forcing all of his consciousness onto the task at hand.

Cory's hand reached again for the coffee cup blindly, but when he tipped it to his mouth, there was nothing. He set it down a bit too hard, sighed, and pushed back his chair.

In the break room, he started a new pot of coffee, taking those moments to reflect. It was dangerous because when he sat still and thought too much, the random, erratic portions of his mind began raising the volume of their incessant refrains. The same two sides of the argument played on repeat. A small committee meeting in his head daily now. Sometimes hourly.

What are you doing, working late again? What for? You don't have to, you know. Now, you can take it easy, enjoy life, and do the things you've always wanted to do.

And the other side of him. *You know why. There's too much at stake at this point. I can't just sit around, raking it in, bored, with nothing to occupy my mind or fill my days. What I want is not the same as before.*

But he wasn't so sure that was true.

The darkness that hovered in the back of his mind threatened to overtake him, and he knew that if it did, he'd be weakened. His resolve would shatter. He would go back to the way he'd lived before, an emotional wrecking ball. A walking personal disaster, despite all the professional success.

So many bad choices. So many decisions were made while waltzing in the alcohol-infused fantasyland that had been his escape, his refuge from dealing with the realities of life. He heard his mom's voice. *You are gifted, Cory—so smart, so brilliant, and because of that, things come too easily for you. But you also have that genetic coding, and I'm sorry for it. I should have chosen better. But your father was an addict, and so are you. You won't find real joy in that bottle or in chasing after women. Slow down, my dear son. Breathe. Look deeper and find yourself; find the way to contentment. It's a far worthier goal than enchantment.*

Why hadn't he spent more time with her? She was gifted, but in ways that were contrary to him. She was wise. She saw things in people, including him, that others didn't. She'd spent most of her life helping people find themselves, but every time she'd tried to do that for him, he'd pushed her away. Brushed off her support.

There's always tomorrow. The refrain of everyone who took their closest relationships for granted. His motto, too. She'd called him that last day. He hadn't called her back, meaning to later—tomorrow, the next day, whenever.

But there wasn't another day because the next day, he'd

gotten the call from her sobbing neighbor, Elvie, or Alvie, or something like that. Telling him his mom was gone forever.

Pain traveled through his chest, sharp and insistent. He coughed and observed, almost outside of himself, the tears that now dripped. *Mom, I'm sorry.*

Seems all he did these days was say, *I'm sorry.* And he was. The regret now unburied dripped through his veins as though he'd been hooked up intravenously to sorrow, loss, and shame. The only relief he had was when he slept at night, thankfully possible.

Another face swam into view in his mind, and he found himself smiling. She was lovely, with eyes that sparkled at the sight of him. A mouth always curving into a smile and arms that warmly encircled him in a love he'd never experienced before. She was his life, his love. She was his now and his future. She was the only hope he truly had.

But... his face fell at the thoughts of all of the problems, the barriers to overcome. The other person who would be hurt. He remembered the sight of his mother after she'd passed, her hand on her chest. Holding an object. A small, framed photo of Cory and his wife on their wedding day. She beaming, he barely smiling. His expression telegraphing the telltale signs of the reality of how they'd married after a night of far too many bourbons. His eyes— puffy and bloodshot. His face flushed unattractively.

A change in air pressure and a small sound interrupted his thoughts. Had the door to the lobby of the offices opened? But he'd locked it, he was sure. Almost sure. Was someone walking down the hallway?

Then, he thought about the notes he'd been getting. *You'll never see me coming.* He hadn't taken them seriously, but now, late at night, all alone, he thought that maybe he should have. Cory thought of his gun, squirreled away in his desk.

"Hello?" A voice called out. A voice Cory immediately recognized because he'd never forget that voice. The voice of someone who had verbally assaulted Cory in court with impunity despite the judge's admonitions. And even as he'd been taken away to spend a few nights in jail, he'd continued hurling his unbridled rage with one target. *Cory.*

"In here," Cory said, turning around. And as the man walked into the room, he asked him calmly, "What are you doing here?" The first thing he noted was the bulge in the man's jacket pocket, the telltale shape of a weapon.

Kevin Bennett gave Cory a look that might have been cold and menacing. Or it could have been simply tired. "I need you to hear what I have to say. I never got that chance in court. We're going to have that discussion now." He slid his hand into his jacket.

"Okay. Let's go to my office," Cory said evenly.

"I'll follow you," Bennett said, his hand remaining in his jacket, resting on the bulge.

And as Cory walked down the hall, he wondered if each breath was his last. Would he feel the bullet go into his back? Would it hit his spine, giving him a torturous death as he became instantly paralyzed?

"Not there," Bennett told him, gesturing toward the small conference table, preventing Cory from sitting behind his desk, within easy reach of his gun. "Over here."

They sat at the conference table. Bennett pulled his hand out of his jacket. In it was the gun Cory had known was there all along.

"That isn't necessary. I'm here, and I'm willing to listen. Put the gun away."

"No way. It's for self-protection. You might decide to attack me."

"Attack *you*? I think it might be the other way around, buddy, don't you think? You've come to my office after hours with no appointment, and now you've got a gun in your lap. Not exactly conducive to a *discussion*. The implied threat makes you guilty of a crime, for which you could go to prison for—"

"*Shut the fuck up*. You're not in court, and you can't get away with your legal tricks, your sneaky manipulations. I'm not falling for it. This time, you get to listen!"

Cory raised his hands. "Whoa, there. Calm down, I'm listening." Against all his instincts, he lowered his hands and took a breath, giving Bennett the space to talk. Or, with Cory's defenses lowered, the time in which to kill him.

Bennett's face was mottled with the intense rosy hue of flushed veins and white spots. His eyes pierced Cory. "Here's how this is going to go. We're going to have a trial, just you and me. No jury, no judge. Matter of fact, I'll be the judge, and you can defend yourself. You can try, anyway." He wiped his forehead with a hand that displayed a slight tremor.

Cory said nothing.

"You are hereby charged with the crime of ruining a man's life by taking away his daughter."

"It's not a crime to represent someone in a custody case. Someone always walks away disappointed at the outcome, and that's not my—"

"Shut up!" Bennett stood up and began pacing. "I'm going to present the case against you first. You'll get a chance to respond, but not now!" He walked a few feet away, turned swiftly, and stood, holding the gun pointing down. He took a breath. "As I said, you are charged with ruining a man's life—*my life*—by taking away my daughter. Here are the elements of the case."

Bennett walked over to the whiteboard Cory used to map out cases. He picked up the dry eraser and removed everything, then picked up a marker. "One, you took a couple of old-history things out of context from my life and twisted them." He wrote, *1. Lied to make me look like a monster.*

"Am I allowed to ask questions?"

Bennett didn't answer right away, seeming to consider. "Yes, but I'll stop you if you try any of your tricks."

"What were the facts about your personal history that were untrue?"

"Objection! Not relevant. The only thing that matters is how you lied and twisted the facts to make me look bad. You brought up an old assault charge from my college days, but you left out the part about how the guy assaulted me first. You used it to make me look like someone who would be a danger to my own daughter!"

Cory was silent.

Bennett turned to the whiteboard again. He wrote, *2. Took the word of my lying, scheming ex-girlfriend without doing a polygraph.*

Cory frowned. "Polygraphs aren't used in custody cases, and anyway, they're never admissible in court because they're—"

"Inaccurate! I know. But you could have required her to do it so you would have seen what a scheming liar she is."

"But she was my client. I had no reason to believe she was lying."

"Do you think I'm stupid? I know how this works. You don't give a shit whether or not your dirtbag client is telling the truth! You care only about raking in your fees while putting on a case, making yourself look smart in front of the judge and jury, and winning. *How it affects a person's life means nothing to you!*"

Cory felt stung by Bennett's words, and he wasn't used to that. But he couldn't deny Bennett's accusation. He almost never tried to find out the truth of a client's story unless it affected how he ran the case or in the likelihood that it might come out in court. He needed to know the truth only so he could prepare for how to respond later.

He'd never cared about how people on the other side of his cases were affected by the ways in which he'd persuaded the jury to see his client's side. Or the methods he'd used to force early settlements or plea bargains.

Or the pieces of evidence he'd sometimes withheld. Like when he'd discovered that Kevin Bennett's ex-girlfriend had done the same thing two previous times, using her partners to get pregnant. In both those cases, she'd lost the babies well before term due to complications. She'd gleefully told Cory that Kevin Bennett had made a great 'sperm donor,' but she wanted no part of him in her and her daughter's life. She'd spoken of *their* daughter as if she were a possession—hers alone, never to be shared with the father.

Cory snapped back to the present when Bennett asked his next question, spit out with sarcasm. "Tell me something, *counselor*. Do you have any kids? Are you a father?"

Cory's middle section tightened. He opened his mouth to speak, but Bennett interrupted.

"Never mind that question; I already know the answer. You're a selfish guy. You have no children. Next question: Have you ever loved someone, anyone?"

"Of course, I have," Cory answered truthfully.

"I know you're married, but being a father is totally different." Bennett paced again, looking down and talking slowly. The gun by his side. "Have you ever loved someone more than your own life? Been willing to give up your life for them? Because that's what being a parent means. It means you would step in front of a bus to save her. There's no other way to say it."

He turned to face Cory. "Do you know how I found out I'm a father? On *social media*. After she had our daughter, she posted pictures from just after delivery. A friend of mine told me. I did the math and knew she was mine. The DNA test I had to spend thousands of dollars in legal fees to obtain proved it." He pulled out his phone and tapped and scrolled. "Here's what she looks like now." He thrust it toward Cory. "Look at her!"

Cory peered at the phone, and the little girl who beamed back at him almost took his breath away. She was bursting with laughter and joy.

"Do you know what my visits with her are like? Huh? Supervised visits only! A social worker has to be there at all times to make sure I don't harm this baby! *My own sweet daughter.*" His breath was ragged. He looked ravaged. "Thanks to you!"

"I'm sorry," Cory said and meant it. Regret trickled down his spine and wrapped him in a blanket of shame and remorse. All of which threatened the small light that had recently entered his life and that beckoned from the far end of a long, dark tunnel toward a new life. But now he wondered if he deserved the joy he might be able to find.

"You're *sorry*. That's just great. Do you know who's tucking her in at night now? Some dude she met on a dating app. A guy who *isn't related to my daughter* gets to act like a dad with her. *Every day.* She barely knows me. I'm this stranger she has to spend a couple of hours with every few weeks, with a social worker present. It's awkward, and I have to work hard to not bust out in tears until I leave." Bennett sat and put his head in his hands, swaying slightly.

The silence enveloped them. The heaviness of the moments

as they dragged on settled over Cory's shoulders. It was a familiar feeling. This time, his life hung in the balance. He didn't feel deserving of a better future, but his wasn't the only life to consider. Cory finally broke the silence. "What do you want, Mr. Bennett?"

"What do I want?" Bennett looked up with a shattered expression. "I want my daughter in my life. I want to take her to school, go to her soccer games, and help her do homework at night. Cook dinner. Take her to Disneyland, settle her in college when she's a freshman. Dance with her at her wedding." He sat quietly again for a moment and took a ragged breath. "I made her a bedroom. I painted the walls, and I bought the furniture. I got my sister to help so it would look exactly like a place for a princess to sleep. Do you know what that bedroom is used for now?"

Cory was silent.

"It sits empty, day after day. I'm not allowed to have her over to spend the night, not even one night." Bennett hung his head again. "I go in there. I can't stop myself. I picture her playing with the stuffed toys. I picture tucking her in at night. It's killing me, but I can't help hoping. But as it stands, I'm going to be the stranger who she sees occasionally until she gets old enough to tell someone she'd rather not."

Cory spoke urgently. "I don't think that's the way it will play out. You can file again, and while I can't represent you because of the conflict of interest, there are others in my firm who can. I'll... see if I can get the fees cut. As long as I'm not in court, I can help with—"

"I know you can't do that," Bennett said. "Again, I'm not stupid. The conflict within your firm is too much. I have to go to a different firm, and the fees won't be cut. I've already taken out a second mortgage on my house to cover the first time. There's no more equity left to borrow against, and I don't have much in savings." He raised his eyes to Cory. "The only thing left is you. I want you to hurt just as much as I'm hurting. I want. Your life. Destroyed."

"I know. I don't blame you. You're right—I was a heartless bastard. I helped my client take your daughter away from you in a terrible way. I'm truly sorry for how I've affected your life. Please, listen before you decide."

He raised the gun back up, and Bennett pointed it at Cory. "Why should I listen to you?"

"Maybe you shouldn't. But it might make a difference. I don't know."

Finally, after what seemed like an eternity, Bennett put the gun back down.

And Cory shared his story. Later, it didn't matter as much what Kevin Bennett did or did not do, whether or not he raised the gun and fired it at Cory. What mattered was how Cory felt—remorseful, sad, and desperate to help the person he'd once callously punished for a college infraction by taking away his child.

Selfishly, Cory hoped their conversation would change the outcome and give him another chance. Forgiveness might be too much to hope for. Hugs and tears? Ridiculous. Maybe he didn't deserve to get off the hook in any way, but nevertheless, he opened up, spoke freely and honestly, even when it made him squirm. This man deserved the truth—the full truth. And maybe, just maybe, Cory would walk away, free to move forward with his life with the hopes and dreams that had sustained him in recent months.

But a few weeks later, Cory lay sunken in the deep end of his own pool with no remaining second chances.

CHAPTER TWENTY-FIVE

DAY SEVEN

"Who are you again?" The man who spoke was grim. His cheeks were lined, his eyes bloodshot with bags underneath, and his discomfort fairly bled from him. His hands were clean, his nails tidy, but his skin was pale. This was no career criminal, and at present, he was far beyond a fish out of water. This was a man suffering one of the worst things that can happen to a person. *Incarceration*. The removal of freedom and autonomy. He'd plunged to a previously unimaginable low rung in life, to a place he couldn't possibly have anticipated a mere year ago. Apparently, for the love of a child and a devastating loss, all perversely twisted and resulting in the ultimate form of revenge.

Kevin Bennett stared through Jill, barely registering her presence. *Disassociation*. Understandable.

She was feeling a bit disassociated as well. Approaching the Lew Sterrett Justice Center earlier, the first impression she had was of a massive, imposing structure. It was a complex of buildings constructed primarily of concrete, with few windows and a heavy security presence. Even from the outside, the atmosphere was stark, devoid of warmth or comfort.

After parking in the designated visitor lot, she'd found the main entrance. A digital sign displayed the visiting hours, and a couple of law enforcement vehicles were parked nearby. Entering the jail, the temperature dropped as the automated doors closed behind her, and she'd shivered involuntarily.

A uniformed guard directed her to a reception desk, where she presented her ID and stated the name of the inmate she was there to visit. She was then asked to empty her pockets, but she'd already made sure to bring nothing inside except her ID, phone, and car keys.

Next, she stood in line, waiting to walk through a metal detector under the watchful eyes of the guards. They were professional but stern, adding to the overall sense of formality and anxiety. The detector beeped, and a guard performed a pat-down search on the hapless woman in front of Jill. After passing through security, she was given a visitor's badge and directed toward the visiting area. Her phone vibrated, and she looked briefly at the screen.

What the hell are you doing? Call me! Nick's text. Someone had leaked that she was going to visit Kevin Bennett. She continued, tucking her phone in her pocket after turning it off.

The walk to the visitation room was a journey through a maze of stark but brightly lit hallways. Each step echoed in the silence, making the journey feel longer than it actually was. The walls were lined with heavy doors, and the occasional window offered glimpses into life inside the facility. The atmosphere was tense and sterile, with the occasional shuffle of a guard's feet or the distant murmur of voices echoing off the hard, plain walls.

Finally, she arrived at the visitation room. She'd waited alone at one of the numerous small tabletops. The room was under continuous surveillance, both by CCTV and by guards stationed at key points throughout the room.

As Jill had waited, she'd been struck by the disparity between this depressing environment and the peaceful, safe atmosphere of her office. Her clients suffered; otherwise, they wouldn't seek her help. But none of them, to her knowledge, had ever been through something as soul-crushing as jail.

Now, she faced Kevin Bennett. Unsure of her own motives but driven nonetheless, she began. "I appreciate you meeting with me. I'm Dr. Jill Rhodes, a psychologist. I've been working on the Cory Holloman murder case."

Kevin Bennett's hand shook, and his face flushed at the mention of Cory. "If you're here to drive another nail in my coffin, forget it." He made to leave—standing and motioning the guard.

"Wait! Please, Mr. Bennett, I'm here because I'm not entirely convinced you killed Cory."

He hesitated.

"Please, just give me a few minutes. You can always leave."

She waited, holding her breath.

He sat down, waving away the guard. "Giving you only a minute or two."

She knew the time she could spend with Bennett was limited. She wasn't a family member or his legal counsel. "Fair enough. I realize you've been charged with Cory's murder. I know this is a terrible intrusion, but can you tell me, is it true? Did you kill him? I'm not trying to trap you or elicit information you wouldn't want to be repeated in court. I'm a licensed psychologist, so anything you tell me is protected. Provided you hire me on the spot." She waited, holding her breath again. This was a long shot and one likely to get her in trouble, both with Nick and the licensing board. But she fiercely hoped that because her motives were pure, it would be okay.

"*Hire* you? I don't even know you. Why would I? Besides, my attorney told me not to talk to anyone. Period."

"I understand. But if you do hire me, you can talk to me freely, and if you say you didn't kill Cory, I believe I can help you."

He sat back, his face working. "Okay." He wiped his face with his free hand. "It's not like I have a lot of other options. They pretty much nailed me, and I don't really understand how or why. I can't afford a good attorney, so they gave me some court-appointed guy who spent all of fifteen minutes with me. The answer is *no*. I did not kill Mr. Holloman."

"And because you've been accused of it, you are suffering from anxiety and depression," Jill fed him.

"Yes." His face changed visibly. His chin wobbled a bit, and he swiped at his eyes.

Relief. Someone was listening to him. Jill felt a thrill of elation, and the unproven intuitive pulse reverberated throughout her system. This man could be innocent, and if so, she aimed to prove it. "You can pay me later. Our session will be $5.00."

He nodded.

"Tell me what happened the night you went to see Cory at his office."

"The first thing you have to understand is that I didn't go there to kill him. I just wanted to scare him."

As Jill listened, she saw in her mind's eye a man obsessed with the loss of his daughter, obsessed with the hurt and hatred, unable to let go of it. How could he have let it go? Every day, peering into the princess-themed bedroom he'd made for his daughter, seeing the absence of what should have been there.

There were no little girl messes—the bedcovers were not in disarray; toys hadn't been played with and discarded. Instead, he was left with the hollow silence of an empty child's room. Feeling despondence again, the sinking feelings of loss, the surge of anger. *Of rage.*

Suppressing the pain and the anger? The pain suppressed and leading to violence?

Empathy surged, and she felt angry with Cory. Yes, he'd done his job. But at what cost? If Cory had been a man of conscience, and Roxanne seemed to think so, then it had to have been very difficult to look at himself in the mirror each day.

"That day in court was the worst day of my life. I couldn't imagine going through something like that—months of depositions, my life ripped apart, and not win. I was so sure the judge would rule in my favor. Who wants a man and his daughter to be separated like that? I felt my whole world crashing down. Do you have children, Dr. Rhodes?"

Why did people who had children always feel compelled to question those who didn't? As if she couldn't quite empathize with them. She could, but maybe not fully. "No."

"Anyway," he continued as if he hadn't heard her answer. "I wanted to hurt him then, right there in front of everyone who had participated in taking my daughter away. At that point, I didn't care what happened to me." His face twisted. "If I'd had a gun that day... I'm grateful I didn't because I would never have seen my daughter again. All I could think of was getting some of the poison out of my system. So, yes, I threatened him in court that day."

"Did you send threatening notes to Cory's office?"

"Huh?" He looked genuinely puzzled. "Don't know what you're talking about."

"Never mind. Please, go on."

"I'm not a violent man. Yes, I took a gun there that night. I wanted him to feel *something*. He was so cold in court. He talked about me like I was *dirt*. He twisted a college assault charge into something that made me look like a monster." He breathed out. "I know what you're thinking—that maybe I did kill him. But I walked into that office that night to scare Mr. Holloman. I wanted to scare him so badly that he would confess to me what a dirtbag attorney he really was."

"So, you only scared him?" she asked. "The police believe you did more than scare Mr. Holloman. They believe you poisoned him, that you sent him a bottle of bourbon laced with something that caused his death." She watched him carefully.

"I did not kill that guy!" He banged his hands on the table, causing the guard to begin advancing toward them. "That is a lie!" His entire demeanor shifted, anger rolling off of him. *Oppressed by the system?* Yes. *Capable of harm, of getting revenge by killing Cory?* Reluctantly, she had to admit the answer was likely yes.

Jill waved away the guard despite her accelerating heart rate. She plunged on. "But how do you explain the fact that the bourbon was mailed from your office with your fingerprints. Mr. Bennett. Our conversation is confidential. Tell me what happened."

Kevin Bennett sat back, shaking his head. "I did send him a bottle of bourbon. Just as a thank you for the conversation we had that night. He... listened," Bennett said. "But I swear, on my daughter's life, it *was not poisoned*. Someone set me up. I have no idea how that happened."

"Who would set you up?" Would he feed her someone else's name? Because he knew something, had an inkling of who else might want to kill Cory? Or simply make something up to divert the accusation away from himself?

Defeat pulled his shoulders down. "I don't know."

This was the truck-sized hole in Kevin Bennett's assertion of innocence. He'd sent the bourbon but claimed to have no idea how the poison got into it. He'd gone to Cory's office with a weapon and revenge in his heart, though he hadn't used it that night. Someone had sent threatening notes to Cory.

Her own belief in Bennett was rapidly slipping away. "Okay. Let's go back to the night you went to Cory's office. To scare him."

"I'm not proud of that."

"What happened?" she prompted.

"Something I never would have imagined."

And when Bennett finished the story of his confrontation with Cory, Jill felt another piece of the puzzle fall into place. It called into question the entire narrative about Cory, revealing something that no one had seen, or at least, she didn't think so. *If it was true.* "I'm glad you told me."

"Right. But what good does that do?" he asked, his face sagging. "Can you talk to the district attorney? The two detectives who arrested me. Someone. Anyone. I mean, what can you really do? I'm still screwed, no matter how you look at it."

His hopelessness tugged at Jill's heart. He wasn't wrong. She had little power in this matter. Additionally, she wasn't at all sure of his innocence, in spite of hearing his story. Now, her heart sank with the stark reality of all the evidence stacked against Kevin Bennett. But she'd committed to helping him, and she would do that.

She spent the rest of the allotted twenty minutes with Bennett, asking more questions, filling in holes. She knew platitudes were not only unnecessary, but they would also be false. She resisted the impulse to offer empty hope. Instead, she committed to seeing him as a client. "While I may be unable to change the situation, I can be a support." Even as she said it, she knew she was in over her head. She'd never had an incarcerated client before. How did a psychologist offer meaning and bolster positivity with someone behind bars?

She had no experience with clients in this position. But there were those who did. She made a mental note to do some research, find someone to guide her so that she could provide real care to Kevin Bennett.

Now, it was time to circle back. To Nick. And to Roxanne. Though they'd apparently succeeded in getting justice for Cory, it felt like there was more going on that had yet to be uncovered.

CHAPTER TWENTY-SIX

Jill was deep in thought as she left Lew Sterrett and headed for her car. Her eyes were down, not watching where she was going. She stopped in her tracks at the familiar voice.

"Did you get a confession out of him?" Nick leaned against her car, arms folded, but he was anything but relaxed. "And where's your situational awareness?"

"Situational—what?"

"Never mind. But we're going to the gun range, and that's not all. Later. Right now, you owe me an explanation. Aren't you the one who said we were working on this case together?"

"How did you find me?"

"I have my sources," he told her, his piercing eyes fixed on her, searching her face. "And you haven't answered my question—are we working together or not?"

"We are."

"And how does your little visit with Kevin Bennett constitute *working together*?" He stopped. "You know what? It doesn't matter. We got the guy, and he's going down for Cory Holloman's murder." He pushed away from her vehicle and turned to go.

"What if I got the opposite of a confession? What if Kevin Bennett isn't the guy who did this? Oh, wait. *You have your man, and you don't care about the truth.*" She pushed her key fob angrily and opened the door of the car, heart thumping. She was tired of defending herself to Nick Webb. "I think we're done here." But before she could close the door, he was there, holding it open. "Wait, Jill."

She glared up at him silently.

He sighed. "If I go around to the passenger door, will you let me in? Or are you gonna drive off and leave me standing here?"

"I don't play games like that."

He rounded the car and got in. She started the car, turning on the air. It was another muggy day in Dallas, and she didn't feel like sitting there roasting.

"What did you find out from Kevin Bennett?" Nick asked, and now, he seemed ready to listen.

"Before we talk about that, let me ask you something. What do you think about a guy who lost his daughter and the rage he might be feeling, acting it out through a twisted poisoning scheme? How often have you seen a case with those elements?"

Nick took his time answering. "I'll admit, it is odd. Most of the time, when a guy goes after another guy with murder in his heart, it's with a weapon—knife or gun. Or a severe beating that results in death." He paused. "But every time I think I know the mind of a killer, someone proves me wrong. There's really no way to fully understand, Jill. And the evidence is overwhelmingly against Kevin Bennett."

"It seems inconsistent to me at this point," she insisted.

He shrugged. "Maybe so. But meanwhile, that's what we have. Why don't you tell me what you talked about with him."

"I want your assurance that this is off the record. I mean it, Nick. I made a promise to the guy."

"Off the record. You got it, and I always mean what I say to you, Jill." His gray-green eyes signaled the truth of his words.

She relaxed a bit. "Okay, I'm going to give you my impressions, but due to confidentiality, I can't tell you the exact content of our conversation."

"Fair enough," he said.

"Here's what I think, and it's based on several threads that I pulled with him. I do think he was angry, enraged at Cory when he lost his daughter in the custody case. I think, like most people, he fantasized about hurting Cory. But I don't believe Kevin Bennett is capable of murder." She turned and looked directly at Nick. "He didn't do it, Nick. I'm sure of it." Even as she spoke the words, she recognized they were far stronger than how she really felt. But that was intentional.

"What makes you so sure? Other than he probably *said* he was innocent, which, by the way, virtually every person I've ever arrested says. At least at first."

"You know he went to Cory's office after his case and before Cory was killed. You know he carried a gun there, right?"

"Right. We can place him there with video. We believe he threatened Cory's life that night. Possibly through the notes sent to his office as well, although we don't have any fingerprints or envelopes to prove that. And don't forget—the bourbon was mailed from Bennett's office, with his fingerprints on the bottle." He paused, his expression shifting to something close to pity. "Honestly, Jill, as much as I respect your insight—and you know I do—the evidence is overwhelming."

Jill sat silently. He was right. The evidence was compelling. How could she explain her doubts to Nick and even to herself?

205

She simply wasn't sure that Kevin Bennett had killed Cory. "I don't have a good explanation except for one thing. The night he went to Cory's office, things didn't go the way we might all think. I found the story of that night, that conversation, to be credible, Nick. And it's a game changer. If it's true, it casts a huge shadow of doubt on the idea that he killed Cory."

"But you can't tell me the details," Nick said, a trace of exasperation leaking into his voice.

"I'm sorry. But I have some ideas for what to do next, where to dig more and, hopefully, prove I'm right." She paused. "If I'm wrong, I'll tell you. There's so much at stake here, Nick. Not only does Bennett's life hang in the balance, but I'm beginning to think there's someone else whose life is at risk."

Kevin Bennett's story of that night in Cory's office tugged at her. She couldn't divulge the specifics to Nick, only the tone. *Candid, raw, and authentic.* Unless Bennett was an incredible actor, he'd told her the truth.

He was making big changes in his life. He was in counseling. He apologized to me, wanted to make amends. I actually forgave him.

But as she drove away, Jill felt deflated. *Bennett's fingerprints were on the bottle mailed from his office.* Maybe Nick was right— she was letting her empathy convince her rather than following the evidence.

Still, she didn't feel settled, and whenever that occurred, she was unable to drop whatever consumed her thoughts. She considered the person she wanted to talk to next, someone who might have nothing but could have something to help her sort out the tangle of emotion, motivation, and deeds that had resulted in the death of Cory Holloman.

"I still can't believe she's gone," said the woman, holding a tissue to her eyes with deeply veined bird-like hands. She blew her nose lightly. "It seems like just yesterday. We were supposed to get together that night and have a glass of wine, our usual routine. It was her turn to host. Well," she laughed briefly, "the truth is she *always* hosted. She has—had—the nicest unit in the building. So beautifully decorated! She loved being surrounded by nice things, but that wasn't what mattered the most. It was her family, her friends, that really mattered to Linda."

Jill had seen clients all day, but in the back of her mind, she'd still been thinking about Cory. Following her latest hunch, she had tracked down Alvie Wardell, friend and neighbor of Cory's deceased mother, Linda Holloman. Since Linda wasn't around to give insight into Cory, it occurred to her that, though one step removed, the next best option might be Linda Holloman's best friend. She'd briefly thought of talking to Erica but quickly surmised that Linda would be far more likely to confide in a best friend than a daughter-in-law.

Someone killed Cory Holloman. If not Kevin Bennett, then who? It wasn't Cory's wife—the widow who stood to inherit nothing. There wasn't any motive for her. Plus, her grief seemed very real. Her attempts to pick up the threads of her life and to help her brother-in-law all struck Jill as plausible.

There were other unanswered questions about Cory and his life, such as his trajectory before his death. Was Cory close enough to his mother for her to have had insights into her son? Maybe.

Alvie, and formerly Linda Holloman, lived in a senior living facility, one of the nicest in the city of Dallas. It featured an extensive array of amenities designed to offer opportunities for social connection for those of an advancing age who no longer wanted to maintain a large home. There was the dining room— beautifully decorated with four and six top tables scattered about, serving three meals daily. The menu, which Jill had perused, resembled that of a 5-star restaurant. There was the game room, with a wet bar, which featured 'free' happy hours daily and activities for the seniors. There was a spa, more than one hair salon, a yoga room, another for aerobic classes, and, of course, a full gym. There was a shuttle that ran multiple times daily, taking them to shopping, local restaurants, sports arenas, and tourist destinations.

The ticket for admission was in the low six figures annually. Plus, a hefty high six-to-seven-figure one-time admission price that was non-refundable until you passed, and then it went into your estate. Jill's conclusion was that Linda Holloman had been a woman of means. Which meant that she'd had substantial wealth during her lifetime. If so, she'd most likely have left an estate of some size. An estate which would have passed to Cory but now belonged to his brother, Travis.

Alvie was more than willing to meet with Jill and talk about her friend. In fact, she seemed eager to have someone to confide in, especially once she heard Jill's credentials.

"Can you tell me what happened that night?" Jill had more pertinent questions to ask but knew Alvie needed to tell her story first. Everyone had a story to tell, and some felt compelled to share it with almost anyone.

"She was my *best* friend. We talked every day, sometimes two or three times a day. My daughter has always been a problem. She married a nice enough guy, but he wasn't Steve Morris, her college sweetheart. Steve owns a company that recently went public! He's a gazillionaire, and my daughter would have had everything she ever wanted if only she'd married Steve."

She stopped and peered at Jill. "Are you married, dear? No, I can see you're not wearing a wedding ring. I hope you know how important it is to marry well. Someone who can take care of you when the babies come. I know you have an important career now, but it's not easy putting a baby in the arms of a stranger to care for them while you go to work. I know—my daughter found out the hard way. Her husband was a *schoolteacher*," she said with obvious distaste, "and that meant my daughter had to keep her much higher-paying job. She's a CFO, you know. Does really well." She beamed with pride, but then her face fell. "Still, though, it would be much better if she could have stayed home with the kids. Her husband is one of those 'stay-at-home dads,' you know." She looked as though she'd taken a bite of something sour.

Jill had to slow down and divert this rant, or she'd be there all day. "And Linda was the person you could go to, to talk about anything that bothered you. That last day, did you see her? Talk to her on the phone?"

"Like I said, we talked every day. Yes, I talked to her that morning on the phone. We made plans for wine time later, and then I had to go because my daughter's husband needed help with the kids. He was taking one of them to the doctor and wanted to drop off the other two. Which didn't happen because—" She stopped and looked a bit confused. Waving a hand, she said, "Oh, well, I've slept since then, can't remember why he didn't drop them off."

"Mrs. Wardell, I'm hoping you can help me understand Linda's son, Cory, a bit better. Actually, both her sons, Cory, *and* Travis."

Alvie perked up. "Well, that's a story, for sure. The first thing you have to know about Linda is that she was a great mom. To two boys who were nothing like her. And who she couldn't save."

CHAPTER TWENTY-SEVEN

"She was a single mom," Alvie began, "and she worked hard to raise her sons, but Cory was a huge problem pretty much since middle school. But things began going sideways, personally, that is, right after he finished law school. She was so proud of him for becoming a lawyer, especially since he didn't have a father to help him. Their dad disappeared when they were little, and she heard years later he'd died young. I think he was a drunk, too. Apple doesn't fall far." Alvie's eyes gleamed as she told the story, relishing the attention.

"But anyway, what bothered her was Cory's drinking. He'd come over to see her after he'd been out at the bars. Making all kinds of noise, keeping her up for hours. She finally had to tell him to quit coming to see her unless he was sober. Well, after that, she didn't see much of him at all. Broke her heart. So sad." Alvie shook her head sorrowfully.

There it was again. Cory's drinking. Roxanne had mentioned it early in the case, but Jill couldn't remember the details. Hadn't he tried to quit? Maybe, but if so, he'd apparently fallen off the wagon enough to drink the bourbon laced with the poison that had killed him. Maybe Alvie would know more. "Did Linda say anything about Cory trying to quit?"

"Oh, he was always trying to quit. He'd say *never again, Mom. I mean it. I'm done with this.* It would last a few weeks, sometimes longer. And the next thing you know, he'd show up drunk again. I can't remember how many times we went around that one. Lather, rinse, and repeat."

A familiar story. The alcoholic's pathway to sobriety. Or death. Until he found his 'bottom,' he'd have never quit. *Bourbon laced with poison.* Often, the alcoholic's bottom was death, though usually not the kind Cory had experienced.

"What about Travis, Cory's brother?" Jill asked.

"You know, poor Linda didn't get the best hand dealt to her when it came to her kids. Travis is a sad case of a kid who was lost and probably always will be. He didn't do well in high school, and after two semesters of college, he dropped out. Lots of little jobs like coffee barista and waiter, but he's never seemed to make enough money to support himself. Plus, he never stayed employed for long. Linda didn't like to admit it, but she supported him financially, or at least, made up for the shortfall." She stopped. "Where are my manners? Can I get you a glass of iced tea, dear?" She checked her watch. "Glass of wine? It's happy hour somewhere, you know." she added mischievously.

"No, thank you. I've got other appointments and will need to finish up soon. Tell me, what else do you know about Travis? What exactly was wrong with him, from Linda's point of view?"

"He called her and came to see her constantly. He couldn't seem to make a move without her advice. More than advice. He wanted her to tell him what to do with his life. He always seemed very... scared. Anxious, I guess you'd call it. No confidence."

Jill thought of the last time she'd seen Erica with Travis. How he'd looked at Erica before answering questions. How hesitant he'd seemed. Insecure. Totally lacking in confidence, as if he was stuck around age fifteen or so. Not quite a fully grown adult, emotionally or psychologically. *Arrested adolescence.* Or so it seemed.

Had his mother, Linda, failed to help him fully develop? Had she hovered over him too much, made decisions for him? Some parents—actually, many parents today—were uncomfortable with the necessity of individuation from their children. They were paranoid about harm coming to their offspring, so they watched over them incessantly, governing their choices far beyond childhood. Had Linda been one of those parents?

"Would you say Linda was over-protective? Did she seem too involved in Travis's life?"

Alvie laughed out loud. "Linda—overprotective? Not at all. She tried everything she could think of to untie the apron strings with Travis. But he wouldn't have it. He wanted her advice about everything—what clothes to wear, whether or not to apply for a job. He seemed to *need* her to tell him how to live his life. Yes, she tried to change it."

"What did she do?"

"Once, she turned off her phone for a day, didn't take his calls or answer his texts."

"What happened?"

"He came over, started ringing her doorbell. When she didn't answer, he just stood there, talking to the closed door as if it was her. I saw him. She was out shopping or something, trying to ignore the fact that her son might be having a meltdown. It was pathetic. When she got home, she just let him in."

Jill felt a tingle. Something about this story didn't make sense.

"It sounds like Travis was very dependent on his mom. It must have been devastating when she passed away."

"I don't know. I never saw him again after Linda passed away."

It clicked in suddenly. Travis must have transferred his dependence from his mother to his sister-in-law. Which explained why Erica had so adamantly stated that she'd have to take care of him.

Jill was accustomed to helping parents and children loosen the ties that bind. That was a normal situation in family counseling. But she'd never treated someone with the diagnosis she now suspected was Travis's. Dependent Personality Disorder, a rare Cluster C disorder. Not a passing stage of life. A condition that was inflexible, pervasive, maladaptive, and lifelong. Like all personality disorders, treatment could extend for years, even decades, with little to no improvement.

She sighed. Erica couldn't possibly know the extent of what she had committed to with Travis at this point.

One more thing she was curious about. "Do you know what Linda did when she was working?"

Alvie beamed. "Linda was so smart. She was a middle school principal. She had a doctorate in education, and she was also an attorney."

That explained a lot in Jill's mind. A picture was forming for her, of Cory's family of origin. An educated, highly intelligent single mom. Who didn't choose from the best end of the genetic pool for the father of her two boys. But who did the best she could to give them what they needed.

One son, an alcoholic.

The second son, a permanent adolescent.

Jill's phone vibrated insistently. It wasn't the first time since she'd arrived at Alvie's. She picked it up and stood abruptly. "I'm sorry, Alvie, I have to run. Thank you for your time."

"But don't you want to hear the rest? I haven't even told you about how we found her. It was terrible—"

"I'm so sorry to interrupt. We'll finish later."

Jill left as fast as she could.

Jade needed her.

CHAPTER TWENTY-EIGHT

Jill rushed to get to her sister, and she didn't really pay much attention to the clues that might have informed her about where she was headed. When she walked in, she was instantly overwhelmed by the vibrant, pulsing energy and the neon rainbow hues that danced across the walls. To the left, there was a long, gleaming bar counter made of polished quartz, reflecting the colors of the room, where bartenders concocted drinks with flair and dexterity. Each one of them could have walked off of a runway—she'd never seen so many beautiful men in one place before. The backlit shelves behind them boasted an impressive array of spirits, liqueurs, and mixers that contributed to the spectrum of colors.

On the large dance floor, gyrating bodies moved to the beats of pop, electronic, and disco music. A mirrored disco ball hanging from the ceiling scattered fragments of light across the moving bodies, creating a kaleidoscope of shimmering colors.

Scanning the room, she spotted Jade on the far side, sitting at a small round table. Her head was thrown back with laughter as she chatted with some guy Jill had never seen before. Jill made her way through the crowd, but by the time she got to Jade, she was alone. "Hey," she greeted her sister, who stood briefly to give her a hug.

This was not their favorite retro jazz haunt. This was an entirely different world. Instead of the relaxed, soulful notes of a saxophone weaving seamlessly with the rhythmic plucking of a double bass and the soft patter of brushes on a snare drum, Jill's head pounded with the rhythmic pulsing of Abba. Which, though not her usual scene, she soon found energizing. Unconsciously, she'd begun tapping the tabletop and swaying a bit. "So, your text sounded urgent," she shouted at her sister. "What's going on?"

"Oh, that!" said Jade, smiling. "It got you here, right?"

A couple of shot glasses landed on the table, and Jade picked up hers, nodding at Jill's. "Cheers, little sis!"

A bit reluctantly, Jill picked up hers. "Cheers, big sis!" She tossed it back. *Tequila.* Her least favorite drink. But she soon felt the warmth of the alcohol spread, and her shoulders relaxed a bit.

Jill leaned over and spoke loudly in her sister's ear. "No, really, what's going on with you? I rushed to get here because of your text. And that voicemail earlier. What's up with that?"

Jade's eyes danced mischievously. "Have you really taken a look at this place, Ms. Observant?"

Not exactly, no. The priority was getting to her sister, who'd been acting strangely. *Where* they met wasn't nearly as important as *when* they met. And, hopefully, talked. *She'd been meaning to talk with her sister.* They were long overdue, and this place wasn't conducive to a heart-to-heart, not the kind she needed right now. But she took a moment to look around.

On the dance floor, the crowd was truly eclectic. People were dressed in everything from casual jeans and t-shirts to flamboyant costumes and even high-fashion ensembles, creating a mosaic of individual styles.

As she looked more closely, Jill's smile grew. There were rhinestones and feathers paired with towering stilettos. There was makeup as a work of art in itself, featuring bold eyeshadows, dramatic false eyelashes, and glossy, vibrant lip colors. Wigs—she assumed—ranged from sleek bobs to voluminous curls dyed in every color of the rainbow.

One patron was dressed in a meticulously tailored superhero outfit, complete with cape and mask. Someone else sporting the iconic cone bra and high ponytail reminiscent of Madonna.

Drag queens.

When she raised a brow to Jade, her sister simply raised her hands and shrugged. "No one's going to hit on me here, right?"

Her sister wanted a wild night out, but she didn't want to have to fight off men the whole time. And she would have. Jade was striking, with her dark, flowing hair, gorgeous figure, and full lips always set in a smile. She had always attracted men, and if she were still single, she'd have had her choice. But she'd made her choice, and she seemed happy with her partner. "No argument there," Jill agreed.

Though it wasn't Jill's scene, it made sense for Jade. Jade was in the art world; she eschewed anything mainstream, and she thrived when she could find a place where self-expression ruled. The more expressive, the better. The atmosphere here was infectious.

Jill relaxed, letting the music, the laughter, and the people-watching work to overcome the stress she'd carried in the door.

Before long, Jade dragged her onto the dance floor. They shook and vibrated to the music, grabbing each other's hands and spinning each other. Huge smiles splitting their faces, the two sisters moved in sync and harmony, occasionally losing their balance but recovering to much giggling. A couple of drag queens nearby applauded them and said, "You go, girl!"

Breathless, they kept going for three music sets until finally, Jill begged off. She made her way to a booth much further away from the dance floor and flopped down, sucking in air rapidly, waiting for her heart rate to slow. Jade quickly joined her, not even fazed. *Amazing.*

"Who was that guy you were with when I got here?" Jill asked after some time, wondering if, maybe even in a gay bar, her sister might be hit on. Wouldn't be a shock.

Jade looked away for a moment, her mouth straightening. "No one. Just some guy." She cut her eyes back to Jill again. "Speaking of guys, what's going on with you and Ethan?"

Jill sighed. "It seems he lost his job. And he forgot to tell me. Plus, he moved in with his mom." She flagged down the waiter and ordered a vodka martini, slightly dirty. If they were going to talk about Ethan, she needed a little more liquid courage.

"Wow. The triumvirate of male ego-crushing. How is he?" Jade looked truly concerned, and that irritated Jill.

"*He* is fine, well maybe not fine, but he'll be okay, I'm sure," Jill bit off. Her martini arrived—frosted glass, tiny ice crystals on top, two olives. *Perfect.* She took a sip. Why did Jade always extend her empathy to the men Jill dated? Less so for her own sister. *Story of her life.*

"You know he really loves you, right? The last thing a guy wants is to lose the respect of the woman he loves. And you're losing respect, aren't you?" Jade shook her head mournfully.

Wow. Jill took a much larger sip of her martini, relishing the cold slide followed by the increasing warmth. At that moment, she could appreciate the pull alcoholics felt. If the second martini felt as good as the first, she'd keep drinking. But for her, the next drink was always a disappointment because it didn't feel as good. If she made it to a third drink, which was likely tonight, it would incite dizziness, followed by drowsiness and disconnection from the matters at hand. The next day, she'd be rewarded with a throbbing headache.

She was a 'cheap date.'

"Maybe he doesn't deserve my respect," she argued. "He *lied* to me, Jade. By omission, but that's the same thing. I had to find out about his job myself. So embarrassing. It's not like this is the first time he's lied to me."

They weren't huge lies.

Just had a couple of drinks with my buddies.

Sorry I'm late—traffic was brutal.

I never dated her—we were just friends.

They were the kind of lies men told to avoid disapproval, nagging, or lectures. Or out of insecurity. But Jill yearned for authenticity.

"So, he lost his job. He's devastated and embarrassed, and you're mad at him because he didn't tell you right away?" Jade's tone conveyed an irritating level of concern. *For Ethan.*

Jill glared at her sister. "I'm entitled to be pissed right now. Just because I'm a therapist doesn't mean I have to be Mother Teresa all the freaking time."

Jade put up her hands. "Peace, sis. Sorry, I poked the hornet's nest. I'm just trying to support you here. You know, encourage you to make up with your man. You've been through a lot—with men, that is—and I know you want a family."

A family. Unspoken was the ticking clock of Jill's age. Late 30s. Another relationship on the brink of implosion. Childbearing years sliding by ever more rapidly. Her ovaries depleting themselves of eggs. A pit formed in Jill's stomach. She took another long drink. Even worse, she couldn't participate in the singles scene like other women her age. It would be potentially disastrous to put herself on a dating app, risking too much personal life exposure to her clients.

Shrink looking for a soulmate.

Wanna lay on my couch?

Free analysis daily for the rest of your life.

She snorted at her own inside joke and almost spewed her drink.

"What's so funny?" Jade asked.

"Nothing. It's just... me. Relationship failure number... what is it, anyway?" She looked at her sister to fill in the blank, the person who'd been a witness to her disastrous single life from day one, starting in high school.

Jade reached over and touched her hand. "Hey. Stop that. I know what you're doing."

Jill's eyes filled with tears. "What is it anyway? There's something wrong with me. You know it, and so do I. I can't seem to pick someone right. If I think he's good, he turns out... not good. If I think he's not good enough, he moves on and makes a wonderful husband for someone else." She wanted to stop talking about it. But now that the gates were open, she couldn't stop.

"Don't," said her sister, concern etching her face.

"No, really. I'm a total loser when it comes to men. The right ones pass me by, and the wrong ones attach themselves to me, sticking around for... way too long. Until *they* can't take it anymore. Then they leave. That's what really hurts. I know when a guy isn't going to be right for me. I see it coming—for weeks, months even, but do I do anything about it? Hell, no. I put up with it. I bend myself into a pretzel trying to take care of him or fix him, neglecting my own needs. And just when *I can't stand it anymore*, he takes off! I don't even get to be the one to break up." She tried to stop. She absolutely *hated* self-pity.

"Let's go, honey," said Jade, throwing cash on the table and standing.

"That's a couple of hundred-dollar bills! There's no way we drank that much. Let's wait and get the tab," said Jill, hiding her face so no one would see her tears.

"No way. Come on," Jade said, tugging Jill's arm. "Besides, I have something else I want to talk about, and it's too noisy in here."

"I'm sorry, so sorry," Jill mumbled as her sister guided her out of the bar. It had been a long time since the cascade of self-pity had caught her unawares. Only Jade understood where it came from. The crowd pressed, people flowing into the bar. It seemed to take forever to get to the door against the tide. Though absolutely no one there could possibly know Jill, she burned with embarrassment, longing to hide.

Finally, they reached the door and stepped out. Her sister reassured her as she walked alongside, her arm tucked into Jill's. But as they made their way into the parking lot, someone grabbed Jade's arm. "Going somewhere?" said a familiar voice.

"Daniel? What are you doing here?" Jill asked.

Her sister's husband. In scrubs. Looking madder than a hornet. "Stay out of it, Jill. This is between me and my wife."

"I thought you were at a conference. And let go!" shouted Jade, struggling to pull away.

He did. "No more running away. You're going to have to deal with me," Daniel said. He turned to Jill. "This is a private matter." But in his voice and eyes was an unspoken plea.

"You have no right to speak to my sister like that!" shouted Jade.

Jill had never seen her sister like this, shrill, incensed. "It's okay, Jade. You two obviously need to talk." She backed off, pulling out her phone for a shared ride. But her finger slipped and pressed a different button.

"No, Jill. He can wait. Let's go," said Jade, following her sister. "I want to make sure you get home okay."

"It's fine, really. I'm okay. Please, go with your husband. We'll talk later."

Jill hugged her sister, noting the rigidity of her body. And as she turned away, she heard them begin talking intensely. She only caught a few words, but they were enough to chill her.

... *saw you with... lying... tired of the games... you, not me, and you know it...*

It wasn't until much later that she realized she'd never gotten an answer about the odd voicemail her sister had left her.

CHAPTER TWENTY-NINE

The ride from the bar to Jill's home was quiet. Not awkward quiet. But, *comforting.* His presence was a safe space, and she felt so relieved she almost started crying again. Later, standing at her door, she tried to thank Nick, but the words wouldn't come.

"You don't have to thank me," he said. He reached over and brushed away a tear on her cheek, which shocked her.

Had she started crying again? *Great.* She'd embarrassed herself, not only at the bar but now, in front of someone she'd have to see again professionally.

How she ever managed to get a date, let alone get into relationships, was a mystery. The awkwardness she felt so much of the time traced back to events she'd rather not think about. Preston had warned her many times that she could run from them, but she couldn't hide. *It is sitting there, affecting you, and like it or not, you'll have to deal with it someday.*

"Feel like talking?" Nick asked.

"Not really," she lied. It would be heavenly to invite him in, make hot tea, put on something comfortable, put up her feet, and unburden herself. She allowed her fantasy to extend further to her feet being rubbed by hands that gradually moved upward...

She looked up. Nick's arm was outstretched, his hand on the wall outside her door, creating a small space of warmth and safety. She couldn't speak. Or move away.

"Uh-huh," he said knowingly. "What is it?"

She sighed. "It's my sister. Something's going on with her, but I can't get her to tell me. Something always interrupts us lately. Her husband showed up as we were leaving the club, and... I've never seen them like that before. Arguing about—"

"Your sister?" Nick said, looking interested. "Didn't know you had a sister."

"There's a lot you don't know," she said, feeling the walls rise again. One tiny bit of shared personal information always led to another.

"Right," he said, taking his arm off the wall and backing up a bit. "Well, if you ever do want to talk..."

"Actually, can we have breakfast tomorrow morning? I have an update on the Holloman case. And maybe another couple of things to look into."

They set up the date, and as she went to shut her door, she watched Nick's back retreating down the hallway, feeling an overwhelming mixture of emotions. Relief. Longing. Embarrassment, guilt.

Grief. *Ethan.*

She was waiting when he arrived. Nick checked his watch. Five minutes early, and still, somehow, she'd gotten there first. As he slid into the booth, he surreptitiously noted the dark smudges

NINA ATWOOD

under her eyes. Still, she looked impeccable. All buttoned up
again, silk blouse, heels, and makeup in place. He resisted the
urge to smile a bit. Dr. Jill Rhodes was back in form, and he would
never object to that.

But last night, her vulnerability had pierced him. How he'd
wanted to take her in his arms, hold her. But she wasn't available.
She was spoken for. And it would be the height of ego to presume
that she would be attracted to him, anyway. She was gorgeous—
she could have anyone. Sure, she seemed to appreciate him
professionally, and there was the fact that she'd called him for a
ride after having a bit too much to drink last night.

But none of it meant she was attracted to him.

Forget it, dude. His rough edges would never mix with her
Park Cities Dallas style, her highly educated professional world.
*You're a cop. Yeah, you made detective, but you're really just a
cop at heart.* He had a couple of things going on the side, a hustle
here and there, but he lived on a modest salary. His home was
just an apartment where his clothes hung, and a comfortable bed
waited for him after a long day. There were a few added touches,
things he'd enjoyed collecting. But it didn't compare with her
luxury condo.

"Good morning," she greeted him somewhat formally. "I
ordered your coffee," she continued. "I wasn't sure what you'd
want to eat, so I waited on that, except I did get some muffins,"
she said, indicating the basket on the table. "Black, no cream,
no sweetener if I'm remembering correctly. Pot on the table
for refills."

It came out like one continuous sentence. Was she flustered?
Feeling awkward after last night? Because she'd had one too many
and needed a ride? Or because she'd been emotional, vulnerable.
Insecure Dr. Rhodes was a new side to her.

226

He distracted himself with the menu and ordered breakfast. Eggs over easy, bacon, toast. It came out quickly, and he dug in. She nibbled at a muffin and sipped a cappuccino.

They were silent. It was difficult to measure which of them was better at the art of letting silence pressure the other person to speak.

"What is this about—" he started to ask.

"I wanted to go over—" she said at the same time. Her gray eyes sparkled for a bit.

They sat back.

"You first," he said.

"How about me first?" Roxanne said cheerily as she slid into the booth, pushing Jill over. "You guys are going to have to catch me up. What did I miss?" She poured coffee and grabbed a muffin out of the basket, slathering it in butter.

Nick felt a twinge of irritation. But quickly shrugged it off. "Nothing. We just started breakfast. By all means, lead off the discussion." He gave Jill a look, as in, *why didn't you tell me Roxanne was joining us?*

She looked puzzled.

Roxanne glanced between the two of them. "Oh, you're wondering how I knew about this little tête-à-tête. I didn't until I saw Jill's car in the parking lot. This is close to the courthouse, you know, and us legal eagles frequent the place." She took a bite of muffin, smirking. "Seriously, though, you guys need to include me if it's about the case." She looked slowly from one to the other. "Unless this really is a private moment."

"Roxanne—" Jill said, her face turning an attractive shade of pink.

Was she embarrassed at the thought of being with him on a personal basis? *Of course, she was.*

227

"It's nothing private at all," Nick threw in. "It's about the case. Strictly professional. Right?" He said to Jill.

"Right," she said, her mouth tightening.

Christ, could he ever say the right thing?

"Speaking of," said Roxanne, her mouth full of muffin. She finished chewing, swallowed, and licked butter off of her fingers. "This place makes the best muffins. Anyway, remember the woman we saw at Cory's funeral? I managed to dig up some information on her. But before we go there, something odd came up in my circles."

"What woman at the funeral?" Nick interrupted.

"The one Roxanne didn't recognize as one of Cory's friends or associates," Jill said.

"I'd like to remind both of you that there is already a person in custody. One who has been arrested and charged with Cory Holloman's murder. The only reason I'm here to talk about it is…" but his mouth had outrun his brain.

Why exactly was he here?

He had other cases waiting for him, legitimate ones. This was a waste of time. Ire overtook him, though he tried to reign it in. He tossed his napkin down and stood. "I'm afraid I've got to get back to my job. I know you're interested in trying to prove Kevin Bennett is innocent, Jill," he said, softening his tone, "but I'm afraid that's not going to go anywhere."

And as he walked away, he wanted to kick himself for acting so immature. He hadn't done anything like that since middle school when he'd stuck his foot out into the aisle and tripped Scott Ventler. He'd meant to tease the guy, but he'd fallen and hit his head on the edge of Carrie Buttes' desk. She'd jumped up and grabbed Scott, cradling him until he recovered. Which wasn't the goal at all since Nick had been yearning for Carrie's attention the entire school year.

"Well, that was an interesting turn of events," said Roxanne. "What the heck got up his—"

"I have no idea," Jill interrupted. She was still in a bit of shock after Nick's abrupt exit. Clearly, he was tired of her in general. About Cory's case, and especially, after calling him last night and getting a ride to her condo. Shame threatened to overtake her. She pushed it aside and focused on Roxanne.

"But he's wrong. I talked to Kevin Bennett, but before I tell you about that, you know something more about Cory, and I want it now." She pinned the other woman with her gaze and waited.

Roxanne blew out a slow breath. "Fair enough. Before I share this, I'd like to hire you as a consultant." She rummaged in her purse and pulled out a five-dollar bill, which she handed to Jill. "There. I believe privilege extends to client relationships that are non-therapeutic, right?"

"Technically, maybe," said Jill, rolling her eyes and tucking away the bill. Unsaid was the full truth. This was a criminal case, and therefore, their conversation could be discoverable.

Which also made her wonder about her 'therapeutic' relationship with Kevin Bennett. Had she compromised him by talking with him? Nick now knew that she had done so and could bring that into play later.

Roxanne waved a hand. "Whatever." She hesitated. "You're right. There is more. A few weeks before Cory was killed, we took a business trip together."

CHAPTER THIRTY

A couple of weeks before Cory's death

"Hi, my name is Roxanne, and I'm an alcoholic," she said almost robotically. The shock as she'd walked into the room and taken her seat had almost sent her right back out the door. Her heart raced, and she worked hard to avert her eyes from the person across the room. The one she knew.

"Hi, Roxanne," the group responded, including *him.*

"It's been a long day on top of a long week, month, and *year,*" she shared. "And, I've gotta tell you, it's been rough. You see, today, I had to sit in the courtroom across from a man who killed a girl. I'm representing the girl's mother for a civil case later. But seeing her—her shattered face, the tears, the impossibility of her having to take the stand and testify."

Roxanne looked down, swallowed hard, and looked up. She couldn't stop the tears from forming. "When they displayed the photo of the girl who was killed, I didn't see her. I saw someone else. My high school best friend, Hayley. Another girl who was murdered." She cleared her throat, feeling the tightening. "And, all I could think about was taking a drink. Anything to make the guilt go away. Because for over two decades, I carried the guilt of not saving Hayley."

Roxanne picked up the glass of water with a shaking hand, took a sip, and set it down carefully. "But that's not what I want to talk about. It's the rest of it, the road to recovery. Frankly, it's been a bit rocky, if I'm honest." She grimaced. "No, it's been *fucking hard*."

People laughed softly and nodded. One guy in the back pumped a tattoo-covered fist in the air, grinning.

She paused, swallowed, then continued. "There's this...this temptation, you know? It's not like a boogeyman hiding under the bed. No, it's more of a shadow, creeping around every corner of my daily life. It springs out when I'm alone, when I'm feeling overwhelmed, or when the past rears its ugly head."

There was a hint of bitterness in her voice as she added, "And the stigma—you guys know what I mean. It's like being poked and prodded every time you try to stand tall. The sideways glances, the judgmental whispers, it's like getting sucker-punched when you're already down."

She looked around the room, meeting the eyes of the other attendees. Though she deliberately avoided one set of eyes. "The biggest battle, though," she said, "is the one that happens inside. This *journey*—it's not just about not drinking. It's about making peace with who I was and accepting who I am now. And let me tell you, understanding that I'm more than my past, more than my addiction... that's a steep climb. *That* takes my breath away at times."

As her words filled the room, she let out a sigh, "But there's this little spark, this hope. And you know where I find it? Right here, with you all, with people like you, when I'm at home with my regular group. But we're all the same, aren't we? It's the stories, the understanding, the shared nods, the encouragement... You keep me grounded. You give me the courage to face the storm."

Her voice grew steadier as she concluded, "I gotta tell you— this is no easy victory tale. I wish it was a story with a beginning, a middle, and an end. In the rearview mirror, one day soon. But it's not that. It's a battle, one I fight every day. One, I know I'll fight for the rest of my life. But it's also filled with these small wins along the way. And I'm not there yet, but I'm closer than I was yesterday."

She turned to sit down but stopped and faced the group again. "Almost forgot. I've been sober for three hundred fifty-eight days. Very close to one year." She paused, feeling the wave of heat, desperate for relief. She swallowed. "I think I'm gonna make it to that chip."

A quiet fell over the room for a moment, and then, almost as if a switch was flipped, the room erupted into spontaneous applause. A chorus of *well done, Roxanne*, and *keep going, we're proud of you*, echoed in the room.

She sat down with a smile on her lips, soaking in the support. *Amazing.* Even though this was a group of strangers, one she'd likely never see again, in a city other than her own, they were connected. There was an instantaneous bond, one forged by walking through the hellish journey of life without the numbing benefit of their former substance of choice. A bond it had taken her months to forge at her regular AA meetings. She'd swum in the river of denial for a very long time, trying desperately to convince herself. *I'm not an alcoholic. These people are different than me. They're losers, and I am NOT that.*

But there was a purpose to the structure of the program,

a requirement to admit the addiction in every single meeting. It took longer for some than others. But in order to recover, alcoholics had to re-arrange their view of themselves—*their very identity*—at some point. From *I'm a regular person who happens to drink* to *I'm an alcoholic who cannot control my behavior with alcohol.*

Identity re-structuring is very hard but essential. Those who don't manage it go back to their substance of choice. Those who do have a shot at maintaining sobriety. This Roxanne had learned. And because of it, she could fly to any city, find a meeting, and quickly put herself in a room wherein the support for her hard-won sobriety would be instantaneous.

But she expected anonymity—it was the core of the program. To walk into the room and know that no one there would ever reveal her identity gave her a sense of safety. And today, that had been disrupted. The vulnerability she'd felt while sharing rocked her, though she'd forced herself through it.

A few minutes later, Roxanne waited outside. For him. "What the hell, Cory. Were you following me? Checking up on me? This is supposed to be confidential, sacrosanct. Even a subpoena in a criminal case can't pierce the privilege of an AA meeting. You know that! I can't believe you would—" But she stopped.

Cory faced her, and what she saw in his face blew her away. *Sadness, openness, vulnerability.*

"I had no idea you would be here, Roxanne. I'm here for me. But I'm glad I saw you."

Later, they shared coffee and common stories in their journey to remain sober. So many things became clear after that. His subdued nature around the office. The downcast eyes at times. The slow melting away of the arrogance and cockiness. His defensiveness pierced. But all of it without ever having told anyone that he was in recovery. Including Roxanne and the other partners.

His explanation resonated with her. *I'm so embarrassed. I hate the guy that I was. I'm trying to be a better person.*

"This is why you were so adamant that Cory didn't just drown, which would have been an act of self-destruction. Without the poison, he would have had to consume an enormous amount of alcohol, enough to produce a stupor. The reflex that kicks in if you start to intake water is so strong... he'd have fought it. Unless he was inebriated to the point of unconsciousness," Jill said.

"Right. But I'm still having a hard time with the idea of him drinking at all, which he clearly did, or he wouldn't have ingested the poison." Roxanne sighed. "I suppose, like Erica said, he fell off the wagon. Which saddens me."

It didn't yet add up to a full picture for Jill, either. But she had another question. "Why didn't you tell me sooner?"

"Technically, I'm never supposed to reveal the fact that I saw someone in a 12-step meeting. It's sacrosanct. You know that." She fiddled with the tableware.

"This isn't just about Cory, is it? Not telling me. Or Nick. It's about *your* sobriety," Jill said. "Almost one year," she mused. "Some people find that first anniversary to be a turning point." She hesitated but plunged on. "Either they fall off the wagon because one year isn't the same as *one day at a time*, and it's overwhelming, impossible, even, to imagine another year. And another, stretching indefinitely into the future. So, they give up."

Roxanne looked up, stricken. *"Or?"*

"Or, they keep going, re-focusing on one day at a time, which is the only way to do it."

"That's almost exactly what my sponsor said." Roxanne shifted uncomfortably. "Enough of that. Where are we with this case? You said you talked to Kevin Bennett."

"Right. I did, and I'm not certain he killed Cory. And there are other issues I've found as well." Jill spent a few minutes sharing the gist of her conversation with Linda Holloman. "I came away understanding more about Cory's family of origin, but I'm not sure it has anything to do with his murder."

"I'm not as convinced as you about Bennett. Maybe he's guilty, or maybe not, but I don't feel settled about it either," said Roxanne.

They both concentrated on food and coffee.

After a few minutes, Roxanne broke the silence. "I wish I knew the terms of the original trust," she said. "The one that passed to Travis when Cory passed away. That might tell us something."

"Such as?" Jill wondered.

"I'm not sure. There could be other beneficiaries we don't know about, people who might have an interest in the estate. Where there's money, there's always someone nearby consumed with envy and greed."

"Then again," Jill said, "we could be talking about a woman who sold all her assets and put them into the purchase of a spot at the very pricey facility where she lived. That's not unusual for people who are aging and want to simplify things, right?" She told Roxanne about Alvie's description of Linda's top-notch unit.

"True," said Roxanne. "Plus, we have no idea whether or not the money she put into that place will be reimbursed to her estate. Lately, there have been stories of these facilities selling to private equity in highly leveraged transactions, which creates

NINA ATWOOD

financial difficulties for them if they have a slump in residents.
The pandemic brought that to the forefront."

"There's one other problem with this whole line of thought,"
added Jill. "If a beneficiary of Linda Holloman's trust wanted
the assets, how could they possibly have known she would pass
when she did? She wasn't that elderly, and she wasn't frail. She
was living a nice lifestyle, still active when she died. That person
could have waited for many years. Cory and Erica were doing
well financially, from all we've learned." Jill couldn't get her mind
around this thread.

"You're right," agreed Roxanne. "I think this is a dead end."
She threw down her napkin and stood. "That means there's
some other motive and, possibly, some other person we haven't
yet found. Which brings me to the woman at the funeral."

Jill's phone buzzed. She didn't recognize the number but
picked it up anyway. After listening carefully and nodding, she
ended the call and turned to Roxanne. "That was Linda Holloman's
neighbor, Alvie. She says she has something important to tell me.
We should probably go see her."

"Wait," said Roxanne. "Before we do that, I want to check
out the woman from the funeral. Something tells me she was
important to Cory." That fierce expression was back. "Maybe
important enough to want him dead."

CHAPTER THIRTY-ONE

DAY EIGHT

"How did you find her? Lindsay Thomas is a rather common name, after all," Jill asked.

"Easy. We have a private detective agency on retainer at the firm. I, uh, kind of used them to find Lindsay. I figured she had a connection with Cory in some kind of way, so in addition to the usual background info, they looked into social media and did some deeper web searches. It was a random, obscure social site, but the connection was there. Cycling hobbyists."

"Social media, huh? And did it show you what kind of connection they had?"

"No, only that they were linked. But they were both linked to lots of other people. It was an online forum—a discussion group. Random photos of group cycling. Nothing too personal, as far as they could find."

Jill felt frustrated, unsure why. They now had the uphill job of trying to get this woman who'd attended Cory's funeral, possibly only because they'd shared a hobby, to disclose... what? "What exactly are we going for here, Roxanne?" Jill glanced at her watch. "I do have clients to see today." She also felt a growing, though puzzling, sense of urgency about going to see Alvie again.

"I'm not sure. But I find it odd that some woman who met Cory on a website for cycling enthusiasts came to his funeral. Isn't the whole point of random, online relationships to avoid the messiness of real life?" Roxanne's biting sarcasm was on display. "She had to have known him in some other way, offline. Let's see if we can find out."

"This is a little awkward," Jill pointed out. "She's at work, and we're just going to barge in?"

"Follow my lead. Barging in is my specialty," Roxanne said with a grin.

Jill hadn't felt so uncomfortable in a long time. To get into the building, Roxanne had flashed a fake law enforcement badge, which, upon close inspection by Jill, turned out to be no more than a toy. That wasn't bad enough, but now, they were going to confront a woman who wouldn't be expecting them and was most likely going to respond with hostility. *Who wouldn't?*

A few minutes later, they surveyed a large space that was gradually filling with people. Voices filled the air, and people lined up at the incredibly large buffet of lunch items—everything from multiple kinds of salads and breads to vegetables, fruits, and several choices of protein. One of the perks of working for a large oil and gas company like this one. They were betting that Lindsay Thomas would avail herself of the convenience of eating here.

"There she is," Roxanne said, tugging Jill's arm and pointing.

Lindsay Thomas headed towards the buffet line, but as they watched her, she began turning away to head back out. *Not hungry, perhaps? Or something else?*

Roxanne hustled over to Lindsay, Jill following reluctantly. "Lindsay! Lindsay Thomas? I thought I recognized you," Roxanne said to the woman, turning on the charm.

Lindsay Thomas turned to them, and Jill registered her stressed appearance. Face paler than it had been at the funeral, her skin drawn, and a baffled expression. "Yes?"

Roxanne took her arm and began steering her to a table in the corner, chattering away. "We met at Cory Holloman's funeral, remember? How are you? The office hasn't been the same without Cory. We all miss him terribly. And you must miss him too since you were cycling buddies. Right?"

As they sat at the table, Lindsay's initially puzzled expression took on alarm. And suspicion. "Wait. How do you know about the—?"

"The cycling? Wasn't hard. We knew he was into it, and when we went into his computer to check for and respond to client emails, we found one about the forum you both belong to. Well, *belonged* to, in his case." Roxanne gave a wry grin, then quickly turned serious. "We're attorneys, so we check everything. I admit, we came here today to see you. We're trying to put together a few missing puzzle pieces about Cory, and we were hoping you could help us." She paused, nodding toward Jill. "This is Jill Rhodes, who I've asked to help out."

Not providing my credentials. Interesting. Roxanne was going somewhere with this, and Jill might as well do as she'd suggested— follow her lead. "Nice to see you again, Lindsay," Jill said. "I'm sorry for the intrusion. But we could really use your help."

Lindsay's shoulders dropped a fraction. "Okay." But her expression remained guarded.

"How long have you known Cory?" Roxanne began. "We just need a little context."

"Maybe a couple of years," Lindsay said.

"And you met online?" Roxanne asked.

"Yes."

"When did you first get together in person?" Roxanne leaned in a bit.

"About a month after we met online." Lindsay's face had settled into a mask, much like the day of the funeral.

Jill touched Roxanne's hand. "You met online, and *a month later*, you met in person." She deliberately didn't fill in any of the blanks; instead, dangled an obvious mirroring statement as bait, emphasizing the timeline as though it held meaning. She let the silence add pressure.

Lindsay shifted. Her mouth opened a bit, then closed.

Impressive. Most people, when confronted with a statement about themselves, followed by silence, would seek to fill the void. The natural thing to do was to share more, either to correct the statement or augment it, add embellishments. But something held Lindsay back. *Natural shyness? Introversion? Or secrets?*

Roxanne shot Jill an impatient look. "Why did you decide to meet in person?" she asked Lindsay pointedly. "Seems like most people like the anonymity of online forums, where they have the freedom to say whatever they want with no social consequences."

Roxanne's impatience broke the moment. Inwardly, Jill rolled her eyes.

"I—we—wanted to have someone to ride with. He told me his wife wasn't into it, so..."

Roxanne's brows raised.

"It's not like it sounds," said Lindsay defensively.

That gave Roxanne an opening. "How it *sounds*?"

"I mean, it was nothing. We just—" and Jill saw it again. The closing off, the shutting down. "We were cycling friends, very casual friends."

"Friends," mused Roxanne. "And how often did you get together? As friends."

Lindsay's face turned pink. "We rode together on weekends mainly."

"Every weekend?"

"Almost. His wife worked on weekends, selling real estate. He didn't want to just sit around. It was too much—" she stopped.

"Too much temptation?" Roxanne guessed. "We know about Cory—he was a recovering alcoholic."

Lindsay looked down, but not before Jill saw the tears in the corners of her eyes. "Yes. He was." She looked back up. "But he was winning that battle. He was *sober*. I don't understand what happened to him."

Jill chose that moment to lean in and speak gently. "Lindsay, we can see that Cory was important to you. He may have been just a friend, but it's apparent your relationship was far more than casual. Friends can become dear, very close, especially if they're opening up about their struggles in life. Cory opened up to you, didn't he? He talked about his struggle to remain sober. What else did he share with you?"

Roxanne's mouth dropped open, but Jill touched her hand. She closed it and waited with Jill.

Lindsay's features twisted as an inner battle took place. "I—yes, we talked about our lives. But I've already told you everything." Her expression solidified. "That's it. I have to get back to work." She shoved her chair out and stood.

"Here we go! There's mommy," cooed a girl who walked up to Lindsay carrying a baby who appeared to be a few months old. She placed the bundle in Lindsay's arms, chatting away. "She's

241

been asleep most of the morning so far. I gave her the milk you left, but she's hungry, and there's not anymore."

Lindsay ignored Roxanne and Jill as she smiled at her baby and covered her face in kisses. "Hi, Sweetie. Mommy missed you this morning."

Complete transformation. From a woman besieged by inner heaviness to a mom totally in love with her child.

Lindsay adjusted the blanket around her baby, touching her tiny fingers, which curled around mom's index finger. The baby smiled and gurgled, kicked her feet, and struggled to move. Lindsay shifted her to an upright position, and the baby smiled and made noises. "Let's go have some lunch, okay, Sweetie?" She began moving away, oblivious to her two guests.

But Roxanne pursued her, touching Lindsay's arm, halting her. "And who is this adorable little one?" She smiled, touching the baby's foot, making her giggle and coo. "It's been so long since my girls were babies. I miss that stage so much! I swear, if Henry would give me the go-ahead, I'd have another in a heartbeat." She made nonsensical noises that sounded a bit like *choo, choo, choo.*

Jill shook her head. Was Roxanne going to try and hold the baby?

But, no, she didn't do that. Instead, she strategically stood in front of Lindsay, essentially blocking her from leaving.

Lindsay stepped to her right to go around Roxanne.

Roxanne stepped casually to her left, blocking Lindsay as she continued babbling to the baby. "I'm guessing by the pink blanket and the little bow on your head that you're a sweet little girl. And what's your name?" She'd directed her question to the baby as if she could answer.

"Her name's Annabelle." Pride filled Lindsay's eyes. Then,

something else. "I have to go. I only have a few more minutes to nurse her." She swerved rapidly around Roxanne and disappeared.

"Let's go," said Jill.

Roxanne stood transfixed, staring after Lindsay. She turned to Jill, a smile spreading. "Did you get a good look at the baby? I know at this age it's hard to tell, but I swear, that baby is a dead ringer for Cory." She raised an eyebrow. "*Friends*, my ass. Ladies and gentlemen, I believe we have just found a living, breathing piece of evidence that Cory was leading a double life. And I wonder if it had something to do with his death. His *murder*."

CHAPTER THIRTY-TWO

Just when it all seemed worked out, things began to unravel. First, while making a visit to Linda's unit, who should show up but that nosey old neighbor—Alvie or something like that. Sticking her nose in everyone's business. Prying, asking questions, spinning ridiculous theories. There was always a busybody like that hanging around, especially in a place like this. *Warehouse for old people.*

Granted, it's a very nicely appointed warehouse. Linda had always liked nice things. Far too much, clearly. What was the old lady doing spending her money investing in a place like this? Over *eight hundred thousand dollars* just to have the right to live here! The information was right there on the website. Then there was the monthly charge she'd shelled out for meals and amenities— over eleven thousand dollars!

How had she accumulated so much wealth, anyway? She'd been a school administrator of some kind. Her pension couldn't be anywhere near large enough to pay the monthly dues for her home. Or buy the antiques scattered about—the Persian rugs, the Baccarat crystal wine glasses. Cory had said something about how she'd inherited some oil and gas royalties from her grandfather, something like that. Who knew?

She didn't deserve all that wealth, and what was she going to do with it, anyway?

The old bat of a neighbor came to mind again. With her papery skin, glasses that made her eyes too large, and her ridiculous smile. She had far too much interest in Linda's life. And death.

With Cory's law partner and that psychologist asking so many questions, poking around in Cory's life so much, it had been time to go back to Linda's unit and make sure nothing was left behind. That day, when the inevitable had been hastened, Linda's surprise had been obvious. It was too bad, but after talking with her, it was clear that she was immovable. There was no concern or pity for her own fragile position, for what had been done to her. The betrayal, the abandonment.

Then there was the baby. So unexpected. Babies were such a blessing, one she'd yearned for. She was meant to be a mom, wasn't she?

Her mouth trembled a bit. She didn't enjoy the things she'd had to do. She wasn't a heartless person. But she also wasn't a fool. She wasn't going to sit by and let her life be ruined.

As for Linda, her days had been numbered anyway. All she'd had to look forward to was a slow, lingering, agonizing death. She'd been merciful, letting her off easy. *Parkinson's.* Her way had been much better for her, hadn't it?

Today, the old lady spotted her and recognized her. Apparently, she'd spotted her the day Linda had passed. Now, she was spreading rumors, asking questions about the last time she was here. *What were you doing that day? I saw you going into Linda's unit, and then, later, she was dead. I didn't say anything, but I couldn't stop thinking about it.*

Too bad the old lady couldn't stop thinking about it because now, she wouldn't have anything to think about. Ever again. Unfortunate, yes. But it had been necessary.

The killer paused just before stepping outside of Alvie's unit, looking both ways to make sure no one was around. She gently closed the door and walked away, thinking of the next person on her list. But also, she wondered where Alvie's cell phone had gone. She hadn't had time to search, but maybe she could come back later. She left the door unlocked.

In the parking lot, she'd just put her car in gear when she spotted two familiar figures walking into Alvie's building. Her fingers tightened on the steering wheel so much that her knuckles turned white.

Roxanne reached out and pressed the doorbell. Silence. They looked at each other. "Are you sure she's here?"

"She just called me only twenty minutes ago," Jill reassured her. "Push it again."

After two more doorbell rings—they could hear it inside— Roxanne began hammering loudly on the door. Frustrated, she grabbed the doorknob and twisted. To both their astonishment, the door swung open. "What the—" Roxanne said, stepping in.

"Alvie? Are you here?" Jill called out.

The silence was heavy—too heavy. Jill pulled out her phone and pushed a button, which was for the last caller—Alvie's number. A cell phone rang nearby, and they quickly tracked it down. It had slipped between the cushions of the sofa, out of sight.

"Something's wrong," Jill said. She moved quickly, and Roxanne followed on her heels, looking in the kitchen and down the hallway. Jill swung open the bedroom door, and they both scanned the guest room, then kept going faster. The last room in the hallway was the master bedroom, and as they entered, they both saw Alvie.

She was lying on the patterned Oriental rug on the floor, her face ashen, her mouth open and slack. Lips blue.

Roxanne pushed past Jill, dropped to her knees, and put her fingers on Alvie's neck. "She still has a pulse. Call 9-1-1!" And while Jill did, Roxanne began CPR.

Roxanne quickly placed one hand on Alvie's forehead, tilting it back to open her airway. With her other hand, she pinched the elderly lady's nose shut. Bending over, she sealed her lips over Alvie's, administering two rescue breaths. She watched as the elderly lady's chest rose and fell in response, a flicker of hope igniting in her own chest.

Next, she moved to chest compressions. Positioning herself directly over Alvie, she interlocked her fingers and placed the heel of her hand in the center of the woman's chest. Using her body weight, she started to perform compressions—rhythmic, steady, but forceful, pressing down hard and fast, her count echoing softly in the room: "One, two, three..."

Her brows furrowed with intense concentration, a sheen of sweat forming on her forehead, droplets trickling down her temples. Her muscles appeared to strain under the effort, and Jill could see her breaths coming out in short, focused puffs. But she didn't stop. Her count was steady, a lifesaving mantra in the stillness of the room, "27, 28, 29, 30..."

Every so often, Roxanne shouted, her voice firm but laced with desperation, "Alvie, can you hear me? Please, stay with me." Each plea punctuated by the rhythm of her compressions.

Jill stood by helplessly, aching to do something. The voice

on her phone asked questions and gave instructions, which she repeated out loud to Roxanne, who seemed to know exactly what to do anyway. In the distance, she heard the wail of a siren growing louder.

Jill was in awe. Roxanne was Superwoman—continuing the rigors of administering CPR, never stopping. Jill felt helpless as she watched Roxanne's efforts, the sweat trickling down her face.

How had this happened? Had the stress of losing her dear friend finally caught up to Alvie in some kind of cardiac event? She'd sounded vibrant on the phone with Jill earlier, her voice strong and strident. Urgently asking for Jill to come over. But she hadn't sounded fearful.

Jill and Roxanne stood outside the ICU, watching Alvie through a glass wall. She was alive but sedated and expected to make a full recovery. Her daughter sat by her bed, holding her hand. The doctor had explained her status in detail since they were the ones who'd gotten help and kept her alive until medics had arrived. *She lost oxygen for a short period of time. You saved her life. Not sure what happened. Possibly a heart attack, but more testing needed.*

But Jill had placed a call on the way to the hospital, and now Detective Nick Webb strode down the hallway.

"What happened?" he asked, stopping in front of Jill. "Who is this?"

"She is Linda Holloman's neighbor and was her best friend. She had something to tell me, but this," Jill pointed to Alvie, "happened just before we could get there."

"And?" he asked.

"I called because I want you to investigate. I believe someone tried to kill her," Jill told him. The sense of urgency she'd felt earlier continued to rise. Someone was pursuing the rest of the agenda that had begun with Cory's murder. She could feel it, and her body tingled with a raw sense of danger. "I also believe this is connected to Cory's murder. It started with Linda Holloman, somehow. Alvie knows something, and someone realized that and came after her."

Nick shifted his feet, looking irritated again. "All right, that seems a bit of a stretch. First, what makes you think someone tried to kill this woman? She looks—a bit on the older side, right? How do you know she didn't have a stroke or heart attack?"

Jill thought of Alvie's bedroom. The pillow on the bed was smeared with lipstick and flecks of something that appeared to be blood. The bedside table in disarray. Items scattered on the floor around it. She was sure Alvie had struggled and, in doing so, swept her hand over the table, knocking things over and on the floor. She relayed all of this to Nick.

"I'm sorry, but this isn't much to go on." Nick gave Jill a pained expression. "She could have struggled during the onset of the heart attack. That's common."

"Someone tried to kill this woman! Please, you've got to help us. I know this is tied to Linda Holloman and to Cory. I don't think you have all the facts yet, Nick."

"Not only that." Roxanne stepped forward impatiently. "But the rest of what you don't know could fill an encyclopedia. For instance, did your fancy detective work turn up the fact that Cory had a love child?"

"A what?" Nick looked shocked.

Jill responded before Roxanne could. "We talked to someone earlier, the woman we saw at the funeral. She has a baby, but we have no idea if it's Cory's. She claims to be a friend—a cycling buddy of Cory's."

"Friends with benefits! And a little *gift with purchase*," Roxanne added, rolling her eyes. "I have a bad feeling about her. She's acted strangely all along. If she was so close to Cory, why didn't she show it at the funeral? We're in the age of *anything goes* when it comes to people's sex lives. No scarlet letter was going to be pasted to her chest. She had no reason to be so secretive with us, Jill. The baby was right there in front of our eyes. Again, why not go ahead and admit it's Cory's?"

"Wait a second. You met with the woman from the funeral, and she had a baby." A myriad of expressions crossed Nick's face. "What makes you think it's Cory's?"

Roxanne pulled out her phone and took the incoming call. She stalked away, mumbling something about the trust.

Jill watched her go, concern growing. "I'm not sure if the baby is Cory's, but if it... *she* is, don't you think that might be significant?"

"Significant how? Having a baby with the guy—help me connect the dots here, Jill. What else do you know?"

"Not much, except what Roxanne alluded to. Cory's cycling buddy was not exactly forthcoming with us. She's hiding something. It could be the baby is his, or it could be something else. All I can tell you is that every time we've seen her, she's been extremely guarded. She spent time with him on weekends for months. I can't imagine they didn't open up about their lives. I think she knows things about Cory."

Roxanne stalked back, eyes blazing. "Hold onto your hats, people. Newsflash. The terms of Linda Holloman's trust stipulate that in the event of her death, everything passes to Cory and his brother, Cory acting as Trustee. But in the event of Cory's death, it all goes to his brother. *Unless he has a child.* In that case, half the trust goes to the mother and child, half to the brother, with an outside Trustee."

"How did you—" Jill started to ask. "Never mind." Confidentiality was a relative term, and that reality was growing fast for her.

"What does that mean exactly?" Nick asked.

"It's obvious. As long as Cory was alive, she wouldn't see a penny from the trust. She wasn't married to him, and for all we know, he viewed her as a fling and was done with her."

"What are you saying?"

"This means the mother of the baby has a really good motive to make sure her child inherits, and the best way to do that was to get rid of Cory."

CHAPTER THIRTY-THREE

"But how much money are we talking about here?" Jill kept circling back to that question.

Roxanne smiled. "Don't ask how I know. Let's just say someone put their ass on the line for me. But apparently, the most significant asset in the trust is oil and gas royalties from producing properties all over Texas, Oklahoma, and Arkansas. Linda Holloman's father was one of the early landmen in the 1930s. He bought mineral rights steadily for decades—not hard to do during the Great Depression and mid-20th century. People sold them for pennies, not knowing what they were giving away. As wells were dug, the money flowed in, and it benefited Linda's parents, then Linda, throughout her life. But she didn't spend it, at least not much of it. My, um... sources... think there's well over twenty-six million dollars sitting in various accounts."

They all stood silently, absorbing the information.

A staggering amount of wealth. Jill tried to imagine Lindsay Thomas, mother to an infant, plotting to kill Cory. *The baby's father.* Who might have been breaking up with Lindsay prior to his death.

The only barrier between her and thirteen million dollars. Half the estate.

Except there was another barrier, and that was Erica, who they'd also learned was working on converting the entire trust to a special needs trust for the benefit of Cory's brother, where she would be the trustee. Once that was accomplished, with all the assets placed in the trust, there might be no way for Lindsay to get her hands on the money.

But why settle for thirteen million when you could obtain twenty-six? What if there was a way to get both Erica and Travis out of the way? Lindsay and her baby would be the beneficiaries of enormous wealth.

Someone opened the door from the ICU unit and stepped out, startling all of them. "Excuse me," Alvie's daughter said. "My mom is awake, and she wants to talk to you." She looked at Jill as she said it, her face white. "She said a woman tried to kill her."

Nick's face hardened. "I'm a police officer. I need to get her statement, ma'am."

"I didn't get a good look at her," Alvie confessed. "I saw someone opening Linda's door. It was definitely a woman, and I think it was that girl her son was seeing." Her mouth twisted a bit. She whispered, "I think they had a baby together." She nodded her head as though that was a huge scandal. "I think it really bothered Linda, Cory having an affair. She felt sorry for Cory's wife, Erica. She was always saying—"

"Ma'am. We need to know what happened to you," Nick said.

Alvie's eyes teared a bit. "It was terrible. I called you because there are things I didn't get to tell you before," she said to Jill. "While I was waiting for you, I heard something. I went into the hallway, and that's when I saw that woman at Linda's door." She held a tissue to her face for a moment, her hand trembling slightly.

"I went down there to see why she was going into Linda's unit. She had no business being there! Anyway, I went in, but I didn't see her. I thought that was odd. I looked around some and left. I went back to my own unit. I was tired, so I decided to take a nap. I don't remember much more except the pillow, and then—" she stopped, her chest heaving. "She must have followed me home!"

Alvie's daughter stepped over. "I think that's about all she can take for now. She needs rest," she told them firmly.

"Wait. I'm okay," said Alvie, struggling to get her breath, tugging on Jill's arm. "I wanted to tell you this before, but you left too quickly. The thing is, I think someone killed Linda. I tried to tell the police that day, but no one would listen. They don't take it seriously when someone like us dies suddenly." She looked pointedly at Nick. "They think just because we're old, it's not worth looking into." She swallowed drily. "Honey," she said to her daughter, "pass me that water?"

Her daughter rushed to get the water, holding it so Alvie could put the straw in her mouth and take a sip.

Alvie leaned back against her pillow, breathing heavily. "I'm telling you, it's a crime in itself the way they blow us off at our age. Anyway, Linda was *healthy*. She was full of life. She ate like a bird, kept her weight down, and worked out every day. Got her regular check-ups—she'd just had one a couple of weeks before! Sure, she had early-stage Parkinson's, but the kind that progresses slowly. Her doctor told her she'd likely die of something else. Anyway, she didn't just drop dead for no reason. I saw that woman sneaking around that day. After she left, that's when I started feeling funny."

"What woman was that?" Nick asked.

"The one Cory was seeing on the side," Alvie said. Then she

looked confused. "At least, I think it was her. It was a woman, I know that."

"If we showed you some photos, would you be able to identify her?" Nick asked. His expression had gone from interested to doubtful to pained.

"Yes. I think so. Maybe."

Roxanne spoke up. "You didn't actually see her face, did you?"

"No, it was the back of her head. But it was her!"

Jill and Nick exchanged glances while Roxanne shifted impatiently.

"Her, who?" Nick asked.

But Alvie was done. She fell back against her pillow and waved them away. "I told you like I told the police before. *That woman killed Linda.* I know that for a fact. And she tried to kill me."

But as Jill turned to go, Alvie tugged her arm. "One more thing, Dr. Rhodes. Linda's diamond ring. It's rather large and valuable—I think something happened to it. Whoever has that—" But Alvie dissolved into a coughing fit, and her daughter practically shoved Jill out of the room.

"There is some truth to what she said," Nick said.

They stood in the hallway outside Alvie's room.

"What do you mean?" Jill asked.

"The part about the police not taking family members seriously when an older person dies suddenly. There are so many murders in a metropolitan area this size, and not enough resources to address them. Sometimes, I'm sorry to admit, we take shortcuts. There was a case, not that long ago, of—"

"Shortcuts?" Roxanne snapped.

"Give him a chance to speak," Jill said to Roxanne, who rolled her eyes.

Nick looked slightly embarrassed on behalf of his law enforcement brethren. "There were several elderly but healthy people who died suddenly. Family members reached out to law enforcement, but their concerns were brushed aside. Eventually, the pieces were put together. Their deaths had elements in common—they all lived in senior living facilities, nice ones; they were healthy prior to their sudden deaths; there were things that were in disarray and jewelry missing. In one case, there were smears of blood on the pillow on the bed." He sighed. "It turned out to be the work of a serial killer who posed as a maintenance worker."

"Dear God," breathed Roxanne, her eyes wide.

"What a nightmare for those families," Jill said, feeling her heart sink.

"Right," said Nick.

They were all quiet for a moment. The inevitability of aging. Losing mobility, control over one's own body. Being seen by others in a different way, as fragile, less competent. Though it crept in slowly, almost unnoticeably, unannounced, it made its way into every life blessed by longevity. None of them could quite grasp it, but the notion of being preyed upon while enjoying those last precious years was chilling.

"What do you think about what Alvie said?" Jill asked Nick.

"I'll look into it. I'll see if I can pull surveillance around the building and in the hallways if they have it there. It's too bad she didn't actually see the woman's face. She's not much of a witness at this point." His mouth twisted. "Maybe if the medical tests come back conclusive that she was smothered, and there's video of someone entering her apartment—" his voice trailed off. "But whatever this is about, none of it explains Kevin Bennett. He sent the poisoned bottle of bourbon to Cory." He looked at his watch. "I have to run, but I'll follow up later about Alvie."

"Thanks for that," Jill said. "I'll catch up with you two later. I have clients to see, and maybe..."

"Maybe what?" Roxanne asked.

"Nothing. Personal matters."

He couldn't shake the feeling that his case against Kevin Bennett was somehow off track. What had seemed like an open-and-shut case now seemed far too messy, with too many tangents that didn't add up.

It made sense that Kevin Bennett killed Cory as an act of revenge, blaming the litigant for the loss of his daughter. His fingerprints were on the bottle, and it was mailed from his office building. He was on video in Cory's office building just a few days prior with a weapon. It all pointed to Kevin as the killer. Nick felt confident he could get a conviction.

Except for the rest of it. There was a fortune that someone would get their hands on because of Cory's death, perhaps a girlfriend with a baby—potentially the beneficiary. Where money flowed in that quantity, there was a strong motive.

Then there was the suspicious death of Cory's mother, followed by the maybe-attempted murder of Linda's best friend down the hall, Alvie.

Coincidences with no relationship to Cory's murder? Nick shook his head. Unlikely. Accepting coincidence was the easy way out of detective work. And that wasn't his style.

This didn't feel done. And he was relentless. There was one interview he'd put off for a long time. *Why not now?*

"What are you shaking your head for?" His partner Rick had somehow gotten behind him without making a sound.

"Nothing. Well, actually, I'd like you to go along with something. It's the Kevin Bennett case. I'd like to eliminate any rabbit trails the defense team might use. You know, a decoy they might point to."

"That case is about as open-and-shut as you could ever wish for," Detective Stone stated flatly.

"Right. Except there are several dangling issues that don't add up. Plus, a whole new motive for Cory Holloman's murder." Nick brought his partner up to speed on the will and trust, the money, and the suspicious death of Linda, as well as the possible attempted murder of Alvie.

"That sounds like a lot of rabbit trails," declared Stone. He dragged over his chair and plopped his considerable weight down. He had a large Subway sandwich clutched in his hand, and he took the opportunity to take an extremely large bite, little pieces of lettuce and breadcrumbs falling on Nick's desk. "But I'll admit that is a shitload of money and a powerful motive," he said while chewing.

"*Dude.* Make a mess on your own desk," Nick said, swiping away the lettuce.

Still chewing, Stone spoke. "Yeah, whatever. But there is one other issue." He swallowed and took a swig of a large diet drink he'd sat on Nick's desk. "I had a little trouble backing up one part of the story. We went to Bennett's company, where the poisoned bottle was supposedly mailed from, and we couldn't find any record of the shipping. So then, we dug into it and discovered they have a centralized mailroom that some of the businesses use. We think that's where it was mailed, which creates a problem with the chain of evidence." He took another large bite, this time dropping the lettuce mess on the floor. "Better? I swear, you're worse than my ex. Always nailing me for leaving fingerprints on the glass tabletop and not using disinfectant everywhere I went. Jeez."

Nick sat up. "Wait. Without that evidence, we don't really know who mailed that bottle, do we?"

Detective Stone shrugged. "At this point, no, we don't. But we've got Kevin Bennett dead-to-rights. He threatened Cory in open court and went to his office with a gun."

Nick pushed his chair out and stood. "Well, that may be, but I'm still going to keep looking. And I want you in on this with me. Unless you have somewhere else to go tonight." He outlined his plan.

"Sounds like fun. I'm in," said Stone, grinning. "Let's go get the guy."

CHAPTER THIRTY-FOUR

Twilight was just beginning to spread as the cruiser made its way down the street. "Hey, Travis," Nick said, startling the slender guy making his way down the sidewalk.

Travis stopped, and his eyes darted around. "Uh, hey. What are you doing here?"

They'd tracked Travis to his friend Ross's house after trying Erica's house to no avail. He continued walking down the street, forcing Rick Stone to slowly coast their vehicle alongside him.

"Travis, we could really use your help. We're still working on Cory's case, and we're very close to making sure he receives justice. We think there are things that you may have forgotten about that day. So, we'd like to use some memory prompts to stimulate your recollection. That way, we'll have a much better case." Nick kept his voice even, non-committal, crossing his fingers. They didn't have to ask—they had enough reason to pick him up, but they'd agreed they would get further by easing his fears.

"Memory prompts? I don't understand," Travis said, cutting his eyes to them but still walking.

"It's kind of like playing a video game," Nick lied, feeling only marginally bad for the deception. "It's a technology that uses images and shapes and colors."

"Video games?" Travis stopped. "How long will this take?"

"Not long. Hop in, and we'll go to the station. We should have you back here in an hour or so. Are you hungry?" And at Travis's nod, Nick sweetened the bait. "We'll grab food on the way. Our treat."

"Good, huh?" Detective Stone asked their quarry when he popped several French fries dipped in catsup in his mouth.

Travis nodded, mouth full. They sat in a small conference room at the station, one typically used for internal meetings. It was more comfortable than an interrogation room. They wanted Travis at ease.

"I guess you skipped breakfast," said Rick.

Travis swallowed. "Yeah." He took a large bite of the hamburger and chewed, looking down self-consciously.

"Is that normal for you?" Nick asked.

"Yeah," he said. "I forget sometimes." He swallowed. "When do we start the video games?"

The two detectives exchanged a look.

"First, we'd like to record the session, only with your permission, of course." Nick placed a recording device on the table. "Is that okay?"

Travis chewed his food for a moment before nodding.

Nick tested the water further. "You mentioned you forget to eat sometimes. What about Erica? Seems like you would eat breakfast together in the morning now that you're living there."

Travis's neck flushed. "She's too busy. She leaves for work before I get up. But it's not her fault. There's food in the house; I just forget to eat sometimes." He laid the hamburger down carefully and placed his hands in his lap, twisting his fingers. He continued to look at the tabletop.

"You must miss your mom," said Nick. "Our condolences on your loss of her and your brother."

Travis nodded, swallowing.

"It's lucky you have Erica to look after you now," Detective Stone said.

Travis's brows drew together, and he nodded just a little. "Yeah."

Nick cleared his throat. "One of the things we wanted to talk about was your mom's death. We got information today that indicates she didn't die of natural causes. We think she may have been murdered."

Travis's head shot up. "Huh?"

"Did you ever meet your mom's neighbor, Alvie?" Stone pressed.

"Miss Alvie? She was Mom's friend. But... what did you mean? Mom died of a heart attack or something like that." His growing alarm drained his face of color. "And my brother drowned!"

"Listen. We know Cory didn't drown. He was poisoned. Travis, that's two people in your immediate family. Because of their deaths, you are going to inherit a tremendous amount of money."

Travis's eyes widened. "Money? I don't know what you're talking about. I have my disability check, and Erica pays the other bills for the house and stuff." His brows pulled together.

Stone leaned in and spoke sternly. "Bullshit. Your mom was wealthy—you had to have known that. Where do you think all that money went after she died? It went to your brother and now, to you."

Travis's head shook back and forth. "Mom never talked to me about money. She gave me some every now and then when I couldn't pay the rent a few times. Um, maybe she gave some to Cory. I don't know. But... my brother, poisoned? No way!"

Detective Stone banged his hand on the table. "Cut out that shit, Travis! Quit acting like some helpless little boy. You're a man. You know more than you're saying, and let me tell you, if you don't talk to us, it's not going to go well for you. Ever hear of obstruction of justice? Your mother and your brother were *murdered*. And you are *rich* now because of it."

Travis's hands twisted more. His eyes shifted rapidly between the two detectives. "No. No. No. No. I don't know anything about any of that. You're both lying to me—there's no video games like you said. I want to leave. Now."

Nick held up a hand to stop Detective Stone just as his mouth opened. "Wait a second." He turned to Travis and spoke kindly. "It's our job to ask questions, to try to get to the truth. We're not lying. Cory was murdered, and we believe your mom was as well. Look." Nick showed Travis a copy of his brother's revised death certificate.

Travis placed a shaking finger on the page. His lips moved as he read carefully. He dropped his hand and looked at his lap again. "I don't know," he mumbled. "That could be fake."

Nick watched him carefully. Either he was genuinely shocked to find out how his mother and brother died, not to mention the money, or he was a brilliant actor. Which sociopaths often were. Time to go to the next revelation.

"Travis, listen," Nick said. "There's something else. Your brother had a girlfriend, didn't he?"

Travis didn't look up. His head moved from side to side while he continued mumbling. It sounded like *no, no, no.*

"Did you ever meet Cory's girlfriend?" Rick Stone pressed.

"*Girlfriend.* I don't know her," Travis said. His leg moved up and down, and his hands twisted. He mumbled some more, then looked up and blurted, "This is all my fault. But it was an accident. I didn't mean to; I swear I didn't—" And his agitation increased, his breaths shortened, and his face paled. He looked back down at his lap, and his lips moved incessantly.

The two detectives looked at each other. "He's gone, isn't he?" Detective Stone said.

Nick shrugged. "He's here. He just doesn't want to deal with the truth right now."

"Whatever," said Stone. "Anyway, he just confessed."

"I'm not so sure about that," said Nick. He touched Travis's arm.

Travis jumped. He looked up, and his eyes were so wide the whites were showing all the way around. It reminded Nick of the horses on his grandpa's ranch and the way their eyes looked when they were spooked.

"Listen, Travis. Do you remember your mom wearing a large diamond ring? Do you know what happened to it after she passed?"

"Uh, yeah. She wore it all the time."

"And?" Detective Stone said impatiently.

Travis said nothing.

They continued the interrogation, questioning relentlessly, pushing Travis. *How did you kill your brother? What did you put in the bourbon?* But to no avail. He clamped his mouth shut.

He was done talking.

CHAPTER THIRTY-FIVE

Jill pulled into her reserved space, stopped, and turned off the engine. She sighed. *Poor Alvie.* Did someone try to kill her? Was it Lindsay? Was she even capable of such a thing? A young mother, her daughter, possibly Cory's love child. Was she driven by greed—aware of Cory's wealth, unwilling to let it slip away?

Could a heart filled with the love of a child also be a heart filled with murder? The darkest of drives alongside the sweetest?

Her mind drifted to her sister, Jade, and niece, Carly. She smiled, remembering the day she brought the two of them home from the hospital.

"She's so tiny," Jill said, leaning over the crib and gently touching the top of the baby's head.

The room was a sanctuary of serenity and warmth, carefully crafted with love and attention to detail. Soft pastel hues adorned the walls, and delicate curtains filtered the sunlight.

The centerpiece of the room was the crib. It stood elegantly against one wall, draped in billowing fabrics that whispered promises of peaceful slumber. Plush toys and stuffed animals adorned the crib. A soft mobile hung from the ceiling, dancing gently to a lullaby.

For weeks, they'd shopped together, haggled over décor, and carefully assembled this space, waiting for the baby's arrival. Maybe she would have her own time of preparation for motherhood down the road. *Maybe not.* So, she'd relished every moment of Jade's journey, almost as if it were her own.

Jill sat cross-legged on the soft rug near Jade. Her sister stood at the crib. Her face broke out in a radiant smile as she kissed the top of Carly's tiny head. "Look at her, sis. I can't believe she's really here. I can't believe how much love... I feel like my chest is going to burst."

Jill rose and stood beside Jade, looking down at the baby. In that moment, a deep sense of responsibility washed over her. She recognized the fragility of life and the uncertainties that lay ahead, but she was resolute in her commitment to protect and nurture this tiny being. She silently pledged to shield her from harm, to be a guiding light in times of darkness, and to provide solace and strength when needed.

She'd fallen completely in love with her niece from the day she was born.

Jade stood beside her, her eyes shimmering with affection. As they exchanged glances, a silent understanding passed between the sisters. Their bond of lifelong devotion and protection. Now extended to include another.

"I love you," Jill breathed to Jade. And to the baby. And she meant it.

THE DEEP END

Jill felt heavy inside. Something was going on with Jade, and for the first time ever, she was keeping secrets from her sister. It didn't seem possible—she was devoted to Daniel—but all the signals indicated she was having an affair.

And Carly seemed to be sensing that something was wrong with her mom. The self-soothing. The comments about not wanting the other person there. *Was Jade introducing her daughter to the other man?*

Judgment washed over Jill. *How could she do that?* She was still married to Daniel. They weren't even separated. Guilt followed the judgment. Who was she to judge her sister?

Jill's phone chimed. She felt a chill as she read the text.

Can you talk?

She called. "Daniel? Is Jade okay?"

"She's fine. Listen, Jill, I don't know what to do. Jade's gotten herself into something. I... it's just... there's no easy way to say it. She's having an affair." He made a choking sound.

The heaviness increased. "I know, Daniel."

Jill opened the door and exited her vehicle, locking it. Only then did her eyes travel around the parking garage, noting the absence of other vehicles. She looked at her watch, noting the time with shock. *No wonder.* All the normal people had left work and headed home hours ago.

She'd talked with Daniel for far longer than she'd been comfortable, listening to him cry and ramble about *her own sister*. Yes, it was clearly painful for him. But why call her? Surely, he had other people to talk to. Couldn't he understand how wildly uncomfortable it was for her to listen to him talk about her sister that way?

He hadn't denigrated her. Or put her down or called her names. Instead, he'd been sad and pitiful and weepy. He'd shared details she hadn't wanted to hear. All of which cast him solidly in the role of victim. To Jade's perpetrator role. And now, pulling Jill into the rescuer role. *Classic drama triangle.*

She began walking briskly toward the elevator, her heels clicking on the concrete.

The evening cast a shadowy veil over the desolate underground parking garage as she progressed. The flickering fluorescent lights above bathed the concrete walls in a sickly pale glow, distorting the surroundings. Her every footfall reverberated through the cold silence, amplifying the tension gathering between her shoulder blades. The rhythmic echoes bounced off the empty parking spaces, intensifying her unease. She picked up her pace, glancing around.

You're being silly. You walk through this garage every day. There's nothing to worry about.

And her own inner voice answered. *But you're never here this late unless the security guard walks you out.*

Then, she heard a rhythmic sound in the distance. *Footsteps?*

Her heart raced, the audible thumping competing with the echoes of her footsteps. Her senses sharpened, and every breath seemed amplified, alerting her to hidden dangers that only her now active mind could conjure. Her eyes darted, searching for any sign of movement, her ears straining to pick up the distant sounds again.

She stopped and forced herself to listen. But there was nothing.

Either she was alone in the garage, or someone was following, stopping when she stopped.

She picked up her pace again, spotting the elevator ahead. Time seemed to stretch, elongating the moments of unease as she made her way as rapidly as possible. Her breaths grew shallow, matching the rising tension that threatened to engulf her. Each step became a battle against her own escalating fear, her willpower straining against the sinister grip of the imagined danger. *This is not like me.*

She strained to hear the movement of another person. But she couldn't be sure.

At last, she reached the elevator and pushed the button. As she waited for the doors to open, she glanced around. There was no one there, and she began to breathe more normally.

Jill stepped into the elevator, turned, pressed the button for her floor, and watched the doors slowly move. Just before completely closing, a hand snaked around one of the doors and stopped them. A scream formed in her throat.

CHAPTER THIRTY-SIX

"What do you think?" asked Nick.

"I think anyone who gets on disability at this guy's age is running a con. Look at him," said Stone with disgust. "There's nothing wrong with him. He's physically able to get a job. If we keep letting everyone who sneezes on the public dole, just so we can buy votes, it's going to bankrupt—"

"I'm well aware of your feelings about that," Nick interrupted impatiently. This wasn't the time for one of his partner's rants about politics and government malfeasance. "I meant, what do you think about his story."

Stone shrugged. "I don't know. He wasn't exactly a font of information. I'm not sure I buy the ignorance act. The fake surprise at the news of his brother's murder and possibly his mother's."

"He looked surprised," said Nick. "That could be real. But what about his statement that he killed his brother?"

"Sounded like crazy talk to me. None of it added up. Come to think of it, maybe he is batshit crazy and deserving to get a disability check."

"Then there's the ring," Nick mused. "Although there's an

easy explanation for that. He might have no clue what happened to it since they didn't live together."

"Yep. Look, I don't think this is going anywhere, and I have to get somewhere." Rick Stone was finished for now. "What do you want to do with him? I say we keep him on ice for a while. I still think Kevin Bennett killed the guy. But who knows? Maybe they did it together for some reason. Two birds with one stone—revenge and money, split the winnings later. Either way, we need to clean up the chain of evidence, and one way to do it is to get this guy to pop."

Nick agreed and moved Travis to an interview room to sweat it out for a bit. As Nick headed back to his desk to do more research, he wondered what could happen to a guy Travis's age who was able-bodied yet so emotionally paralyzed that he couldn't even hold down an entry-level job. He shrugged. It wasn't his main concern right now. He owed Jill a follow-up on the surveillance in Linda Holloman's building.

An hour or so later, Nick sat back. He shoved back his chair. It was time to talk to Travis again.

"I'm sorry! I didn't mean to scare you," Ethan said.

The palpitations in her chest were gradually diminishing, and in their place rose anger. "If you wanted to talk, you could have called or texted. It's not okay to just show up here like this, especially late at night, following me like that. This garage is creepy enough without you—"

"What are you talking about? I just got here. I parked a few spaces away and saw you."

"Forget it." Jill punched the floor number in the elevator, and they stood silently as it rose. Stepping off, they made their way to Jill's office.

Twisting the doorknob to her office, Jill stopped. *Unlocked again.* The next conversation with Lauren would be very different. This was a security risk she couldn't afford. Client files couldn't be compromised like this. Not to mention the laptop sitting in plain view on her desk. That made her pulse kick up a bit. What if someone had found it? Taken it and cracked the security password?

Lauren was still new and didn't quite understand the imperative for confidentiality in her and Dr. Kelly's line of work, even though she had been trained. Was it time to look for a new assistant? Someone further along in a graduate program, perhaps older, with more maturity?

Her mind flashed to, just a couple of nights ago, to her client. *His wife, with a gun.* Lauren walking in the door, directly into the line of fire. Later, the relief, the hugs. No, there was no way Jill could fire her. More training—that was all that was needed. Maybe a security camera either in the hallway or the reception room. Or both.

Ethan was saying something. But she stopped in the hallway, mind made up. "Listen, Ethan, now is not the time. I've had a super long day, and my work isn't done. I have to prepare for tomorrow before I can leave. Please, just go home."

"But I've been waiting all day, Jill. I can't believe you're just blowing me off like this. I need to tell you the whole story. There are things you don't know and—" He shifted from foot to foot. "It's just—there are so many things I want to tell you. You don't really know the truth." His eyes begged her to give him... something.

But she didn't have anything to give at the moment. "You're

right. You deserve to have a chance to explain yourself." She sighed. "But I just can't right now. I know this is painful for you, the waiting, but I'm afraid you'll have to—"

His face reddened. "*Really?* Oh, my God. You know what? This is exactly why I didn't tell you everything when it happened. I'm the last priority in your life, and it's very obvious what's really going on." His voice turned nasty. "You have time for your ridiculous amateur sleuthing with that *detective*, what's his name, but not for me, for our so-called *relationship*. Well, forget it. I'm done." He turned and stalked away, stopped, and turned back. Hurled his last words at her before leaving. "Don't bother calling me."

So many secrets. So much anger. Had she caused it? With neglect, with passivity, maybe even with a trace of apathy. Was Ethan really jealous of Nick? Or was that a smoke screen, a defense mechanism thrown up to distract her from his own issues. It was understandable. Jade's words rose in her mind. *The triumvirate of male ego-crushing.*

Add the loss of respect from the woman he loves, a man's worst fear. It might have all been too much.

Sitting in her office later, Jill tapped the keyboard, closed the document she'd been working on, and leaned back, exhausted. Though she'd been focused on her clients, in the back of her mind, Cory Holloman haunted her.

So young, with so much life ahead. A biking friend who may have been a girlfriend. *A fling?* Or someone he'd fallen for while indulging in a mutual interest. Someone in whom he'd confided his struggles to attain and maintain sobriety. Confided his marital problems? Emotional intimacy that evolved into a deeper attraction. Perhaps love.

A baby. Annabelle, a tiny daughter, a new life, and new love abundant. For Lindsay. *For Cory?*

Then there was Erica, the wife who perhaps didn't know about the friend/girlfriend her husband had been seeing. That thought sparked others, and Jill pulled the thread in her mind, drifting.

The air pressure changed slightly, and tiny hairs rose on the back of her neck. *Ethan, again*. The trace of fear was replaced by a surge of irritation. "You might as well come in." She'd have to deal with the destruction of her latest relationship at some point. Might as well be now.

She heard footsteps approaching, but they were light. *Not Ethan's.*

Her door opened slowly. Jill's eyebrows rose.

"I'm sorry for showing up like this, but I was desperate. Please, Dr. Rhodes, you have to help Travis." Erica stood in Jill's doorway hesitantly. "The police, I think that detective Webb guy picked him up."

At Jill's indication, Erica came in and sat at Jill's desk. Her shoulders slumped. "I can't believe this. Travis was gone when I got home. I called Ross, but he'd left there hours earlier. Then, Ross told me he saw a cruiser pick up Travis and drive away. Why would they do that?" She lifted a bewildered expression to Jill. She swallowed and fiddled with her handbag. The diamond ring winked in the lamplight.

"How do you know it was Ni—Detective Webb—who picked him up?"

"I called the station and got someone to tell me. They said I couldn't go see him, not yet. They wouldn't give me any information. This isn't right, Dr. Rhodes. He's not represented by legal counsel. He didn't do anything, but that never really matters, does it? He won't understand he has to *ask* for counsel. I know how these things work! My husband was an attorney." Tears filled her eyes. "A good one." Her voice dropped. "I know what this means. Please, you have to help him… call that detective." She coughed. "Um, could I have some water?"

"Sure," Jill said, rising, grateful for the distraction to think.

Why would Nick pick up Travis?

Jill filled two glasses of water from the filtered cooler, brought them back, and set them on her desk.

Erica picked her glass up, held it to her lips, then set it back down. She leaned forward and spoke quickly. "The thing is, Travis has severe anxiety like I said. When he gets in stressful situations, he says whatever he thinks the other person wants to hear. Especially if he has to deal with questions. They're questioning him, aren't they? Though I can't understand why. But they are, aren't they?"

Jill allowed that it was likely. She pictured shy, anxious Travis in an interrogation room, a cold, unfamiliar space. No one there to advocate on his behalf. Not knowing why he was there, perhaps not even understanding the nature of the questions.

Nick was only doing his job. But what was he doing with Travis? He'd seemed completely convinced that Kevin Bennett had killed Cory. Only mildly interested in what may have happened to Linda Holloman, to Alvie.

Jill took a long drink of water to cover her puzzlement. Maybe she should call him, try to get him to tell her what he was doing. But the blue line was hard to cross. Most likely, she'd argue with him and still come away empty-handed.

"Dr. Rhodes? Did you hear me?" *Erica.* "I said. His therapist

275

called it *confabulating*. He makes up things when he's under stress, and his anxiety goes up. I'm sure you know what that means."

"Yes, of course I do," said Jill. Confabulation was not the same as lying. It was a distortion, an overlap between real memories and fabricated ones. Certain mental health conditions triggered it. So did alcohol and drugs, and sometimes, dementia.

"He could be saying *anything* right now," Erica said. "Don't you see that? And with no attorney... he's too vulnerable. They won't know he's just confused and filling in blanks. They will believe him! He could be arrested." She twisted the diamond ring anxiously.

"Arrested for what?" Jill asked. She took another drink of water, feeling the dryness in her mouth, noticing an odd taste.

Erica dropped her eyes. "I don't know. For whatever they think he did that made them pick him up." She peered up at Jill. "What are we going to do?"

As if on cue, Jill's phone rang, and she answered it. "Yes?" She swiveled away from Erica's watchful stare and listened.

Jill felt an odd metallic taste in her mouth as if she had been sucking on a fistful of old pennies. Her mouth twisted. Words tumbled out. "Yes, of course. I'm getting close to wrapping up at the office now. I know. Tomorrow will be a better time to talk." She pulled the phone slightly away, covered the mouthpiece, and apologized to Erica. "My boyfriend, dating troubles. I'll just be a minute." She returned to the call and listened more. "Okay. Got it. See you later, sweetheart." She disconnected and felt a wave of nausea.

"Was that really your boyfriend?" Erica asked suspiciously.

Jill rolled her eyes. "It's nothing, really. He's a little insecure, maybe jealous of... a friendship. We'll work it out. We always do."

And as she said the words, her heart sank, knowing there wasn't going to be a shining resolution to her problems with Ethan.

Erica stared at Jill, and something changed in her expression. "I don't believe you. I think that was someone else. Who was it?"

Jill fumbled under her desk and reached for her phone at the same time. "I don't know what kind of game you're playing, Erica, but I don't have time for it. How about we call Detective Webb right now and find out what's happened with Travis. Unless you have something else." She used her most authoritative voice, and it seemed to mollify Erica, who sat back again.

A throb of pain rose in Jill's head. "I'm wondering about something, Erica. I had an interesting call today from Cory's mom's neighbor, Alvie. I'm sure you know who I'm talking about."

"Sure, I know who you're talking about. Alvie, the queen of butting into other people's business." Suspicion fell over Erica's features. "Why on earth would she call you?"

"She seemed to think that Linda Holloman didn't die of natural causes, that she was killed."

"What? That's crazy. She's not in her right mind, Dr. Rhodes. Linda used to complain about Alvie all the time—always intruding, making up stories. You can't believe that nonsense."

"I'm not sure," said Jill carefully. Warmth spread into her chest, followed by a sudden chill. "I think something did happen to Linda, and I think because of it, someone attacked Alvie today." She swallowed again, looking at the glass of water but leaving it untouched. "I think you know something about that, Erica. And about Cory's girlfriend, who I also saw today." She pushed back a tendril of hair with a shaking hand. "Why don't you tell me what really happened."

CHAPTER THIRTY-SEVEN

A strange smile played over Erica's lips. "Where would you like me to start?"

"Why don't you start with the ring," Jill said, nodding at the flashing jewel on Erica's hand. "Cory didn't give it to you, did he?"

Erica's expression hardened. "No. He did not. But he should have."

"It was Linda Holloman's, wasn't it?"

"Yes. He thought he was so smart, hiding it. I found it one day, in his underwear drawer. It was in one of those nice ring boxes, the kind you get with a new ring. It was wrapped in a red ribbon." She gave a brief, hollow laugh. "I thought he was saving it to give to me on our anniversary. But our anniversary passed, and that's when I started noticing things."

Weeks earlier

"Where are you going?" Erica spoke to Cory as he crept toward the bedroom door.

Cory started. He stopped and turned, a neutral expression on his face. "Just out riding. Go back to bed and get some sleep. I'll be back later."

She yawned and stretched, watching him carefully. "I'm not sleepy. How about I go with you? Give me just a couple of minutes, and I'll be ready."

Did his face just fall?

"Um, I'm not sure how far I'm going to ride. It could be hours, and you don't like it that much. Plus, it's hot out there, and I know how you feel about that. But thanks for the offer." He turned as if to leave again.

"No problem. I'll turn back when I've gone far enough. Who knows? I might be able to keep up with you. I've been doing spin classes and really worked up my stamina." She gave him a mischievous smile—but on the inside, it was more like a jeer.

Cory froze. She could almost see the wheels turning. "Listen, Erica, I really need some alone time this morning. I'm sorry, and I don't mean anything by it, but you know, with the changes I've been making, it's not easy, and sometimes I—"

"Really," she interrupted, sitting up in bed. "I don't think it's alone time you want." She let one shoulder strap fall from her scant nightgown as she reached for the bedside table and pulled out a small box. She slid off the ribbon as Cory's mouth dropped open. She pulled out the ring and slipped it onto her left ring finger, holding it up to the light and smiling. "Thank you, darling! I couldn't help myself. I know you were going to surprise me later, and I'm sorry I spoiled it." She crooked a finger at him with a sly grin. "Now, come over here and get your reward for being so sweet."

He edged toward the door.

Her eyes opened wide with innocent surprise. "Cory? What

are you doing? Come here." She pulled the covers aside and exposed more of her form. She tousled her hair and lowered her lids alluringly. "Now, babe. I'm so ready for you."

Cory drew himself up. Resolve painted his expression. "I'm sorry, Erica. I'm just not in the right headspace for sex."

She dropped the act and leaped out of bed. "You're not in the right *headspace*? To make love to your wife? What the hell is *wrong* with you?" She stared at him. "By the way, exactly when were you going to give me the ring? Our anniversary was weeks ago, yet the box was still in the drawer."

"I don't want to get into this right now, Erica." Cory opened the door, walked out.

She followed him, the boiling waters of rage threatening to spill over. "Stop right there! You're going to deal with me now. I've had it, Cory! I know what's going on. Who is she? WHO IS SHE?"

But he continued walking away, and soon, he was gone. To his retreating back she hurled every accusation, laced with the worst language she could conjure. But it did no good.

After he was gone and the house was quiet, the emptiness in her chest expanded to the size of the sky.

Nick had spoken rapidly, trying to tell Jill about the startling developments from the interview with Travis. The surveillance video feed from Linda and Alvie's floor, outside their units. The ring—which seemed to tie several things together. He'd asked her questions, but she hadn't answered. Instead, she'd indicated she thought he was Ethan. And she'd sounded odd.

He bolted for the parking lot as soon as the call was disconnected. Jill wasn't alone, and she wanted him to know that.

THE DEEP END

Earlier

"Can I go home now?" Travis asked Nick, who'd stepped back into the interview room.

"Soon. But first," Nick said, as he clicked on the recorder, "I need to hear more about your sister-in-law. Where did she get the big diamond ring she's wearing?"

Travis looked up in fear. "I'm not supposed to talk about that."

"Why not?"

"She didn't want me to talk about it because she said it made her sad."

"It's your mom's ring, isn't it, Travis?"

Travis looked down. "Yes."

"Your mom died, and Cory wanted to give her ring to Erica?"

Travis shook his head slowly. "I don't think so."

"What do you mean?"

Travis looked up sadly. "They had a fight about it. He said it was a family heirloom. He told me he wanted it to go to someone else."

"Who?"

"I don't know how to get it back. She says it's hers now. But I told her Cory wanted the baby's mom to have it. She got really mad at me." He looked up at Nick, and his eyes were weary. "She's good to me and all that. But sometimes, she's scary."

Nick leaned forward. "Tell me about the baby."

"That must have been terrible. What did you find out? About Cory and the... the secrets he was keeping." She pushed her hair off her face as a wave of heat swept upward from her chest. She panted for a moment, and her vision wavered a bit. "I'm not feeling great, so we have to finish this soon."

Erica seemed unconcerned. "I found out everything except who she is. Not until today, that is. He was cheating on me!"

"You found out about the girlfriend and the baby, and all of a sudden, you weren't so sure about being able to get your hands on the trust." Jill's voice sounded far away, as though someone else was speaking.

Erica frowned. "What are you talking about? Yeah, there's a trust, and it was a nice surprise to find out about it." She cut her eyes to Jill. "It's Travis's anyway," she said. "For now. But that's just icing." She shoved back her chair and began pacing while keeping a watchful eye on Jill. "I could have handled the cheating as long as he got out of it and dropped her. But he didn't! And, the ring... it was *mine*. His mother wasn't going to need it anymore." Her pace picked up.

"What happened to Linda? Did you have something to do with her death?"

"She was old! She had Parkinson's, you know. She was going to lose it, go slowly downhill. It was for the best, anyway. And after that, we were supposed to start our own family. The money was going to be Cory's way out of having to work so much. He *promised* me." She turned a haggard face to Jill. "Have you ever had anyone promise you everything—to love you, take care of you—and then *abandon* you?"

For a moment, vulnerability softened her features. But it was swiftly gone. Her eyes glinted. "No, of course not. Look at you." Her hand swept the air. "You have it all. A career. Men to pick and choose from. You get to sit here, and people pay you to listen to their problems. How hard can that be? I saw you with that guy, cute as can be, but you're throwing him away for that detective.

Women like you make me sick. You just look around, see a guy you want, and it doesn't matter if he's already taken, if he's married."

Jill was vaguely aware that Erica had begun talking to someone else, not her. *Projection.* The real person wasn't here, so she'd projected that person onto Jill with all the ancillary rage. She touched her temple. Her head pounded with a persistent ache. It was unrelenting and intense as if someone was drumming an incessant beat against her skull.

All along, they'd suspected the enraged father who'd lost his daughter in a custody battle. A father who'd sought revenge. Then, they'd wondered about Linda Holloman's wealth, a powerful motive.

But they'd been wrong. The real motive was a jealous rage triggered by the devastation of emotional rejection. When combined with certain personality disorders, and now, she suspected Erica of narcissism, emotional rejection could be the spark that ignited the tinder that led to the explosion of murder. Rejection often fueled active shooters. It had fueled Erica, driven her to commit unspeakable acts. "What about Alvie? What could she have possibly done to make you so... angry with her?"

Erica shrugged. "She was in the wrong place at the wrong time, spying on me. I heard her tell someone on the phone about seeing me at Linda's. I couldn't have that." She peered at Jill. "Too bad for her."

"She's still alive, Erica. She survived, and she's talking to the police now."

Erica laughed. "No way. I made sure she wouldn't know it was me." She reached into her bag and pulled out a wig, dangling it in front of Jill. "It's human nature to see the familiar. All you have to do is change things up a little, and all of a sudden, people see what you want them to see."

The wig was a replica of Lindsay's hair, very different from Erica's. No wonder Alvie had thought it was Cory's girlfriend.

"How did you do it, Erica? I know you poisoned Cory," said Jill. And as she said the words, something clicked in. "But how did you manage to get Kevin Bennett's fingerprints on the bottle?"

Erica waved that away. "So easy. The bottle arrived at the house with a handwritten card from him. I didn't even have to do anything. I simply stowed it away so I would have something to divert attention away from looking into me further. I knew the investigation would go in that direction once I steered it that way. Again, human nature is to follow the easy, familiar path."

"But it was delivered to the house, the day he died. While you were away."

"Right. By me, from Bennett's office mailroom. Ta-da. Chain of evidence complete." She gave Jill a distorted grin.

Her narcissism was running the show now. In her zeal to brag about her cleverness, Erica was giving Jill everything she'd need later. "But how did you get Cory to drink the bourbon? Wasn't he sober at that point?" Jill deliberately put on an expression of awe.

"Cory kept bottles of electrolyte water. Easy enough to put the selenium in the only remaining bottle before I left for the spa. I made sure Travis gave it to him. Poor kid is probably confessing right now." But her eyes held anything but pity.

"You sent the notes to Cory's office, didn't you?"

"Just a little extra insurance. Cory told me about Kevin Bennett threatening him in open court, so I put his exact words into those notes." She smiled at her own cleverness.

"Cory... sober and trying so hard to move on with his life. Why not just divorce him? No one deserves to die over..." *What was it?* "Infidelity." Jill's focus on Erica was fading fast, and along with it went her normal verbal dexterity. Sadness washed over her. Cory—finally cleaning up his life, getting sober, moving forward. But the trail of destruction he'd left behind had caught up to him.

"Don't feel sorry for Cory, Dr. Rhodes. He was about to dump me. He was a bad person. Just ask the people who went up against him in court. There are a dozen people who wanted him to suffer, who wanted him dead." She wandered away, and her voice fell. "He destroyed my life. He doesn't deserve your pity."

CHAPTER THIRTY-EIGHT

Nick pressed on the gas, blasting his siren to get people to move out of the way. He'd called for backup, not knowing what kind of scenario he'd be facing. What was happening? He thought of Jill, sitting there, alone in her office. And someone showing up. *Erica?* Had she escalated from poisoning to something else? Was she even now pointing a gun at Jill, or had she already shot her? His stomach felt hollowed out.

He'd wasted far too much time on Kevin Bennett, ignoring the burgeoning signs that Erica Holloman was the real killer. The most basic rule of thumb. First, check out the spouse/partner/ lover. Intimate relationships gone awry were often the catalyst to violence.

He thought of Jill, with her intuition, telling him *Kevin Bennett is innocent, and I am going to prove it.*

He, with his skepticism, doubting her. Not moving fast enough to pick up Travis, question him. If only he'd done so, none of whatever was happening to Jill would have taken place. He gripped the steering wheel in frustration.

He floored it again, and suddenly, a truck swerved in front

of him. He slammed on the brakes, but the vehicle went into a slide. Time slowed down as he watched the side of the truck rapidly approach his front bumper. Then, he braced himself for the impact and listened as the sickening crunch filled his ears, followed by the deafening explosion of air bags.

Jill's breathing had become shallow. Each intake of air felt like a herculean task. Her heart pounded in her chest like a wild beast, erratic and without rhythm.

She tried to reach for her phone, to call for help, but her hands trembled like leaves in a violent storm. Her movements had become slower, like moving underwater. The world around her dipped in a surreal haze. She looked up, tried to focus on Erica, who now resembled a cutout figure. "What's happening to me?" she asked in Erica's direction.

"Just relax. It will be over soon," the blurred figure said from across the room.

"But everyone will know you did this," Jill said, knowing that it wouldn't matter. Erica would be gone, and so would Jill. "How did you do it?" She closed her eyes, and for a moment, she lost track of where she was, who she was talking to.

"You really should keep your door locked," a voice said. "Your water dispenser was an easy target. Since it's Friday night, no one will find you until Monday, and by then, it will look like you had a heart attack."

"But that's crazy. Someone will—" but she stopped herself. Was Nick coming? He would be in danger. She had to warn him, but how? *Who was that?* There was a voice across the room, but it was difficult to determine to whom it belonged.

A fever had set in, an intense heat flooding through her veins, sweat trickling between her shoulder blades and down her back. She felt lightheaded, and the world began to spin uncontrollably around her. The room dimmed with every blink of her heavy eyelids.

Nick disentangled himself from the airbag, checking his body for injuries. Other than a cut on his forehead that was delivering an irritating, slow trickle of blood into his left eye, he was okay. He wiped away the blood and tried to open the door. *Stuck*.

Nick's heart pounded in his chest as he desperately tried the handle of his cruiser's door again. His knuckles were turning white from the strain, the cold metal of the handle unyielding under his efforts. The force of the impact had jammed the door.

His mind was abuzz with irritation, with worry, with urgency. He could feel the adrenaline pumping through his veins, fueling the intensity of his effort to get out. Every moment he wasted in this car was a moment during which the threat to Jill intensified. The sirens in the distance felt like a mockery, a painful reminder of his incapacitation.

His initial panic subsided as training kicked in. He knew he needed to get out; he needed to regain control. Grabbing the radio, he relayed his predicament to dispatch, his voice calm despite his situation. The familiar click and static a welcome anchor in the storm.

Unbuckling his seatbelt, he threw his weight against the door one last time, a vain effort before abandoning the path. Groaning with the effort, he shifted towards the passenger side of the vehicle.

Carefully, he crawled over the center console, the radio equipment and computer terminal becoming inconvenient obstacles. The scent of spilled coffee and hot metal filled the air, a stark contrast to the sterile chill of the air conditioning he'd been enjoying moments before. He tried to avoid breathing in the powdery residue from the airbags, but he coughed, nonetheless.

Finally, after what felt like an eternity, Nick reached the passenger door. He gritted his teeth, praying it was not as uncooperative as its twin. With a sigh of relief, he pushed the door open.

He hauled himself out of the cruiser. Turning back to survey the damage, the twisted mess of metal and glass that was once his vehicle felt surreal. His gaze then shifted to the truck, concern replacing anger for a moment. Immediately, he felt torn. But he knew he couldn't just sprint away.

He would check on the other driver, then he'd get to Jill.

Her head pounded as waves of nausea swept over her. Someone was talking nearby.

"It's all his fault, really. If he'd just given me the ring, I would have known it was just a fling. Someone who didn't mean anything to him. Of course, I could have just ripped that thing off of Linda's hand that day. But then I wouldn't have been able to wear it. He *knew* I wanted that ring. How many times had I told him how beautiful it was? But he was going to give it to *her*!"

Jill grabbed the trash can next to her desk and heaved. It was agonizing, but nothing came up. She slowly slid to the floor and lay prone to try to keep the room from spinning so much. "What about the baby?" She wasn't sure whose baby she meant, but it seemed important to ask.

"Like I said, it's probably not his since she's such a skank. But either way, there won't be any issues. I'm taking care of that later."

Jill's head swam more, but inside her skull, alarms rang alongside the piercing pain. "What do you mean, you're taking care of it? What did you do?"

"Did you know you can buy selenium on the internet? Unlike other dangerous substances, this one hides in plain sight and isn't regulated. It's a supplement, after all. So easy to slip into someone's drink. Tastes a bit weird at first, but again, no one sees it coming." A giggle escaped. "No one sees *me* coming. I'm afraid Cory's girlfriend is going to be at the top of the suspect list when they follow my latest trail of breadcrumbs right to her. To her house, which they will search. *Murder/suicide*. She killed Cory because he refused to leave me. Then, unable to live with the remorse, she took her own life. The baby will go to foster care. Although, maybe I could step in as the long-suffering widow of the baby-daddy and take the baby. Yes, that's perfect!"

Jill heard a sniffle or two, followed by a nose being blown.

"I *wanted* a baby. I tried to get pregnant—threw away all the birth control. Do you know what it's like to want something so badly, Dr. Rhodes, but you just can't—and *she* has a baby. Just like that. It's not fair!"

Something crashed across the room. Somewhere in her consciousness, Jill was aware that the voice droning on belonged to someone who'd left logic and sanity in the rearview mirror, someone who was rapidly coming apart. How crazy was it to poison someone, then poison someone else, and then plant evidence in… *whose house was that?*

A baby's face entered her consciousness. *Annabelle*. This

insane person wanted to take Annabelle after killing her mother. Jill reached up and pulled herself back into her chair, panting with the effort. "You can't do that," she said into the swirl of her office toward the woman who continued to talk to herself and to no one.

CHAPTER THIRTY-NINE

For a few moments, there was some clarity. In the back of Jill's mind, she remembered the handwritten notes discovered in Cory's files.

Look behind you. I'm there. But you'll never see me coming.

The notes were intended as a diversion, a way of pointing to Kevin Bennett. But in their format, in the language itself, was the true message, written by Erica herself. She hadn't been able to stop herself from revealing her motive. *Rage*—born of a deep emotional wound, that of sexual and emotional rejection, intolerable to the shallow psyche of the narcissistic personality.

You'll never see me coming.

Most people didn't see the person coming who secretly plotted their death. Certainly not when it was a spouse or significant other. The person who shared their bed, who drank coffee with them in the mornings, and who sat across from them at dinner. It was too close, too personal, and far too unfathomable.

"Dr. Rhodes? Dr. Rhodes," said Erica. "Are you okay?"

The voice was nearby, and she vaguely recognized it. Jill's head was on her desk, and it felt unbelievably heavy, too heavy to lift.

Still, she attempted to do so, and the room immediately swam. Nausea rose, and this time, she heaved productively. Where it went, she had no idea. Her eyelids were mostly closed. Too difficult to open them. The buzz in her head rose to a crescendo as if a swarm of bees had entered her office and sought to find an exit. "Help," she whispered weakly.

The voice across the room was almost too soft to hear. "Don't worry, Dr. Rhodes. I'm sure help is on the way."

Her office door closed softly just after the lights were dimmed. *Was it bedtime?* She let out a slow breath, praying for relief from the overwhelming sickness that spread throughout her system. The sharpness of the pain in her skull was unbearable.

Jade... always there for me... "Help me," Jill murmured to her sister, whose face swam before her. So much like her own face, yet so different. She drifted into darkness, hearing a bell or a buzzing nearby.

"Hang in there, buddy. We're going to get you out." Nick found the driver of the truck slumped and initially unresponsive. Blood flowed, albeit slowly, from his forehead. *Not a deep wound.* But his left arm hung in an unnatural way.

"I can't breathe," the guy wheezed. He clearly struggled to draw a breath. *A collapsed lung? Or the aftereffect of the airbags?*

Nick talked to the emergency operator as he stood waiting, unable to help the driver. *Still miles away from helping Jill.* Would the emergency vehicles ever get here? "He says he can't breathe," he reported. He listened, shaking his head, then spoke again. "I can't tell what the problem is! I'm a cop, not a paramedic. How far away are they?" Hearing the answer, he leaned into the door of the truck again and spoke reassuringly to the driver. "They're almost here. You're going to be just fine."

He tried Jill's cell again, but it rang repeatedly before going to her voicemail.

The world had tilted. As Jill lay on the scratchy carpeting of her office, her vision swam in and out of focus. The white of the ceiling blurred into a haze of indistinct gray as if seen through a frosted pane of glass. Her eyelids fluttered, heavy, threatening to close. It felt as if she was adrift on the open sea, the room spinning and pitching with each agonizing heartbeat. She fought to stay awake, to stay present, but consciousness was a slippery eel, wriggling away from her desperate grasp.

There was a sudden noise as her door was flung open. The lights brightened. Someone knelt close to her, touching her neck, pulling open her eyelids. She felt her eyes twirl.

"Thank God," someone said, a familiar voice. That same voice spoke urgently to someone else. Then, again, to her. "Hang on, Jill. You're going to be okay. I promise."

She felt instantly reassured and drifted again, still in agonizing pain that couldn't be endured consciously. So, her body let her go into the darkness.

Sirens wailed in the distance, piercing through the unnerving quiet and awakened her. A sudden flurry of noise heralded the arrival of others. Footsteps thundered in the corridor, drawing closer like the beat of war drums in her disoriented mind. The slam of a door echoed and reverberated in her skull, making her wince. There was a frantic, urgent quality to the sounds that deepened the churning pit of nausea in her stomach.

Time stretched as they approached, their shapes vague and indistinct, masked by the halo of harsh light from the hallway that silhouetted them. Their uniforms, dark against the luminous backdrop, blurred and shifted as if seen through rippling water.

There was a constant, indistinct chatter of voices, words, and phrases washing over her in a broken tide. It sounded as if they were underwater, their voices garbled and muted. "Poisoning or drugs of some kind," they said. "Unresponsive," they noted. The words wormed their way through the fog of her thoughts, filling her with a strange sense of detachment.

One of the shapes knelt beside her, gloved hands touching her skin, cold and impersonal. They checked her pulse, the pressure against her throat a stark reminder of the reality she was barely clinging to.

She felt the prick of a needle then—sharp and sudden— against her skin. It was a brief moment of pain, tangible and real, that momentarily overtook the pounding in her head. The sensation was almost welcome. It was the introduction of an IV line, one she vaguely understood would flush out the poison in her system.

Her world began to tilt again, and she felt hands, many hands, slide under her, lifting her up. The sensation was disorientating, the world swaying as they moved her onto a stretcher. Her head lolled to the side, the room spinning out of control as her body was bundled and secured.

The wheels of the stretcher squeaked against the cold hallway floor, a high-pitched noise that echoed, bouncing off the walls and piercing through the dull throb in her skull. The movement was jarring, making her stomach lurch.

"Hang in there, Jill. We've got you. You're going to be okay," the familiar voice told her.

The journey out of her office seemed to take an eternity, each second stretching out into infinity. The hallway was a blur of beige and white, a stark contrast to the dim, surreal world she'd been trapped in.

The final journey into the ambulance was a hazy memory, her consciousness waning, slipping away with each passing second. The doors slammed shut, the sound echoing around her, muted and distant. The wailing of the sirens began anew.

And then the slow crawl of time abruptly accelerated, and the last thing she remembered was the rhythmic humming of the ambulance, the sway as it sped along. The fading voices of her rescuers became a distant echo, whispering reassurances, fighting the encroaching silence.

As her world faded to black, the words registered. "She's crashing. We're losing her!"

CHAPTER FORTY

A chill raced down Jill's spine, as jagged as the shadows cast by the gnarled trees in the woodland depths. The eerie darkness of the forest enveloped her, its murky depths reaching out with skeletal fingers, obscuring the path ahead. All around her, the wind whispered, rustling through the leaves, and creaking the branches. The blue specter of her sister's dress fluttered just out of reach like a wisp of vibrant smoke in the gloom.

Her heart pounded a furious rhythm in her chest, each beat a sharp reminder of the task at hand; she had to reach Jade, had to keep her in sight.

Her little legs ached, protesting each leap over a gnarled root, each stumble on the uneven, leaf-littered path. But she forced herself on, breath coming in short, sharp gasps, each one fogging the chilly air. She could see the vibrant shock of blue, Jade's dress, flit between the trees. But each time she reached the spot where she had last seen it, Jade was gone, her girlish laughter echoing through the forest like a chilling melody.

The wind picked up, howling through the twisted boughs, sending a flurry of leaves spiraling to the forest floor. A sudden rustle in the bushes to her left sent her heart into her throat. A bird took flight, its shrill cry piercing the eerie quiet. Jill jumped, her eyes wide in fear, but she did not stop running.

Jade's laughter echoed once more, a flash of her blue dress winking at Jill from the depths of the forest. Jill made a beeline for it, the world around her blurring into shades of black and green as she ran.

She slipped, her foot finding an unsteady rock instead of solid earth. She tumbled, a gasp escaping her lips as she met the cold, damp forest floor. For a moment, she lay still, the taste of leaf-littered earth bitter in her mouth. Her knee throbbed in pain, but she pushed it aside.

With a grunt, she pushed herself up and stumbled forward, her small hands swiping away the moisture from her cheeks. She was scared, yes, but also determined to catch her sister.

The last vestiges of her fear seemed to give her strength, propelling her forward, her breaths coming in hard pants. Jade was near; she knew it. And with every step she took, every leap over a fallen log, every brush against a thorny bush, she felt herself drawing closer to her elusive quarry.

The flashes of blue that punctuated the night were getting brighter, closer. She could almost hear Jade's panting breaths, almost touch the blue fabric of her dress. She was near. Very close.

And then, silence. There were no more flashes of blue, no childish laughter echoing ahead. Jill stopped, and for a moment, all she could hear was the pounding of her own heart. But that slowed, and all she could hear was silence. She looked all around. A scream of frustration and fear rose in her throat.

The following morning

Nick sat hunched on the edge of the sterile, starch-white hospital chair. His gaze was fixed on Jill's pallid face, the fluorescent lights overhead casting shadows that gave her features an ethereal quality. The constant hum of medical machinery served as a disquieting soundtrack, each beep and blip a reminder of the frail thread upon which her life had hung just a few hours before.

He studied her face, each line, each curve etched deep in his mind. Her eyes were closed, and her lips were slightly parted as she took shallow, uneven breaths.

Nick's heart throbbed in his chest, its rhythm syncopating with the monotonous blips from the monitor. Every rise and fall of Jill's chest felt like a small victory, a silent rebellion against the cold clutches of uncertainty. He took her hand, knowing he had no right to do so.

Luckily, he'd been able to convince the medical personnel that she needed police protection, which had given him access to her bedside. He'd been there all night, alternately sleeping on the uncomfortable sofa in the room and checking on Jill.

Suddenly, a moan slipped through her lips. A sigh so soft yet loaded with pain. It pierced Nick's heart. His gaze snapped to her face, searching for any sign of consciousness.

The moan morphed into a small scream, a plea that cut through the sterile silence of the hospital room. His hand tightened around hers as if he could anchor her, draw her back from the torment she was clearly experiencing.

He felt helpless, powerless in not being able to alleviate her distress. He longed to journey into her dreams, to face her fears and banish them, but he could only sit there, holding her hand, offering silent support.

Instead, he leaned over, whispering words of reassurance. Her scream faded into a whimper, the sound dying in the chilling air of the hospital room. He bent to press his lips against her cold hand, then quickly dropped it as the door flew open.

Jill's assistant, Lauren, rushed to Jill's bedside. "Oh. My. God! What happened?"

Behind her trailed an attractive woman; traces of Jill's own delicate features echoed in hers. "Oh, dear God! Jill! Oh, dear." Her voice was panicked, almost shrill. "What's wrong with my baby?" She put her fist to her mouth. "Who are you?" She'd abruptly turned to Nick accusingly. "What happened to my daughter? Where are the doctors? *What are you doing here?*"

"Now, Crystal, calm down," said the man with her. His calm demeanor contrasted sharply with the agitation currently exhibited by his companion. "We'll talk to the doctors. But first, let's introduce ourselves to this young man."

Doing the math, Nick surmised Crystal was around sixty, but she had the smooth, translucent skin and luxurious hair of a much younger woman. The man reminded Nick of a college professor with his carefully combed hair and closely clipped white beard. He gave Nick an intelligent, curious expression as he touched his wife's shoulder reassuringly. *Jill's parents.*

Nick stood. "I'm Detective Nick Webb." He shook hands with Jill's father, who introduced himself as Daryl Schaffer. Jill's mother merely nodded. "I work with Jill—Dr. Rhodes—periodically. She ingested something that made her seriously ill, but we got to her in time. I'll go find the doctor to update you. Excuse me."

A few minutes later, Nick re-entered the room, physician in tow, just in time to see Jill's eyes begin to flutter. Relief washed over him. As Jill slowly awakened, he waited to find out if questioning her now would be appropriate. But her disorientation told him that would have to wait. He slipped quietly out of the room.

Now that Jill was in the care of her family, he felt free to finish the work from the previous day. His partner had been working since late the previous night to try to track down the loose threads of the case. They'd continued to hold Travis, uncertain of his role.

The room slowly swam into view, but Jill's eyes couldn't focus. Shapes—people, some tall and standing, others sitting nearby. Her eyes searched for the one person she wanted to see, straining to focus through the blur. "Jade?"

One shape separated itself from the others and came close. "I'm here, honey." A soft hand stroked hers.

"What happened?" Jill asked, unable to recall why she was here, feeling so tired. Unable to see clearly. *Where was here?* "Uh, where am I?" Memories tugged, but she couldn't make sense of them. Sadness washed over her. "*Jade,*" she said, voice cracking with desperation, not knowing why.

"Oh, Jill, sweetie. I'm here," said her sister, crawling into the bed alongside her. "You've been sick, and you're in the hospital, but you're going to be fine."

Then, she was enveloped in her sister's warm embrace, and the tears flowed. "I don't remember what happened! Why do I feel so bad?" She shook with something—fear, or sadness, or the echoes of a memory that wasn't really a memory. "I couldn't find you..."

"Shh. I'm here."

Other voices spoke nearby, but she didn't care. She only wanted her sister's love and comfort. She was, after all, the only person who had given her comfort all those years ago. She drifted into a peaceful sleep.

Later, Jill's eyes flew open, and this time, she saw clearly. Jade was asleep next to her, scrunched into the impossibly narrow hospital bed, snoring slightly. No one else was in the room. "Jade." She jostled her sister. "Jade! I remember everything." She looked around frantically, but there was no one else there. "Where's Nick? I have to tell him!" She tried to sit up but felt far too weak.

"Welcome back, sleepy head," said Jade, stretching next to her. "Wait. I brought something for you." She sprang out of the hospital bed, grabbed her bag from a chair, and dug around in it. "I know it's here." She pulled out her cell phone and pushed a few buttons. A moment later, she held it up to Jill.

"Hi, Aunt Jill! Mommy said you're sick, so I drew something for you." Carly, her niece, held up a large piece of construction paper. The drawing was beautiful, stylistic—a sinuous gray cat with long fur. "It's Tiger!" Carly fairly shouted, referencing their cat. Jill was struck again by her niece's budding artistic talent, far beyond her years.

"Hi, sweetie," Jill managed to croak, doing her best to look more energetic than she felt.

"Mommy! When can I go see Aunt Jill?" Carly asked. That sparked a conversation between Jade and her daughter, with Jill quietly watching. Carly seemed like her old self, with none of the anxiety she'd exhibited recently.

But where was Nick? He needed to know who had been there when she collapsed. Sooner rather than later. "Jade? I need to talk to you," she whispered so Carly wouldn't hear. "Now," she insisted as Jade continued talking to her daughter.

"What? Hold on," said Jade, finishing the call with Carly. She turned to Jill, all smiles. "What can I get you, honey? How about some water?"

"Thanks, but right now, the main thing I need is to talk to Ni—Detective Webb. He needs to know what happened before I got sick."

CHAPTER FORTY-ONE

Lindsay shifted Annabelle from her right hip to her left, pulling open the door with her right hand. Her breath caught in her throat at the sight of Cory's wife.

"Lindsay. So nice to meet you," said Erica, smiling in a way that was anything but nice. She pushed her way into the house and looked around. "So, this is where you screwed my husband? I mean, it's okay, but it's nothing special." She turned to Annabelle and smiled again. "I'll admit, the baby is adorable." She gestured for Lindsay to precede her to the family room.

Lindsay walked ahead of Erica, her heart thumping. She took deep breaths to try to calm down. Her arms wrapped Annabelle protectively. She bounced her lightly to help herself calm down and to distract the baby from the anxiety radiating through her body.

Sitting across from each other, the two women silently took stock of one another. Lindsay felt Erica's eyes traveling up and down her body, but not in appraisal of her physical appearance. Instead, she felt emotionally naked under the woman's surveillance.

There was no kindness in Erica's stare, no sense of compassion or empathy. Instead, it was as if she were being studied by a predator. Unconsciously, she touched her own throat then pulled her daughter even closer. Gathering her courage, Lindsay spoke up. "What's on your mind, Erica?"

"What's on my mind? I'll let you know when I'm ready. Right now, I need *you* to talk, Lindsay. Tell me all about you and Cory."

Lindsay swallowed. "I don't think that's going to do anyone any good. It's in the past, and Cory is... well, he's not here. We all need to move on." It sounded thin to her own ears. *Would it be enough?*

Erica leaned toward her. "I know you seduced him. Obviously." She waved her hand and sat back. "I want to know what he *told* you. What did he say about me? Married guys who cheat never admit that *they* are to blame. They always blame the wife. So, tell me. What was his excuse for cheating? Did he say I was too old, or too fat, or not interested in sex? Because we were lovers all the way until he... died tragically." She smiled. "If he told you we weren't having sex, he lied. Did he tell you he gave me his mother's big, fat diamond ring for our anniversary?" She held her hand out to Lindsay and cackled. "After he gave me the ring, we screwed like rabbits."

Lindsay gulped. Her chest felt heavy for the thousandth time over the last couple of weeks. She missed him so badly at times it was a physical pain. The emptiness of the future stretched before her in a never-ending ribbon of loneliness. Without Annabelle, it would be unendurable. She stroked the top of the baby's soft, down-covered head.

"Cat got your tongue, I see. Not what you expected to find out, is it?" Erica's eyes narrowed. "Oh, stop with the crocodile tears. I know what you wanted, what this was all about. You wanted the money, the trust." She rolled her eyes. "Well, you can forget that. You're not going to be able to lay claim to the trust. You're not entitled, anyway. I'm Cory's *wife*."

Gathering her courage, Lindsay spoke up again. "What did you do to Cory?" Her mouth was unbelievably dry. "He didn't drown. He was a champion swimmer," she added as a deliberate challenge. She tried her best to check the corners of the room without shifting her eyes.

"What did *I* do? You really are naïve, aren't you? Cory got what he deserved. He destroyed my life just so he could get a little sex on the side. But he didn't love you. He loved *me*," she added. Her mouth quivered for a moment. Then froze. The predatory gaze returned.

"What did he deserve?" Lindsay heard herself ask.

Erica studied Lindsay, her head tilting for a moment. "It's like this. He deserved a slow, lingering, painful death while wondering what happened to him, where he went wrong. And that's what he got. You reap what you sow."

"You poisoned him, didn't you," stated Lindsay, swallowing drily.

"I think you know the answer to that," said Erica lightly. "Why are you asking me all these questions, anyway?" Her eyes narrowed with suspicion. "Are you setting me up?" She wandered across the room. "Is there someone else here?" She opened her bag and drew out a gun, holding it to her side casually.

Lindsay pulled Annabelle to her side, as far away from Erica as possible. "Please, put the gun away. There's no one here but me and the baby." This wasn't supposed to be happening. Her mind searched frantically for a way out.

Erica walked through the open kitchen and pulled open the pantry door. She closed it and came back to sit across from

Lindsay. "There'd better not be. Now, it's time to get on with things." She put the gun on the seat next to her and opened her bag, pulling out a water bottle filled with liquid. "This is what you're going to do. Drink this." She placed it on the coffee table between them.

Lindsay stalled for time. "What is that?"

"You don't need to know. Drink it." Erica turned her gaze to Annabelle. "I know you don't want anything to happen to the baby. But it will if you don't drink that now." Then her eyes strayed to the gun.

Could she get to the gun before Erica? Lindsay felt her throat closing with fear. *Think.* "Please, don't hurt my baby. You can do whatever else you want, but please... take care of Annabelle." She drew herself up with false confidence. "Please! Promise me you will." She forced out the next words, feeling the nausea that rose. "She won't have a father, and you're her only chance. You could be... her mother."

Erica's eyes softened as she focused on the baby. "Yes. I deserve that, after all. I was supposed to have a baby. That's one more thing he took away from me, with his... rather untimely death."

Was Erica blaming Cory for his own murder? *Unbelievable.* She pressed on. "And one more thing," Lindsay said. "I at least deserve to know what happened to Cory before I... drink that. Please," she begged.

"I made sure he got the same thing you're about to drink. I made sure he suffered. I made sure he *died* painfully," Erica ended viciously. "You know, he really wasn't a good guy. He cheated on me. He screwed over anyone he went up against in court with dirty tactics." She grinned. "He cheated on you! With me." But even as she said the words, her eyes welled up with tears.

"I'm sure he loved you," Lindsay whispered. "I'm sorry you got hurt."

"Shut up! If you were so sorry, you would have stayed away from him. He was married, for God's sake! Women today have no scruples, no decency. Everyone in Hollywood cheats, has children without the benefit of marriage, and then they parade it all in the media like it's nothing! *No one* says anything about it. Well, it's not nothing, and I have something to say about it." She swiped away a tear angrily, picked up the gun, and aimed it at Lindsay. "Now, drink!"

Several things happened at once, and later, Lindsay would swear it all happened in slow motion. It was distorted, and her ears roared with adrenaline the entire time and for hours afterward.

The door banged open, and footsteps thundered. "Police! Put the gun down! Get down *now*!" A male voice shouted.

Erica turned with the gun toward the two figures on the far side of the room. Her finger tightened on the trigger.

Lindsay froze as her eyes flashed to the figures. She opened her mouth, trying to find words to warn them. She reached out an arm, knowing she couldn't possibly stop Erica, not with Annabelle in her arms.

Erica fired.

Lindsay dove to the floor with Annabelle, who began emitting an ear-piercing cry. She rolled toward the sofa so that her back was to the room, and Annabelle was against the sofa, shielded by her mother's body. She began praying, whispering in desperation, an old prayer springing to mind. *The Lord is my Shepherd...*

Lindsay heard Erica scream in defiance and fire again. Other shots echoed in her living room.

Then, it was quiet. An odd smell hung in the air. She sobbed, holding Annabelle tight against the sofa. The baby continued to cry in distress. She whispered soothing words, rubbing the baby's back.

"It's okay, now." A hand touched her shoulder, and she jerked in fear. "It's okay, you're safe now."

Slowly, she rolled away from the sofa and sat up, still holding Annabelle tightly. She looked up into kind eyes, an unusual gray green in color. Very good-looking in a rugged sort of way.

"I'm sorry that turned out to be so dangerous. You did a great job." Detective Nick Webb held out a hand, wincing.

Lindsay took the offered hand and allowed herself to be pulled to her feet. "Shh," she said to Annabelle. "I can't believe she had a gun," she said to Detective Webb.

"We didn't expect that, I'm sorry to say," said Detective Webb. "We expected she would try the poison, but not... this."

Lindsay was afraid to look but dared to scan the room. Erica lay moaning on the floor, clutching her right arm, which slowly leaked blood. "Is she okay?"

"It's a flesh wound. The EMTs are on the way," said Detective Webb, gesturing toward his partner, Detective Stone, on his cell phone, talking. Webb quickly cuffed Erica's good arm to the leg of a large, heavy table as she blasted him with colorful language.

"Are you okay?" Lindsay asked Webb as she wriggled uncomfortably.

"I'm fine except for one hit." He pointed to a hole in his protective vest, grimacing. "Here, let me help you with that."

"No, it's okay. Here. Hold Annabelle?" She handed him the baby, who looked startled. Almost as startled as the expression on Detective Webb's face. But she smiled inwardly, noting how easily he took the baby, instinctively having her straddle his hip. He gave Annabelle a goofy smile, which made the baby laugh.

Lindsay turned away, unbuttoned her blouse, and pulled off the hidden microphone that had been attached to her body earlier. She buttoned her blouse and turned back, handing the equipment to Detective Stone, who'd walked over. *Was he checking out her body?* That was when she noticed the woman who'd come into the room. *Cory's legal partner.*

"Wow, that was a total cluster," said Roxanne, giving Detective Webb a glare. "What the hell happened to *it will be okay. We'll just get her on record, and that's it.* But I suppose all's well that ends well. Unfortunately, though, we are all witnesses to another crime." She paused. "Attempted murder."

"Which is why everyone will stay put until we can get back-up, someone to document the scene and interview everyone," said Detective Stone. "Meanwhile." And he read Erica her rights.

"There's one more issue," said Roxanne, giving a heavy sigh. "I am still Erica's legal counsel, and in that capacity, I have to do something. Until I can refer her due to conflict of interest." She walked over to Erica's prone body. "Do not talk to these guys or to any other cops who show up, Erica. I'm getting a colleague for you now. Until you get further advice from him or her, do not talk. Period." No one in the room missed the note of disgust in Roxanne's voice as she advised her client.

"Nice," said Detective Stone. "Once again, the bottom-feeding criminal defense attorney makes hay helping a killer get..."

"That's enough," Detective Webb told his partner. "She helped us avoid putting an innocent guy in prison. Who we now have to get out of jail. We have a lot to focus on," he finished.

Detective Stone rolled his eyes. "Sure. Why don't we let out a few other scumbags and sociopaths while we're at it?"

"Kevin Bennett isn't a... never mind." Webb pulled out his phone and made a quick call.

At that point, Lindsay tuned out of the conversation. She had only one focus. *Annabelle.* "Excuse me, everyone, but I have to get my daughter away from all this." She fled to the bedroom.

"Thanks for letting me know." She hung up and turned to Jade. "That was Detective Webb. They were able to pull off the plan and get plenty of evidence. The scary part is Erica brought a gun..."

"To a poison party," said Jade darkly. "Is Lindsay okay?"

"She and the baby are fine, though shaken. No one saw that coming. Erica has a gunshot wound, but it's minor. They've taken her into custody." She pursed her lips thoughtfully. "I'm wondering what will happen to Travis. I'm not sure how well he can function on his own." She struggled to sit up.

"Stop that! You're supposed to be resting," said Jade, pulling the covers up and gently pressing Jill back against the pillow.

"I have got to get out of this hospital," said Jill. "By the way, have we gotten any of the tests back to find out what I ingested?"

"Oh, I almost forgot. While you were asleep, the doctor came in and confirmed it's selenium poisoning, just like Cory. Also, Detective Webb confirmed they found Erica's fingerprints on the water dispenser at your office. Just one that she apparently missed when she was wiping it down."

Jill sighed and sat back again. "All the pieces have come together into one sad portrait of a woman who will now spend the rest of her life in prison. And now, Cory's brother will have to learn to be independent. If he can."

Suddenly, from the fog of her memory, Jill remembered the call from Daniel about Jade. "Um, listen. Daniel called me last night. About you."

"I know," said Jade, looking away.

An uncomfortable silence stretched. Since that had almost never happened in their entire lives, Jill was stunned.

Jade looked at Jill and sighed. "It's complicated. I'm not trying to be mysterious, but there are things I can't... I just can't talk about it right now. Daniel and I aren't getting along, and I have my suspicions, but they're not facts at this point." She brushed away a strand of Jill's hair. "Anyway, none of that stuff is important right now. Your health, your recovery, is important. I had a chance to talk to the doctor earlier while you were asleep. You might as well get Lauren to cancel your clients for a while. Recovery from this kind of poison isn't easy."

And as Jill sank into the pillow and pulled the covers up, she felt it—a heaviness like none she'd ever felt before. She drifted away, soothed by Jade's closeness.

CHAPTER FORTY-TWO

Six weeks later

A mosquito landed on Jill's forearm, and she brushed it away languidly. Twilight in April was a soothing wash of colors that gradually deepened as Jill sank into the lounge chair, her eyes half-closed in contentment. The cobalt sky faded to darker shades of gray and navy as the patio party lights twinkled and the firepit added a special glow. It was just chilly enough to warrant the soft throw over her legs.

The aroma of hamburgers cooking on the grill, along with the bowls of guacamole and chips sitting in front of her, should have been wildly tempting, but she was still struggling with her appetite. She smiled to herself, knowing Jade would soon be hounding her to *take another bite, even if you don't want it. You have to get your strength back.*

Jade had become a permanent fixture in her life since the poisoning, and she felt it again—that deep-down tug of devotion, of the treasure of her sister, who tethered her own heart. But of late, there had been another feeling, one of quiet dread. With clients, she identified it as *waiting for the other shoe to drop*, the hallmark of those who struggled with generalized anxiety.

Her gaze strayed to the guests whom Roxanne had invited over to celebrate Jill's recovery. Not that she was entirely recovered, but she was no longer confined to her bed or sofa for most of the day. She walked short distances in the mornings, forced herself to the gym two times per week for light strength training, and adhered to a strict diet and supplement regimen designed to regain her health.

Roxanne's outdoor entertainment space was beautiful and peaceful, affording them a comfortable environment for friends and family to gather. Jill wondered, not for the first time, about finding a house and moving out of her high-rise condo. She'd always assumed that would be with Ethan after the wedding. The wedding that would never take place.

Ever since the poisoning, issues like her disastrous relationship with Ethan had taken a back seat to her recovery, as well as to an emerging perspective, one which both calmed her and caused some apprehension. It wasn't like her to brush aside a break-up so easily, but she'd found that the pain had quickly receded far into the background of her consciousness. Her gaze drifted to an unlikely tableau taking place nearby. Oddly, she felt unaffected, detached from the absurdity of it.

Ethan—invited by Roxanne—sat near Nick Webb. They were engaged in a lively conversation about sports. Her attention strayed to the two men, and she began picking up the tone of their words, not overtly hostile but not friendly either.

"You're getting it all wrong," Ethan scoffed, his gaze never leaving the Cowboys' highlights playing on the flatscreen TV that hung in the covered patio. "The Eagles will be the thorn in the Cowboys' side this season, not the Commanders. That new quarterback, Hurts, he's got talent, mark my words."

"I'm telling you, man, the Eagles aren't our main problem this season," Nick disagreed, pointing his beer bottle at the TV. "They're always a threat, sure, but after their performance last season, I don't see them bouncing back quickly. Look at how their new quarterback played after Wentz left; he struggled."

Ethan shook his head. "The Eagles' quarterback is still green, sure, but he showed promise towards the end of the last season. Besides, they've had a solid offseason. Don't forget, they got that wide receiver from Alabama in the draft. That's a game-changer."

"Yeah, but it's more than just individual players," Nick argued. "The Eagles have a new coach and a new offensive system, which could give them some early problems, but let's not overlook the Washington Commanders."

Ethan shrugged, crossing his arms. "The Commanders? Seriously? They barely made .500 last season."

"Yeah, but you're missing the point. They have consistency with Ron Rivera. They're returning with a more experienced Taylor Heinicke, who has shown some serious talent, plus they've beefed up their offensive line in the off-season. The Commanders' defensive line was already monstrous, and with Heinicke getting comfortable in the pocket, they could easily outperform the Eagles."

Ethan glanced back at the TV, frowning. "I'll give you that Heinicke has potential. He pulled out some surprises last season, and his arm strength has been impressive, but he's still not a top-tier quarterback. If he can't elevate his game this season, the Commanders don't stand a chance against us."

"But that's just it," Nick argued. A smile played across his face as he seemed to be having fun poking at Ethan. "It's a team game.

Yes, a quarterback is important, but look at the Cowboys. We have Dak Prescott, one of the top quarterbacks in the league, but we didn't manage to clinch the division last season. We do have a strong team, but we've got to watch out for the Commanders, especially when we've got both offense and defense to worry about." Nick smiled at Ethan, who scowled back.

Ethan shrugged, feigning indifference, his expression tense. Then he glanced over at Jill and quickly looked away, taking a large pull of beer. As the sun set and the glow from the flat-screen TV illuminated their competitive faces, the conversation of the two men died.

Jill wondered what they were really arguing about. *Football?* Or something else.

She moved her attention elsewhere. Her niece Carly and Roxanne's two daughters, Annie and Rose, splashed about in the pool, occasionally shrieking with laughter. Roxanne's husband, Henry, tended the grill with Daniel, both dads talking quietly while they kept a watchful eye on the kids.

Roxanne sat closest to Jill, sipping sparkling soda, making sure Jill's glass of the same remained full. "You sure you don't need anything else?"

"No, I really don't. Except to get back to work. That's what I really need," said Jill.

Her practice partner, Preston, sat on the other side of Roxanne. Having heard Jill's comment, he waved it away. "Not a chance. Not until you get medical clearance." His clear-eyed gaze and knowing look took in Jill's small tribe. But he smiled easily and carried on conversations with his usual wry sense of humor, putting others at ease.

One of Jill's pet peeves was trying to be social with others in her profession, only to be met with far too much analysis, cold observation, and lack of warmth. She smiled inwardly, feeling again her deep appreciation for Preston—his brilliance as a psychologist, grounded with genuine empathy and warmth.

"Right on," said Roxanne and fist-bumped Preston. Soon, the two of them were engaged in a lively debate about the role of mental health in law. Preston's wife, Donna, listened, smiling indulgently.

Lauren, her assistant, was out on a date, having texted that the guy was too hot to pass up. One of these days, she would have a talk with Lauren about easing back on the tad-too-much desperation vibe she often telegraphed in her dating life.

Crystal, Jill's mom, stood near the pool, a glass of wine in her hand, talking animatedly to her husband, Daryl, who wore a patient expression, nodding periodically.

Jill closed her eyes briefly, listening to the quiet conversations that swirled around her. Almost everyone significant in her life was present. All of them gathered to make her feel cared for. Contentment washed over her. She began to drift off.

"Hello? Is everyone out here?"

All heads swiveled to the newcomer. Lindsay, carrying Annabelle, stepped through the sliding glass doors, looking shy and uncertain. Roxanne leaped up to greet her, and Henry quickly offered a drink while grinning ridiculously at the baby. Soon, Annabelle was in Henry's arms. He was a natural stay-at-home dad, devoted and doting with his two daughters. And, apparently, with any child that entered his immediate presence.

Lindsay joined the group with Jill, ending up next to Detective Webb. She gave him a warm smile, which he returned. They talked softly, Lindsay occasionally throwing her head back and smiling. Her long neck and tendrils of blond hair seemed to have caught Nick's full attention.

An unwelcome feeling of tension stole Jill's contentment as she watched his eyes, his easy smile. All aimed at Lindsay. Then she thought of something. "Lindsay, I was wondering—how are things going with Travis?"

Following Erica's arrest, Roxanne made sure there was an introduction between Lindsay and Travis. From all she'd heard, Jill was pleased to learn that there was a relationship forming between the mother of Cory's daughter and his brother.

"Really well," said Lindsay. "He wants to live on his own, so we found an apartment nearby. He comes over for dinner a few nights every week, and Annabelle absolutely loves him." She gave a genuine smile. Then, speaking seriously. "But he has ground rules. He has to remain in counseling. So do I, and thanks for your referral, Dr. Kelly," she said, nodding to Preston. "We both have a lot to work through."

Jill felt good about Travis, Lindsay, and Annabelle. Family could show up in the most unusual ways and be formed by the unlikeliest of bonds. And bizarre events—even unusual circumstances such as these.

Then, there were the family bonds that couldn't be tightened. Possibly never healed. Her glance wandered to Crystal, the mom she'd gotten, who wasn't the mom she'd needed. Still, she felt a tug of affection. Crystal presented problems on a regular basis, but she was also charming and endearing at other times.

Jill picked up her phone and checked the time for perhaps the eighth time. *An hour and a half late.* Daniel had arrived with Carly, explaining that Jade was finishing up a piece she'd been working on all day and couldn't tear herself away from. Since then, he'd shown no concern over his wife's whereabouts, perhaps because this wasn't an unusual scenario. Jade was usually late for everything.

Except that lately, Jade had been glued to Jill's side. And she'd told Jill the day before that she would be there early to check the dietary offerings, make sure her sister got the right selections to support her recovery. Jill frowned and picked up her phone again.

Hello. You have almost reached Jade Rhodes Webber. Leave a message, and maybe I'll call you back.

"Hey, Sis. Where are you? I thought you were going to be here early. Anyway, here's the address again, just in case. Call me, even if you're coming later. Or not coming because you need to finish your piece. Just call, okay?"

Jill disconnected and felt that sense of dread wash over her again. While still in the hospital, she'd pondered the vividly realistic nightmare about herself and Jade as little girls, the terrifying pursuit through the forest. Since then, she'd re-lived it several times in memory, each time shaking her to the core. Her doctor had assured her that the disturbing realism of the dream was an artifact of the opiates and her brief stint on a respirator.

She wasn't reassured. Her mind was a labyrinth of uncertainties of late, and anxiety gnawed at her. There was something unsettling about the unknown, about what lay ahead in the uncharted territory of her life.

As she reflected *on Jade's newfound secretiveness, her own breakup with Ethan, and her minimal pain about it*, the weight in her chest grew. Her thoughts raced, making it difficult to focus on anything else. She absentmindedly swirled the ice-cold glass of soda, her thoughts mirroring the motion—a constant swirl with no direction. Questions without answers spun around in her head, creating a greater sense of impending doom.

Jill realized that she was allowing her mind to construct a narrative of dread, the fear of the unknown turning her into an architect of her own anxiety. But she also understood that

319

this fear was born from caring deeply about the outcome, from wanting the best for herself and those she loved.

As she sat there, surrounded by people who seemed so engrossed in their own worlds, she felt isolated. She longed for someone to understand the heaviness that burdened her soul, but she couldn't find the words to articulate her fears. They were nameless, formless, and yet so potent.

At that moment, she felt someone watching her. She looked up and saw Nick studying her with concern. As he caught her eye, he gave her a reassuring smile. Warmth spread throughout Jill's chest and up her throat. Her cheeks warmed, and she felt calmer.

With a conscious effort, she shifted her focus back to the present moment. She took another deep breath, forcing herself to relax and focus on the murmurs of conversation around her. And as the evening wore on, the orange glow of the spring sunset gave way to darkness, and everyone chowed down on the savory offerings from the grill. Jill realized that the feeling of dread might not completely disappear, but she could learn to coexist with it, to acknowledge it without letting it paralyze her.

The future may be uncertain, but the present was still within her control.

The End

TITLES BY NINA ATWOOD

The Expert Witness: Jill Rhodes Mystery/Thriller Series, Book One, is available on Amazon.

About Roxanne: A Psychological Thriller, is available on Amazon.

Free Fall: A Psychological Thriller, is available on Amazon.

Unlikely Return: A Novel, is available on Amazon.

For more of Nina's books, visit Nina's author page on Amazon.

Join Nina's VIP Reader Club for FREE fiction, notification of author inside stories plus upcoming titles in the series, and discounted book deals, here.

Copy/paste:

https://www.ninaatwoodauthor.com/freenovella/

Reward Special note: *If you introduce me to someone in the moviemaking industry [big screen, streaming content] that results in a signed contract and paid advance on any of my books, I will pay you a reward of $10,000.*

– Nina Atwood

Contact: nina@ninaatwoodauthor.com

About the Author

Nina Atwood is a licensed psychotherapist and award-winning executive coach. A published self-help author since 1996, Nina now writes fiction. She lives in Dallas, Texas, with her husband and their adorable fur babies.

To my readers: I am an independent author. I publish and market my books on my own. Your review on Amazon is one of the main ways that authors like me gain traction with our books. If you enjoyed reading this book, please take a moment and write a positive review. Or simply provide a starred review. It makes a huge difference, and for that, I thank you in advance!

Nina

Made in the USA
Las Vegas, NV
19 September 2024

95513426R00184